UNIVERSE JOURNEY:
LOVE'S LUST LOST

JEROME WETZEL

IT'S ALL BEEN DONE PRESENTS
COLUMBUS, OHIO

LOVE'S LUST LOST

Jerome Wetzel

It's All Been Done Presents
Columbus, OH

This book is a work of fiction. All names, characters, places, events are used fictitiously. Any resemblance to actual people or incidents, living or dead, are entirely coincidental.

Copyright © 2017 by Jerome Wetzel

All rights reserved. No portion of this book may be reproduced without the express, written permission of the author. For further information, please contact books@iabdpresents.com

It's All Been Done Presents is an entertainment content provider of works created in or created by peoples connected to Columbus, Ohio. To contact the published, either to enter into a business or publishing arrangement, or to engage the services of any of our artists, please contact us at iabd@iabdpresents.com or 614-916-6043.

Cover art used copyright free from NASA images. Cover design by Jerome Wetzel.
Names: Wetzel, Jerome, author
Title: Universe journey: Love's lust lost / Jerome Wetzel
Description: First ebook edition from It's All Been Done Presents, 2017.

This novel is dedicated to the memory of Jack Overfield.
A greater character than any in this book.

PROLOGUE
EARTH, MAY 2416

Cadet Richard F. Kahkay woke up with a groan. Everything on his body ached, from his dry throat, to his swimming head, to his nauseated digestive tract, to his well-used penis. Even his hair, which seemed to be trying to pull its way out of his head, caused him pain.

Where am I, anyway, Kahkay wondered, forcing his eyes open against the blazing sun as he sat up slowly, grabbing something soft to help pull himself up.

"Ouch!" exclaimed a feminine voice, followed by sharper pain than the rest of the discomfort Kahkay was feeling. If he had to guess what brought the newest sensation to his stinging cheek, Kahkay would have hypothesized that a woman had smacked him. Which made sense, since he had just tried to right himself by yanking on a large, supple, purple boob. He could vaguely see, through his fluttering eyelids, the angry-looking female whom said boob belonged to lying naked beside him, propped up against his bed, which they apparently didn't make it into last night. Rookie mistake.

Kahkay was no rookie. In fact, it had been four years since he'd been one. Today, he was going to be graduating from the Associated Starsheep Services Academy, a fully seasoned officer, the pride of the fleet, and among the initial batch of Earth cadets to ever serve on a starsheep, the first of which would launch from Earth this summer. But before that, he had to graduate.

Kahkay would actually be giving the valedictorian speech at the ceremony. Which is why he had been celebrating so hard last night with...

"Garry!" exclaimed Kahkay, then immediately cringed, unhappy about the loud sound his voice had just made. He put a hand to his head, though that did nothing to ease the pain.

"Dick?" asked an equally groggy voice from a short distance away. Kahkay forced his eyes open once more as he took in the figure of his best friend, only inches away. As naked as Kahkay and the purple woman were, Cadet Garry Marshall was on full display, two women of various hues and equal nudity on either side of him.

Garry and Kahkay had met their first day at the Academy, nearly four years ago. With a shared love of females and liquor, it didn't take long for the two to bond and become wingmen as well as buddies.

Although the two men shared certain tastes, they differed in nearly everything else. While Kahkay was incredibly smart and had terrific instincts, which led to his place at the top of the class, despite his lackadaisical attitude, Garry barely scraped by, studying when he could around the antics Kahkay dragged him into.

Kahkay always included Garry anyway, though, because Garry was the life of any party. Brilliant at spinning a yarn, Garry could suck in those few females who didn't respond to Kahkay's movie-star looks and chiseled abs. Garry's shaggy hair and grey eyes weren't classically handsome, but in combination with his skills and the dashing Aryan Adonis beside him, he got them plenty of attention. Which usually led to a booze-fueled orgy of flesh much like the one that had taken place here, until a few short hours ago, on the floor of their shared dorm room.

"What time is it?" asked Garry, looking only slightly more alert than Kahkay felt.

"Do I look like a clock?" asked Kahkay.

"Well, you do have a face and hands," quipped Garry.

"Har, har, Gare," said Kahkay, now fully awake. He wiped his eyes, uncaring about his own manhood being fully in view of his friend. They'd seen each other's phalli often enough, though only touched them on that one occasion both had vowed never to speak of again.

"Oh, shit!" exclaimed Garry, looking at his watch.

"Gare, quieter, please!" begged Kahkay, wincing.

"We're late!" said Garry.

"For a very important date?" asked Kahkay. "Hehe. I rhymed."

"Seriously, Dick, we're late! Graduation starts in five minutes!"

"Oh, it's just across campus," said Kahkay. "Plenty of time."

"Only if we run!" said Garry, jumping up and pulling on a pair of pants.

"Wha...?" asked a yellow beauty with fiery orange hair, whom Kahkay hadn't noticed behind him until right this minute, and whom he had absolutely no recollection of before this instant, even though she was definitely on his side of the room, not Garry's.

"I love to run," said Kahkay, grabbing his graduation robe from the back of a chair and putting it on, not bothering to add anything else underneath.

"When you're this hung over?" asked Garry, who pulled his own robe over his bare, hairy chest and looked around, under tangled sheets and splayed limbs, for his left shoe.

"Well... maybe not," admitted Kahkay, who was already at the door, not even bothering to secure footwear. "Let's go!"

"Did you finish your speech last night before you passed out?" asked Garry as the two jogged out onto the bright green quad, the air already humid on this warm, May day in central Ohio.

"If by speech you mean making love to my one-thousandth woman, then yes," said Kahkay smugly, proud at having thought of that gem of a comeback in the five second pause before he answered.

"Wow!" said Garry, almost skidding to a stop before running on. "You really did it! A thousand women in four years! That has to be some sort of record."

"Oh, it definitely is," said Kahkay, smiling. Then he remembered the yellow-skinned vixen and wondered if maybe he'd slept with his one thousand-and-first last night, too, and had already forgotten about it. Oh, well. Only round numbers meant anything, and that privilege (probably?) belonged to the purple-skinned beauty whose breast he had inadvertently (that time) honked moments ago.

"You two are sexist pigs," came a voice in their ears. Not for the first time, Kahkay regretted giving Cadet Grace Thomas his comm code. Of course she would butt in on his moment of triumph.

"Grace?" asked Garry, cocking his head. Grace must have initiated a three-way call.

"Yes, it's me," said Grace. "Where are you two? The ceremony is starting!"

"We're in our seats, Gracie," said Kahkay.

"No, you're not!" said Grace.

"Well, we will be in just a minute," admitted Kahkay. "I can see the stadium."

"Did you finish your speech, Dick?" asked Grace.

"No," said Garry. "But get this! Dick slept with..."

"...his thousandth bimbo. Yes, I heard," said Grace. "Glad I wasn't one of them."

"You always were, in my mind," returned Kahkay. He'd long had a thing for Grace Thomas, which is why he had given her the comm code in the first place. She was intelligent, pretty, and with a commanding attitude that intimidated most of their peers, men and women alike. But she hadn't h with anyone, as far as Kahkay knew, save maybe a couple of long-term boyfriends she'd had when she wasn't giving him a run for his money at being number one in their class. Boring!

"But I didn't sleep with you," protested Grace.

"Not physically, no," said Kahkay. "But in my heart, we did it lots of times." He knew that would drive her crazy, and the thought of her lips pouting made him smile all the more.

"That would be sweet if it wasn't so gross," said Grace, not sounding amused. If Kahkay had to pinpoint why he liked her so much, the fact that she didn't find him charming would probably be the primary reason, a rare quality in a woman. "So you're really getting up in front of hundreds of your classmates and their families and the brass without anything prepared?"

"When have I ever prepared?" returned Kahkay. "I'll wing it! It'll be fine!"

"Uh, oh. Roddenberry's waiting. Gotta go, Grace," said Garry, touching his earlobe and ending the connection.

"Thanks, Gare," said Kahkay, relieved to escape her judgment, if only temporarily. "Good thinking."

"No, Roddenberry really is at the door waiting for us," said Garry.

"Oh," said Kahkay, catching site of the severe Commander, Kahkay's least favorite instructor, standing by the stadium gate, tapping his foot impatiently. Roddenberry taught history, and considering how gray his hair was, he had probably lived through the subject, too, at least in Kahkay's estimation. His sense of humor seemed to lean towards the outdated, never finding Kahkay as amusing as most of the faculty did.

"Commander, we-," began Kahkay.

"Save it, Cadet," said Roddenberry with a frown, his forehead wrinkles adding more wrinkles on top of themselves. "I'm not your professor anymore so I don't have to hear it. Get in there and deliver your speech so we can graduate you and be done with it."

"Yes, sir!" said Kahkay smartly, snapping off a salute as he jogged past the commander, Garry falling back to follow behind him through the narrow door. Roddenberry answered them with an eye roll.

Up on the stage, Kahkay could see Admiral Brooks at the podium and instinctively yawned. Brooks was even older than Roddenberry, and twice as boring, if that was possible. But at least Brooks liked Kahkay. Which is probably why he smiled when he saw Kahkay enter fashionably late and gestured to him.

"...and to deliver the commencement address, our valedictorian of the class of 2416, Richard A. Kahkay!" said Brooks, stepping back and smiling broadly.

Kahkay's classmates stood to applaud him. Kahkay enjoyed his victory lap, waving and grinning as he continued his jog straight down the middle aisle and up to the temporary wooden stage, his bare feet appreciating the relief a red rug rolled out brought to them after slapping rough pavement for the past several minutes.

"My fellow cadets," began Kahkay, looking out over the see of maroon caps and gowns, all of which appeared to have shirts peeping out from under them. Lame, thought Kahkay. What was the point of a graduation robe if you couldn't go nude under it? That had been his plan all along, even if he hadn't been rushing to make it on time.

"You all know me. Richard O. Kahkay, top of the class, number one in the A.S.S., best looking cadet, and sure-to-be youngest captain in the fleet, in a decade or less. Also, I'm pretty sure I just broke the record for most women slept with while at the Academy. One thousand." The crowd stared at him without making a sound.

"I know you're impressed with me; I don't blame you. I even shock myself into silence sometimes," said Kahkay, flashing his signature pearly whites, then going on, not caring if a few of those gathered might be thinking less than flattering thoughts about him, as some scattered scowls indicated. Those people were just jealous, he reasoned.

"But today isn't just about me. It sort of is, because I'm up here giving the speech. But it's really about all of us, and all we've accomplished. Maybe you all didn't have the best grades or sleep with the most members of the opposite sex, like I did, but you all accomplished something terrific in your time here. That's why we're the best class to ever come out of the A.S.S. The envy of all other classes that have come before us and that will come after us.

"After today, we go our separate ways. (Kinda rhymes.) I know each and every one of us is destined for greatness. We're going to change this galaxy in ways big and small. We'll explore new worlds, discover new life forms, defend the helpless, and defeat the bad guys. I know mankind has not yet left this planet in an official capacity, but we're so close, and we'll be among the first to do it.

"I've seen what you all can do, and you've wowed me. I'd be proud to have each and every one of you on my crew someday. So go out there, where no men or women have yet gone before, and be awesome!"

As Kahkay finished his speech, he could tell he'd won over the doubters. Almost every student had leapt to their feet and was applauding him. All were smiling, many were laughing. Some of the parents looked confused, but that was OK; they didn't know him the way his fellow students did. Kahkay was happy to represent his peers on this momentous day.

Kahkay hopped off the front of the stage, forgoing the stairs, and strode triumphantly over to his empty seat in the front row next to Grace Thomas, who had even cracked a little bit of a grin, in spite of her best efforts not to.

"How was I?" asked Kahkay.

"Not bad," admitted Grace. "You *do* know how to work a crowd."

"Of course I do. Feel up to a little valedictorian-salutatorian celebration sex?"

"Not even if you had already made captain," returned Grace. Kahkay couldn't help but smile. Only with her did being rejected feel like scoring.

CHAPTER ONE
EARTH ORBIT, 2424

Commander Garry Marshall was nervous. He was a grown man; he'd turned thirty last month. He didn't get nervous much anymore. But today, he was definitely nervous.

Garry wasn't nervous because this would be the first time he set foot on a starsheep; it was actually the second. His first experience had been three years ago, and he'd been away from Earth for most of the time since then. Shipping out as a Lieutenant Commander in charge of communications, he'd recently, finally earned the rank of Commander and the right to be Executive Officer of a starsheep.

But being a freshly-minted XO wasn't why he was nervous, either. After all, he'd trained for this for a long time. Four years at the academy, five serving the A.S.S. on Earth in various capacities, and finally a starsheep rotation on the *A.S.S. Budget*, a modest, but respectable, ship. He felt fully prepared to take on this new professional challenge.

No, the reason Garry was nervous was because his best friend, Dick, would be his new captain.

Garry hadn't seen Richard "Dick" Kahkay in person in eight years. They'd been inseparable in their academy days, of course, but then drifted apart. Dick had been assigned to the very first Earth starsheep shortly after graduation, and Garry had been left behind. They'd tried to get together when Dick had shore leave, but it just never happened, something always inevitably coming up, either Dick's ship being called away or Garry having duties he couldn't get out of.

Sure, there'd been an annual Christmas card, and Garry always sent Dick a shot glass on his birthday, Halloween, New Year's, St. Patrick's Day, and Cinco de Mayo to remind him of old times. But Dick had stopped returning his messages years ago, except for very occasionally, and never answered his calls.

Garry understood, or at least, he tried to. Dick was a busy man, rapidly rising through the ranks and doing great things. But a single memento back or a quick note would have been nice. For his part, Garry was rising, too, albeit a bit more slowly. Still, XO at the mere age of thirty was rare, an accomplishment to be proud of.

It's not like Garry had had much else to do other than throw himself into his work. He still loved liquor and women, his main hobbies from his academy days, but without Dick by his side, Garry was lucky to, every once in a while, get a sole female to take him home. It was nothing like the orgies and fun Garry had become accustomed to in his younger years, and it paled in comparison, leaving him unfulfilled.

Garry consoled himself by doubling down on his work. He'd also discovered an old television and movie producer that shared his name, and he'd studied up on him, watching everything the guy had ever made in his free time. Garry had even become so obsessed that he'd taken to slipping references to the other Garry into conversation, perhaps a bit too often, according to some, and much more frequently when he was nervous or excited. Between those two things, and a fair amount of continued drinking, he'd had a pretty full life thus far.

Ah, who was he kidding? Garry missed his glory days and longed to get back to them. That's why, when he'd heard Dick was taking command of his own starsheep, Garry fought hard to be his first officer. Garry had been offered other postings, including a prestigious one back at the academy, but what he really wanted was to recapture what he'd lost from his youth, and he saw Dick as the only way to do that.

Could things possibly be the same between them? Would they fall back into old patterns? Maybe Dick had moved on, like Garry had tried to. Maybe Dick wouldn't be glad to see him, Garry having managed to convince Admiral Jamieson not to reveal that he'd been assigned to Dick's ship. Their surprise reunion was sure be awkward. Maybe it wasn't too late to accept that academy posting...

"Hello," said a pretty voice. Garry looked up from his drink, shaking away the thoughts of doubt. He was glad he did. The pretty voice belonged to an equally pretty lady.

Standing five foot three, with long, straight blond hair, Garry knew at once who this was. He'd made a point of reading every officer's personnel file before serving with them. But the picture in this particular case did not at all live up to the reality. It was as if he'd only seen the Mona Lisa drawn in crayon, and now she was standing right in front of him.

The fact that she was scowling did nothing to detract from her beauty.

"Why, hello, Lieutenant Tokaladie!" said Garry appreciatively. "Aren't you just one of Blansky's Beauties? Sit down. Let me buy you a drink."

"It's not even nine in the morning," said Tokaladie, her scowl deepening.

"Exactly. A little hair of the dog that bit you," said Garry.

"Excuse me?" asked Tokaladie.

"It's an expression. Means I drink to erase the hangover from last night," offered Garry helpfully.

"I didn't drink last night," said Tokaladie. "It was a Monday."

"Sure, sure, I know," said Garry. "I never miss Margarita Mondays. Or, I didn't miss the inaugural one, anyway. Our new ship's bartender makes a mean drink. I didn't see you here, though."

"Of course not. Margarita Mondays isn't a thing," said Tokaladie.

"Sure it is. Why, back in the academy, Dick and I-," began Garry, launching into his favorite topic: tales from college.

"I don't know who Dick is, and I don't want to know," interrupted Tokaladie. "The captain's coming; you're needed on the bridge. If you're not too drunk to drive."

"Hold on just a second," said Garry, starting to get a little offended. "This is only my first beer of the morning, so yes, I'm perfectly fine to drive the ship. And second, the rest of the crew won't be in until this afternoon, so I'm sure I'll be completely sober by then. Unless Dick lets me buy him a drink to welcome him on board. And you should totally join us."

"Dick? Wait, are you talking about Captain Richard Y. Kahkay?" asked Tokaladie, head tilting to the side quizzically. If anything, that only made her sexier in Garry's estimation.

"Of course!" said Garry.

"You shouldn't refer to the captain by his first name, let alone a nickname," said Tokaladie.

"I've known Dick for more than a decade! Of course I call him by his first name," said Garry.

"You'd better not do it while on duty," scolded Tokaladie.

Garry didn't like her haughty attitude, which was almost enough to distract him from how nicely she filled out the purple-and-black uniform; just like him, she'd opted for the version with the skirt and lower neckline. So he did what he always did when he got uncomfortable: change the subject.

"What's your first name?" asked Garry.

"Why do you want to know?" asked Tokaladie, eyes narrowing.

"I thought maybe you and I could...," began Garry.

"Oh, no, no, no, no, no," said Tokaladie quickly, interrupting him. "That isn't happening. Besides, you knew my last name and rank when I entered. I assume that's because you read my personnel file, which contains my first name. That means you're only asking in an attempt to hit on me, and like I just said, that isn't happening."

"Why not?" asked Garry, hurt.

"Because I don't date co-workers," said Tokaladie.

"Why not?" asked Garry again.

"For oh so many reasons that we don't have time to get into right now," said Tokaladie. "We have to get up to the bridge, remember?"

"Right, right," said Garry. "Just let me finish my beer here..."

"You don't have time for that," said Tokaladie.

"Sure I do. If Dick was already on his way up, the bridge would have paged me by now," said Garry, taking a long swig.

"I have been repeatedly paging you for the last ten minutes," said Tokaladie. "Why do you think I came down here to find you?"

"Oh," said Garry, slipping his phone out of his pocket, flipping it open, and seeing several missed pages. "Looks like I left it on silent." He usually did that while in the bar in the hopes he'd be having a conversation with a lovely lady that he didn't want interrupted. Such as this one right now. The ability to shut it off was the main reason why Garry had switched to the pocket model, away from the customary implanted ear piece.

"Come on!" said Tokaladie insistently, tapping her foot.

"Fine, fine, darlin'," said Garry, chugging the rest of the bottle and standing up. Unfortunately, in his hurry, he spilled a bit down the front of his dress.

"Don't call me darling," said Tokaladie, eyeing the spreading wet spot on Garry's chest.

Garry answered her with a belch. It seemed appropriate. He started forward for the elevator. She followed quickly.

"You *are* going to change first," said Tokaladie. It was not a question.

"You think I should?" asked Garry, looking down. "It's just a little spot. It'll dry."

"That won't erase the smell," said Tokaladie.

"Fine, fine. I'll stop by my quarters real quick and meet you up there," said Garry.

Women. He would never understand them.

Admiral Jamie Jamieson glanced over at the tall, handsome, confident, egotistical asshole next to him and tried not to grimace at the stupid grin on the man's face. Though, were their positions reversed, Jamieson probably would have had a similar expression. After all, a majestic beauty had just become visible through the window of their transport, and even Jamieson had to admit to being impressed by it. "There she is, son, the A.S.S. *Thrifty*," said Jamieson.

"Wow, boy, she is *hot*!" exclaimed Kahkay. Jamieson rolled his eyes. A few months of having Kahkay serve in the office beside him while waiting for the *Thrifty* to be ready for launch had been all of the young man Jamieson cared to take, and more. He couldn't wait to be rid of him.

"It's a metal ship. How can metal be hot?" asked Jamieson. He immediately regretted his choice of words. Of course metal could be hot, but not in the way that Kahkay meant it, and there had to have been a better way to phrase it. He hoped that the captain wouldn't notice the awkward answer, and thankfully, he didn't. Or if he did, Kahkay showed rare restraint by not pointing out the mistake.

"Thank you, Admiral Jamieson," said Kahkay formally, and Jamieson was grateful to move on.

"No need to thank me, *Captain* Kahkay. You've earned it," said Jamieson, and indeed Kahkay had. Whatever feelings Jamieson might have about Kahkay personally, there was no denying his professional track record.

Kahkay had been an ensign on the *A.S.S. Enterprise*, the first starsheep sent away from Earth, right after he had graduated, one of only sixteen members of his class to earn that distinction. His record hadn't been perfect since then, but overall Kahkay had served admirably, bravely, and always with great loyalty to his crew, at least according to several letters of recommendation, including one from his most recent captain.

It's too bad Kahkay had had to take a brief respite on Earth because of ships' duty schedules between this assignment and his last, leading to Jamieson's two months of hell, sharing an office wall that Kahkay had frequently used as a surface for recreational intercourse, and a kitchenette that the new captain had never once so much as rinsed a coffee cup in. Though he drank from them often enough, usually in the Irish fashion.

"Woo, look at those lines!" breathed Kahkay. "It must be the best ship in the fleet!"

"No," said Jamieson, refusing to share Kahkay's enthusiasm, tempted as he might be to do so, lest they end up bonding, leading to Kahkay feeling comfortable enough to call upon Jamieson socially in the future.

"Uh, the fastest?" queried Kahkay.

"No," said Jamieson, though he suspected it might be once Chief Engineer Foley, who had nearly as illustrious a resume as Kahkay, but was far less showy about it, tinkered a bit with the engines.

"The biggest?" asked Kahkay.

"Not by a long shot," said Jamieson, knowing the *Thrifty* to be thirteen inches shy of that record. Arguably, thirteen inches wasn't much of a long shot, but again, he refused to give Kahkay any satisfaction.

"Well, she's mine, and that's all that matters," said Kahkay, seemingly unfazed by Jamieson's continual negativity. That irked Jamieson enough that he felt he had to respond with another dig, just for principle's sake.

"Yes, you being the one to lead this crew far, far away from us here on Earth is definitely all that matters."

"I intend to make my mark with her and on her," said Kahkay. Now he was just being gross.

"That's disgusting," said Jamieson. "Are you ready to meet your crew?"

"Do the green-throated whores of Persi Alpha VII give the best blowies?" asked Kahkay.

"I have no idea," said Jamieson, suddenly not sure he could take another moment with this crass man. The sooner he dropped Kahkay off and got back to Earth, the better.

"Yes, yes, I'm ready to meet the crew," said Kahkay. He looked back at the ship and there was no denying the awe in the younger man's expression.

No further words were spoken as the shuttle docked at the airlock on the front of the bridge, a convenience for meetings and drop-offs such as this one. If the big screen on the command deck were replaced with a window, the crew would be able to see the smaller vessel. As it was, Jamieson knew they'd hear the clunking without bearing witness to their approach.

The doors opened and Jamieson looked around at the bridge crew, none of whom he knew very well. He could see Kahkay pulling his shoulders back beside him and sensed the younger man would soon be launching into a prepared speech or ice-breaking activity. Just the thought of that was enough to make Jamieson want to depart as quickly as possible even more.

Giving Kahkay a little nudge through the airlock, Jamieson delivered a brief, "*Thrifty* crew, this is your new captain, Richard T. Kahkay. Kahlay, this is your crew. Buh-bye," then closed the door.

Jamieson was halfway back to Earth before Kahkay could open his mouth.

Chief Engineer Colm Foley was sitting on the bridge, absently thumbing the engineering panel, trying to appear just a little bit busy.

Foley was a brilliant engineer, and it was odd for him to be on the command deck. Usually, he was elbow deep in the ship's bowels, working his magic to coax the machinery to go far beyond its manufacturer's specifications. In fact, after only a few days on board, he was confident that his modifications to the engine would make the *Thrifty* nearly forty percent faster than any other starsheep in the A.S.S. fleet, even though it would cost them dearly in energy usage. But that was a problem for another day.

This morning, Foley tore himself away from his passion in order to be present when the new commanding officer arrived. It was important to him to make a good first impression on Richard I. Kahkay, and he couldn't do that if he was hidden away.

Foley was enamored with the captain. It wasn't a crush, strictly speaking, as Foley was completely heterosexual. But there was something about Kahkay that was magnetic to Foley. He couldn't help but want to be in the captain's orbit.

They'd met twice before, not counting Kahkay's graduation at the Academy, during which they hadn't met, but when Foley, a second-year cadet at the time, had first become aware of the other man. Both meetings involved a lot of liquor, and Foley had been one of many in Kahkay's company. The engineer wasn't even sure Kahkay would remember him. That was OK, though, as now that Foley would be serving on Kahkay's starsheep (a post he'd eagerly requested), he would have plenty of chances to make friends with the slightly older man.

The clunking sounds of the shuttle docking at the bridge port were audible and Foley sat a little straighter in his seat. The moment had arrived.

As the doors to the bridge slid open, Foley smiled at the wooshing sound. Strictly speaking, as had become common in this era, many of the *Thrifty*'s functions were virtually silent. However, Foley was a student of history, and he appreciated the noises computers and simpler equipment used to make. As such, he'd started to add sound effects throughout the vessel, some set to go off automatically, some triggered manually by himself.

So far, no one had commented on it, and he took that as a point of pride, satisfied that he'd just made things sound the way he thought they naturally should. Though, he suspected some crewman might just think the materials on the *Thrifty* were substandard. That was a risk he was willing to take; if nothing else, that false impression would give him job security when he 'upgraded' various components.

Then, thoughts of sound effects fled Foley's brain because Captain Kahkay appeared in the doorway. Six-foot-one, a muscular build, hair peaking from the plunging tunic, chiseled jaw, Kahkay was what Foley imagined to be the perfect specimen, far more impressive than Foley's own five-foot-six, scrawny frame (which admittedly did make it easier to crawl between the walls of the starsheep). "Manly" was the word that came to mind regarding Kahkay, followed closely by "stud."

Kahkay flashed a pearly white grin that almost blinded Foley when the light from the big screen flickered off of it. Foley couldn't help but return the happy visage.

Behind Kahkay, Admiral Jamieson didn't look nearly so impressive. His dark features betrayed his uncomfortableness as he shoved Kahkay forward, and Foley got merely a glimpse of his black, curly hair, visible a few inches above Kahkay's left shoulder, before the door slid shut again. Foley was pretty sure Jamieson said something, but realized he had missed exactly what, entranced as he was by the new commanding officer.

Without even thinking about it, Foley's hands drummed on his panel and the distant sound of the admiral's shuttle zooming away sounded through the room, even though, of course, the shuttle made no audible noise in the vacuum of space. The corner of Foley's mouth twitched with appreciation.

"Boy, was he in a hurry or what?" asked Kahkay, looking over his crew. Foley perked up when the captain's eyes landed on him, but Kahkay's gaze didn't betray any flicker of recognition. Foley's heart dropped slightly, but only slightly.

"So, uh," began Kahkay after a brief awkward silence and a quick throat clearing. "Since this is like the first day of school here, I mean, why don't we go around the room and introduce ourselves? Say your name, where you're from, and one interesting fact about you."

Kahkay glanced back over the assembled group, and Foley followed his eyes. There was the reptilian Lieutenant Commander M- at the science station, whom sort of looked like a dinosaur, specifically a velociraptor, but with longer arms and a more vertical stance, at the science station. The short, blonde Lieutenant Tokaladie, who had hurriedly pulled her long hair up into a bun just before Kahkay appeared, was at communications. A couple of ensigns whom Foley didn't know staffed the auxiliary stations. But none of these, including Foley himself, opened their mouths to go first.

All of this happened in just a few seconds, and then Kahkay took control of the conversation back, exemplifying the take-charge attitude Foley expected his captain to have. "I'll start. I'm Captain Richard G. Kahkay, and I'm from a beautiful little hamlet known as Buffalo, New York. A fun fact is that I am, objectively speaking, the handsomest captain the fleet. Who's next?"

Foley couldn't help but agree, eyeing the bulky chest and thin waist, the bulging biceps and the near-perfect swoop of hair that was imperfect in the exact right way to make it even more attractive. God, Foley wished, not for the first time that day, that he came from Richard X. Kahkay's gene pool.

The bridge officers looked at one another in confusion, perhaps not quite having expected this opening. Lieutenant Commander M-, tied with Foley for the highest ranking being present after Kahkay himself, stepped forward.

"I am Lieutenant Commander M-. I am from the planet-," and here M- made some screeching sounds that Foley couldn't possibly hope to recreate, "-and I am the science officer. And a fun fact about me is that I am not evil."

"Did someone accuse you of being evil?" asked Kahkay, narrowing his eyes at the being whose name sounded to human ears like Meow-meow, though Foley knew that didn't quite capture the true sounds, and it certainly wasn't spellable with the Earth alphabet. Hence why official records listed his moniker as an M followed by a dash.

"Not lately," replied M-, tone as cool as the ooze flowing beneath his scaly, green skin, or so Foley assumed, based on his limited knowledge of Earth reptiles. He wasn't a doctor; he didn't know what other species had in place of blood.

"Seems like a strange thing to bring up, and your voice sounds a little sinister to me. Tell me the truth: were you lying before, and are you actually, in fact, evil?" asked Kahkay. The captain stared M- down in such a way that, were Foley the one being grilled, he surely would have immediately broke and told Kahkay what he wanted to hear, whether it was the truth or not.

M- was non-plussed, though, and instead came back with a retort tinged with anger and frustration. "No, and I resent your rassssist implications. Not all reptilian beings are evil."

"Um, sorry, I guess," said Kahkay, who didn't sound apologetic at all. "OK, who's next then?"

Foley recovered his wits enough to speak up. "Whoop-whoo-whoo-whoop-whoop. Chief Engineer Foley here, sir! I'm from Ireland, land of the leprechauns." Foley freely admitted, he loved to let out some nonsense syllables from time to time; it was probably related to his sound effect hobby. But he chose that particular burst in an attempt to jog Kahkay's memory, knowing he'd uttered it before in the captain's presence.

"Yes, yes, we're all familiar with Scotland, Engineer. Why aren't you down in the engine room?" asked Kahkay, still showing no sign of recognizing Foley.

Foley's heart dropped to his feet, but he immediately decided to play it off with a quip, his go-to way of dealing with pain and disappointment. "I like the view from up here. Nyuk-yuk-yuk-yuk-yuk." Except, there was no view, as there were no windows on the bridge. Foley winced, but Kahkay was unfazed.

"All right," said Kahkay, moving on to the person who had received the vast majority of his attention thus far, his eyes frequently stealing glances at her throughout the other answers. Foley wondered if Kahkay was paying attention to anyone else at all. "Uh, how about you, gorgeous? What's your name?"

"I'm Lieutenant Tokaladie," returned Tokaladie, as lukewarm on Kahkay as Kahkay was towards the rest of the crew. From what little Foley knew about Tokaladie, Foley assumed their captain wasn't her type, though he couldn't, for the life of him, figure out why.

"Tokaladie, huh? I'll bet there's a beautiful story behind that name. Is it African?"

African? Seriously? Foley could maybe see confusing Ireland and Scotland, if you had no knowledge of that part of the world, but how in the world did Kahkay think her name sounded African? Especially when coupled with her lily-white skin and blonde locks? Sure, there were parts of Africa she could conceivably be from, but...

No," said Tokaladie flatly, unmoved.

"And where are you from, Lieutenant? Heaven?" asked Kahkay, chuckling to himself. Foley had to smile a bit at that one, too. The pick-up line was old and cheesy, to be sure, but somehow, it sounded smooth when delivered with Kahkay's honey voice.

"Gary. Indiana," said Tokaladie. Foley could practically hear her eyes roll in her response, but to her credit, she didn't physically do that in front of their new commanding officer.

Before Kahkay could muster a comeback, the doors to the bridge opened and deposited Commander Garry Marshall, their new XO, whom Foley had only met briefly in the bar the night before while celebrating Margarita Mondays. They didn't really hit it off, Marshall not holding his booze all that well and being a bit of a bore, so Foley had given him a wide berth.

It didn't look like Marshall had stopped drinking much before this moment. His green uniform skirt was wrinkled, clearly having just been pulled off the floor. His hair, just a bit too long, was mussed, and stubble poked from his chin and cheeks a little further than would be considered sexy on a man.

"Hey, Landlord Dick! How you been, you old son of a gun?" asked Marshall, way too familiarly for Foley's taste, and with an upbeat spirit that didn't match his disheveled appearance.

Kahkay didn't notice any of this, a broad grin breaking out as he turned and embraced the man, practically lifting Marshall off the floor. "Garry! Garry Marshall! My best friend that I haven't seen in eight years! I've been awesome. Got my own ship now. How are you?"

"I'm great, happy days, like New Year's Eve or Valentine's Day! Dear god, I'm the executive officer of a starsheep," said Marshall in that strange speech pattern Foley had found so off-putting the previous evening.

"Really?" asked Kahkay with happy surprise. "Which one? The *A.S.S. Hertz*?"

"No, the *Thrifty*," said Marshall proudly. "She's a pretty woman."

"Why, that's my ship!" exclaimed Kahkay.

"I know. Hence why I'm here, Dick Van Dyke," said Marshall.

Foley inwardly shuddered at Marshall's continued informality, but made a mental note that maybe befriending Marshall would be a good way to get in with Kahkay. To do that, Foley would have to learn to like the man. Foley liked almost everyone, but there was something about Marshall that didn't sit well with the engineer. What was it?

"So my best friend is my XO?" asked Kahkay. "That's fantastic! It's going to be just like college, planet hopping, getting wasted, picking up alien women. It'll be a blast!"

"I'm looking forward to it," said Marshall. "We'll be the odd couple. That'd make a heck of a show. And I can do several spin-offs featuring the aliens we meet, like Blansky's beauties. Nanoo nanoo."

What in the heck was Commander Marshall talking about, wondered Foley. Was he stable?

"Right," said Kahkay, finally echoing Foley's feelings of doubt about the man, even if only a little. "So... how do we start this thing?"

"Oh, I'm also the pilot," said Marshall. "Where do you want to go, Angie?"

Angie? Was that a college nickname, wondered Foley.

"Second star to the right and straight on 'til morning," said Kahkay, and Foley marveled at just how cool that answer sounded.

"I wouldn't recommend that, ssssir," broke in M-. Foley breathed a sigh of relief, having been about to open his own mouth after glancing at the navigational panel. M- would be the parent who kept them out of danger, Foley decided, which every party ship needed, especially if he and Marshall and Kahkay were going to have as much fun as Foley hoped they would.

"Why not?" asked Kahkay, bristling.

"That would take us right into the middle of a supernova," returned M-.

"OK," said Kahkay, unbothered. "Third star to the right?"

"A perfect exit to Eden. Setting course now," said Marshall.

"Ah, Captain, perhaps we should...," began M-.

"What is it now?" asked Kahkay a bit testily. Foley could see why Kahkay would be annoyed with M-, who was coming across as a bit of a buzzkill, but Foley also appreciated that the science officer was looking out for the safety of the crew. Foley hoped the two wouldn't argue; that would be a terrible start to Kahkay's reign.

"Mmm, never mind," said M-, respectfully backing down.

"OK. Go!" said Kahkay, settling back into his chair in the middle of the room, a smile on his face. As the ship sped up, leaving Earth far behind, Foley matched his expression. There were few things more pleasurable than rocketing through the empty void, on their way to a grand adventure!

As the starsheep surged forward, Foley's stomach suddenly lurched. He knew it wasn't space sickness; he'd spent plenty of time on ships with a much rougher ride than this one. His heart joined his stomach in his feet. He couldn't possibly be getting sick now, today of all days, on his first mission with Kahkay, could he?

Kahkay shifted in his chair. It didn't make the seat any more comfortable, but he decided not to shift again. He needed to issue an air of command and confidence, and not even being able to pick a sitting position did not support that image.

He had to admit, he was nervous. He hoped it didn't show. He thought he handled the introductions well enough, setting a tone and sticking to it. He let each of the crew speak, taking an active part of the proceedings. Well, except the ensigns, who didn't matter anyway. But he also kept control of the conversation, just like he'd been taught to in command school.

Kahkay didn't actually think he would be this nervous when his turn at the helm of the ship finally came. After all, this was what he had been preparing for all his career. He'd had an eye on the captain's chair since he was a teenager, and getting it before anyone else ever had was always the plan.

Why then, did it not feel quite right? Why was he having these negative feelings, a tingling in the pit of his stomach, like he'd eaten sushi a bit past the expiration date? Why wasn't he enjoying this more?

It had to be the circumstances through which he'd gained this position. What he'd done to rocket his career forward over the past few years did not sit right with him. He hadn't broken any rules, he hadn't betrayed any trusts, and yet, it felt like he did. He couldn't help but feel that someone else should be sitting in this chair instead of him.

There was a time when Kahkay had lost sight of this dream and never thought it would come true. In a way, it was still surprising that it had, given how far Kahkay had drifted off course. But he'd righted himself again, with a fair amount of help, and while it felt a little surreal to be sitting here, he couldn't say he didn't still want it.

Kahkay looked over at Garry. This was not the man Kahkay remembered from school. The familiar bond between them still existed, as easy to slip back into as his favorite pair of slippers, sitting in the suitcase delivered to his apartment just below the bridge earlier, not even unpacked.

And yet, there was something markedly different. Perhaps it was the grey shadows beneath Garry's eyes, the hollowness behind his cheery voice, the spring that was no longer in the commander's step. Something about Garry had changed.

Or maybe it was Kahkay himself. He still went on his liquor-fueled binges, sleeping with woman after woman, and he still had fun doing it. But lately, Kahkay had begun to wonder if he had almost outgrown it. Not yet, of course; being captain would give him untold opportunities to take his antics to new heights. But now that he'd achieved this position, he'd begun to wonder what would come after. He couldn't just enjoy the now.

Perhaps Kahkay was wrong. With Garry here, maybe the two of them could get back to what they were. Maybe they could conquer the galaxy like they'd always talked about, metaphorically speaking, those late nights in the bars. Maybe these were just first day jitters, and Kahkay's bright future had arrived, full of everything it had always promised.

Or maybe the part of his gut that told Kahkay he was wrong was exactly right.

CHAPTER TWO
EARTH ORBIT, 2416

"Wow, boy, she is *hot!*" exclaimed Ensign Richard N. Kahkay. He couldn't tear his eyes off the sleek, grey beauty, visible through the wide window on the side of the shuttle. Her curves were in all the right places, and the lights shining through scattered windows in the hull glistened like glitter. Kahkay had seen pictures, of course, but to finally glimpse her in person took his breath away.

The *A.S.S. Enterprise* was the first starsheep to ever leave the planet Earth. There had been smaller vessels over the years, including the NASA shuttle of the same name. But this was the first large-scale, space-faring behemoth that Earth had ever built, holding more than seven hundred souls when fully staffed. Kahkay couldn't believe he'd get to be one of the very first to serve on her.

It was a funny story how the fleet vessels got to be called starsheep instead of starships, which involved a heavy accent, a dictation secretary's malfunctioning hearing aide, and a penchant for typos. In fact...

"Put it back in your pants, Dick," said Ensign Grace Thomas, her long, brown hair pulled back into a bun as severe as her expression, both to Kahkay's disappointment, knocking him out of his reverie. He didn't see the far side of her mouth flitting into and out of a smirk. "You're ruining the moment for the rest of us."

"Sorry, Gracie, I just can't help it!" exclaimed Kahkay. She winced, hating the nickname, which he knew and called her anyway. "Have you ever seen anything so beautiful? Besides every time you look in the mirror, that is?"

"Four seconds," said Grace.

"Excuse me?" asked Kahkay, finally looking over to the seat next to him to see Grace equally entranced by the sight, even if her tone of voice wasn't beholden with rapture the way his was.

"I was wondering how long I'd be able to stand serving with you before asking for a transfer," said Grace. "Turns out, the magic limit is four seconds."

"You're not transferring back to Earth before you even get aboard?" asked Kahkay in surprise.

Grace rolled her eyes. "Of course not. But if *you* want to, I won't stop you."

"Why would I-," began Kahkay.

"You two need to get a room," interrupted Ensign Hannah Myers, another one of the sixteen recent graduates that would be serving on the *Enterprise*.

"Not if he was the last rozit on Kremulon," said Grace, making a disgusted face.

"How about you and I get a room instead?" asked Kahkay, slipping an arm around Hannah, a petite blond as short and curvy as Grace was tall and athletic.

"Oh!" said Hannah, blushing a little, not pushing him off. This was how Kahkay was used to being treated, but despite the feel of her firm breast on his side, he kept finding his attention shifting to Grace, who shot Kahkay a brief, disapproving glance before looking back at the starsheep.

What was it about Grace Thomas that Kahkay found so fascinating? She was beautiful, sure, even if her above average height, which had set in too fast, still made her a little awkward in her movements. She was charming and intelligent. She challenged him, setting a high bar he almost had to exert effort to surpass. And unlike almost every other woman Kahkay had met, she was wholly uninterested. Which didn't stop Kahkay from hitting on her every chance he got.

"It's a big ship," breathed Ensign Willis Frier, a plug of a man whose dark expression was always the same.

"We could explore it together," Kahkay suggested to Grace, causing Hannah to pout and pull away ever so slightly. But just slightly. Kahkay had an innate talent for knowing how much he could ignore and push a girl towards jealousy before she gave up and left him sleeping alone, and Hannah still had quite a ways to go.

"I'm counting on it being big enough that I rarely see you," said Grace.

"We've spent nearly every waking moment together for like the past four years. Wouldn't you miss me?" asked Kahkay, giving her his best 'cute' face, the one that had worked on more than three dozen species of females, now that Earth had become a galactic tourist destination.

"No," said Grace flatly, turning away.

Kahkay shrugged and turned back to Hannah. While he would have rather engaged Grace with more witty banter, he didn't want to run Hannah off, lest he have an empty bed tonight. He hadn't yet gotten the lay (hehe) of the *Enterprise* to know where the best spots to pick up women were, and he'd only slept with Hannah twice at the Academy, so she was an acceptable option. If he remembered correctly, she had this one move...

This time it was the *Enterprise* herself that interrupted Kahkay's train of thought, not Grace, who had moved to the other side of Willis to put some distance between them. The shuttle had just come around the bottom, and now he got to see her backside for the first time. He couldn't stop himself from letting out an audible whistle, not that he did much to try.

"One day, I'm going to have me one of these," said Kahkay dreamily. "I'll bet I'll be the youngest captain in the fleet."

"I'll take that bet," said Grace, peeking around Willis. Kahkay smiled inwardly. She never could just let his boasts stand. If nothing else, that showed he got to her, even if it wasn't quite in the way that he wanted to. "A hundred gouda says I'll be the youngest."

"Impossible," said Kahkay.

"Why is that?" asked Grace, hands on her hips, frown deepening.

"Because you're a month older than me," said Kahkay. "And there's no way you'll make captain before I do."

"So take the bet," said Grace.

Kahkay sensed Hannah shift next to him and knew he was getting dangerously close to losing her for the day. Still, he couldn't turn down a challenge, especially not from someone that was a formidable challenger, and that he enjoyed beating so much.

"Deal," said Kahkay, reaching out to shake her hand. Grace looked at him for a minute, as if wondering what he was doing, then extended her own arm and gave his a firm, brief shake.

"Now, gorgeous, what are you up to after the tour?" asked Kahkay, turning to give Hannah his full attention. She had already turned to Ensign Brian Matthews, a strapping lad in security, captain of the Academy bricking team, but she turned back, unable to resist the hundred-watt smile.

Kahkay's sheets did not remain unsoiled that night. Nor twice the next morning.

"Over here!" shouted Grace. Commander Roddenberry jogged slowly over to join her, out of breath after only a few meters, his heavy middle section jiggling in the most unattractive way possible, highlighted by the green shirt that wrapped it so snugly. Not for the first time, Grace questioned the A.S.S.'s process for picking officers for its first starsheep. There had to be a more appropriate choice for XO than the former history professor.

"Yes. Ensign?" asked Roddenberry, trying not to let his gasps for oxygen be audible and failing miserably.

"I think this might be what we're looking for," said Grace, showing her portable instrument panel to the senior officer.

"It's a slug," said Kahkay, coming up behind them and making a face like a baby tasting mashed spinach for the first time.

"Yes, it's a slug," said Grace impatiently, wishing he would leave her alone.

"I thought we were looking for a cure?" asked Kahkay.

"What do you think a cure looks like?" returned Grace. "A syringe labeled 'antidote?'"

"No. I don't know. Maybe a pink flower, or a... a....," Kahkay stammered, unable to think of another example. Grace rolled her eyes. This was the guy who finished only one point behind her in their alien pathogens class? Had he slept with Professor Simpson to earn that grade? It was certainly possible. Although Simpson was married, she wasn't ugly and, in her late thirties, far below Kahkay's age limit. If he even had one.

"Good work, Ensign Thomas," said Commander Roddenberry. "If these readings are correct, we may have the good people of Benji III out of bed and back to work by the weekend. A very successful mission."

Grace smiled proudly. At the Academy, she had done well, but had worked incredibly hard to do so. Only a few months into her first tour in space, she was quickly establishing herself as someone the senior officers could count on. She'd only completed a few missions thus far, but she figured finding a cure for a horrible disease, even if it wasn't a fatal one, should look very good on her resume. How many upset stomachs had Dick Kahkay fixed?

That wasn't fair, Grace realized, pushing those petty feelings back down. Kahkay annoyed the hell out of her, but he was a good officer. He had managed to talk that war lord down from a massacre on their last stop. Granted, the war lord in question was female, and Kahkay had brokered peace largely through sexual manipulation; but still, he had saved the day.

Grace knew that Kahkay liked her, and if she was being totally honest, she didn't mind his presence. Sure, almost everything he said was incredibly idiotic, and his ego was larger than her parents' hovervan, and he seemed to not actually have to try at anything. However, if he had not frustrated her so much, she probably wouldn't have soared as high as she had.

Grace had had an easy time of things growing up. Her parents were wealthy, she had private tutors, and academically and athletically, she'd always performed well. But the A.S.S. was about more than academics. The best A.S.S. officers had an instinct and presence that Grace lacked, or at least, she had lacked it when she arrived at the Academy. After years of watching Kahkay, though, analyzing where he beat her, and learning from her mistakes, she was developing it.

Not that Grace would ever tell Kahkay any of these things. Just because she secretly credited him for motivating her didn't mean anything romantic. Dick would only take that as validation, and he didn't need any more of that. And there was no way she would ever give him the satisfaction of making her another notch on his bedpost, even if he did have abs to die for.

What? She was human; she had eyes. And he took off his shirt, like, *a lot*. Ridiculously often. One would not be blamed for thinking that he was allergic to cotton-like polymers.

Roddenberry took the slug, secured tightly in a plastic jar, back towards Doctor Smokin, their chief medical officer. Grace stood up and wiped her dirt-covered hands on her black slacks, knocking the dust to the ground and leaving a slight slime trail where she'd touched the creature.

Kahkay was still standing a foot away, grinning like an idiot.

"What?" asked Grace testily, hating when he just looked at her like that and didn't say anything, even though a moment without Kahkay's mouth being open was a rare moment indeed, and she appreciated his silence. He was so much easier to take when he wasn't speaking.

"It was just a slug," said Kahkay, shaking his head, his sandy hair flopping slightly across his forehead, a couple of weeks past when he should have gone to the barber.

"So?" asked Grace.

"So, it was just a slug," said Kahkay again.

"I don't understand," said Grace, temper rising.

"It. Was. Just. A. Slug," said Kahkay, delighting in each word.

"You're not funny," said Grace, picking up her equipment and striding away quickly.

"I'm not trying to be, Gracie!" said Kahkay, jogging to catch up with her, which he did far too easily for her taste. "Don't you remember?"

"Remember what?" asked Grace, not missing a step and keeping her eyes forward.

"Professor McFarlane? He thought that-," began Kahkay.

"Oh!" said Grace, interrupting him. She stopped and turned, but looked down instead of at his face. She could feel her cheeks reddening slightly, feeling like a fool for having missed an inside joke they'd shared in a boring lecture three years ago. "Sorry. I'd forgotten."

"It's all right, Gracie," said Kahkay affectionately. Sometimes, he could be so sweet, so caring. Like remembering a shared moment she'd forgotten. It was times like those that she wondered if maybe she shut him down too quickly. She'd never be willing to share him with all the other women, of course, but maybe if he had one substantial one, he'd give up his horn dog ways.

Or maybe not. What had Grace's mother always said? A punta cat doesn't change its spots. And just like that, the spell Kahkay had over her, which had embarrassed and stunned her for a full ten seconds, broke and she turned to walk away again.

"See you back on the ship!" called Kahkay, not following her this time. Without turning around to see it, she knew he had stuck his hands in his pockets and was striding away whistling, that irritating, smug look on his face. Even with her substantial work-related triumph, he'd won the day between them. As he always did.

"Battle stations! Captain to the bridge!" shouted Commander Roddenberry, his pudgy form a little too big for the seat at the center of the room, which he currently occupied. Sweat dripped from the man's brow, and Kahkay spared a brief thought of sympathy for the captain, who would soon be plopping down in a pool of some other guy's perspiration.

Kahkay's fingers danced across his panel, making sure power was routing correctly to weapons and shields. Only being an ensign, he wasn't trusted to man the *Enterprise*'s weapons or raise the shields himself, but his bridge shift did include looking for problems before they began. And while a fight didn't make the task itself any more interesting, Kahkay was glad to be up here when the action went down.

The elevator doors opened and deposited Lieutenant Karla Trinity, a trim brunette that was a bit less traditionally feminine than most with her short hair, broad shoulders, and strong jawline, which seemed to fit with her specialty of engineering, in Kahkay's opinion. Her being a tomboy was something of a turn-on for Kahkay. He didn't know why, but he was attracted to a certain type of personality. A girl didn't have to be hot to turn his head if she had an attitude of confidence and conviction. Or if she just radiated sexuality, as Karla did.

To his surprise, he saw Grace exit behind Trinity, tucking a strand of hair that had come loose from her bun behind her ear. Grace looked flushed, her clothes a little rumpled, which was something she usually was not. Kahkay's interest was now fully piqued. Could the two of them be...?

"Ensign Thomas, what are you doing up here?" asked Roddenberry, probably the harshest he had ever spoken to her. He normally reserved that type of tone for Kahkay.

"I was... um... I was close and just got off duty, so I thought I'd see if you needed a hand up here," stammered Grace, not nearly as put together as she usually was.

"That's not protocol," said Roddenberry, glancing distractedly back towards the big screen, which showed a huge, dangerous-looking craft, its details slowly becoming visible as it approached. It was bronze in color, with at least a dozen spikes sticking from it that had to be guns or laser cannons or something along those lines. There were very few lights visible, and the whole thing had the overarching shape of a crab closing in on its prey.

Grace nodded nervously and turned back towards the elevator doors. They opened for her, but before she could get on, Captain Roberts strode forcefully out, almost knocking her over.

"To your station, Ensign," snapped Roberts, who wasted no time in taking the seat that Roddenberry hastily evacuated. There really wasn't a place for the first officer on the bridge when the captain was present, so Roddenberry stood nervously behind Roberts' seat, leaning a bit on a nearby wall.

"Scoot over," said Grace testily to Kahkay. Kahkay shot her a conspiratorial grin as he made room at the one station on the bridge the recent graduates shared rotation at.

"So you and Karla, huh?" asked Kahkay suggestively, almost at a whisper.

"My engineering rotation is coming up. *Lieutenant Trinity* was just showing me some, um, interesting equipment on the ship," said Grace just as quietly, eyes on the panel, looking much busier than either of them needed to be, even if the station hadn't been double-staffed.

"Yeah, she showed me some interesting *equipment* last month, too," said Kahkay, smiling at the memory. Karla Trinity had been very adventurous in the bedroom. It didn't surprise Kahkay at all that the engineer would go both ways. "Maybe we should compare notes."

"You're a pig," shot back Grace.

"So is this why we never happened? You like women?" asked Kahkay, genuinely curious.

"I don't... I mean, Lieutenant Trinity is a friend. That's all," said Grace. Kahkay wasn't convinced, but the threatening vessel was getting awfully close so he decided to drop it for now. He could always press her for details later. Though, this might explain a lot.

"Have you tried to radio her?" Captain Roberts was asking Lieutenant Commander Larry Johnson at communications.

"Yes, sir," said Johnson, a man who had gone bald and grey way too young, leaving him looking much older than his thirty-seven years. Kahkay briefly wondered why, with all the personal care products and medical procedurals available these days, making it easier than ever to be attractive, Johnson didn't fix that? Maybe the same reason Roddenberry remained overweight; it just wasn't important to them. Kahkay found the notion ridiculous, but was glad he'd never had to bother with such things, being a naturally sexy stud.

"And?" asked Roberts impatiently.

"No respon- Wait. They're calling us," said Johnson.

"Put them on the big screen," said Roberts. The large rectangle at the front of the bridge, which had up until now been showing a starscape with the other ship in the center, flickered to a different image entirely. Kahkay flinched at the sight, and could sense Grace's disapproval of his reaction without needing to turn and look at her.

There were two aliens of equal prominence in the middle of the big screen, which showed from what Kahkay assumed was mid-torso up past their antenna. Assumed, because the Earth creature they most resembled was a cockroach, though they were completely blood red, and it was kind of hard to tell how far down their body went. It was also hard to tell where their mouths were until they moved them, the line of what passed for lips blending in with other crevices on their bodies, which were unclothed; or at least the parts visible of them were.

"Yessssss?" asked the one on the left, the hiss of his (?) voice coming through, despite the built-in translation software.

"How can we...," asked the other one, who looked nearly identical to Kahkay's untrained eyes, save for a couple extra creases.

"...help you?" finished the first.

"I'm Captain Gene Roberts of the *A.S.S. Enterprise*. Please identify yourselves," said Roberts, cool and collected as he nearly lounged in his chair, one elbow on the wide armrest.

"We are..."

"...Orso."

"Your name is Orso, or your species is Orso?" asked Roberts, confused.

"We are..."

"...Orso."

"That... didn't answer my question," said Roberts.

Both Orso made clicking noises that made Kahkay's skin crawl, reminding him of the insects that infested his Buffalo, New York home most winters. He wondered how Grace could appear so unaffected by them.

"We don't..."

"...understand. We..."

"...are Orso."

"OK," said Roberts, taking it in stride and moving on. Kahkay marveled at the captain's demeanor. He wasn't sure he'd be so cool when faced with something so far away from his frame of reference. Kahkay was eager to see strange new worlds, sure, but he wanted to understand them, and wasn't sure he'd be able to push the conversation forward until he at least got the basic info that Roberts was seeking.

"We have..."

"...never seen..."

"...a vessel..."

"...like yours," said Orso.

"This is the first vessel to ever leave Earth," said Roberts proudly.

"Earth?"

"Earth," stated the other Orso. "We have..."

"...heard of..."

"...you from..."

"...the Thrillians."

"Oh, yes. The Thrillians are lovely people," said Roberts. Kahkay did see Grace's expression change now. Leave it to an uptight woman like her to fail to appreciate everything the Thrillians had to offer. Kahkay found them a very entertaining species, and their women were some of the most pleasing in just about every way possible.

"Not..."

"...really."

"Are you at war with the Thrillians?" asked Roberts.

The clicking sounds from earlier got louder and went on for several seconds. Grace smiled beside him.

"What?" Kahkay asked her in confusion.

"They're laughing," she whispered back.

"How can you tell?" asked Kahkay.

"Look at their body movements," she said. The Orso were shaking up and down slightly and turned towards one another, the way humans did when they shared a joke. Was Grace right? Was that awful sound their way of showing amusement?

"We do..."

"...not have..."

"...weapons. We are..."

"...a science vessel..."

"...only."

"Oh," said Roberts. "I apologize. It looks like your starsheep has a great many guns."

"No, those..."

"...are scanners and..."

"...scientific instruments."

"Captain?" inquired Lieutenant Commander Johnson.

"One moment, Orso," said Roberts, who signaled to Johnson to cut the feed. "What is it, Johnson?"

"I did a query in the Thrillian database. The Orso is sort of a hive-mind species, with each consciousness being shared between two to six individuals. Apparently, all of them go by the name Orso, but have ways other than names to distinguish themselves."

"Are they telling the truth about the weapons?" asked Roddenberry. "Those don't look like scientific instruments to me."

"They are, sir," said Johnson. "The Thrillians are a business and entertainment-heavy society, so they don't get along well with the Orso, who only care about research and study to advance their understanding of the universe. The Thrillians report never having been attacked by them, and have found them very easy marks any time they've had actual scientific artifacts to pique the Orso's interest."

"Great. Unmute the call," said Roberts, turning back towards the screen. "Sorry about that, Orso. We were just looking you up in our database. I'm sorry we weren't familiar with you before. We humans also place great value in science and new understandings. Perhaps we can get together and see if we have any knowledge to offer one another?"

"That would…"

"…be most appreciated…"

"…and exciting for…"

"…us."

"Wonderful. Transmit a list of your dietary needs to us, and we'll prepare a dinner for you," said Roberts.

"Dinner?" asked the Orso.

"Food. Sustenance," said Roberts.

"Oh. Most…"

"…other species…"

"…find our eating…"

"…habits unpleasant."

"I'm always up for new experiences," said Roberts. "Let's give it a shot."

"We look…"

"…forward…"

"…to it."

Kahkay was also looking forward to it. As disturbing as he found the Orso, he was fascinated to find out what they ate.

"I can't believe we had to eat that," said Grace, feeling something very much like hung over the morning after the feast with the Orso. She slid into the seat across from Kahkay in the mess hall and put her head on the table.

"Eggs?" asked Kahkay, forking another chunk of the fluffy yellow substance from his plate. Grace groaned and felt the bile rise in her throat.

"How can you eat those after…?" she asked, not even able to finish her questions.

"Those weren't chicken eggs they had," said Kahkay, shrugging. "Besides, I feel like once you spend a few minutes with the Orso, you get used to them pretty quickly."

"Really?" asked Grace. "I don't see how. That was the worst evening I've spent since we left Earth! The mess, the smells…"

"Eh, I've seen worse," said Kahkay. He reached across the table for the bottle of ketchup, with which he practically drowned his scrambled eggs.

"Really? When?" asked Grace, flummoxed.

"Um, first breakfast this morning," said Kahkay absent-mindedly.

"First breakfast? It's seven a.m. When did you get up?" asked Grace.

"Only an hour ago. But you do not want to eat breakfast on the Orso ship. Trust me!" said Kahkay. "They went easy on us when they put in their dinner request."

"Wait a second. Why did you have breakfast on the Orso ship?" asked Grace, raising her head and narrowing her eyes. A disturbing thought occurred to her. "Oh, no. You didn't..."

"Yep," said Kahkay, smiling proudly.

"Not those two leaders?" asked Grace.

"Of course not," said Kahkay. "The foursome from the end of the table. You know, the ones getting drunk and handsy, er, pincery all night?" They were interested in some, um, research on human sexuality, and I was happy to oblige."

"Oh, you have got to be kidding me!" exclaimed Grace, and this time she didn't think she could hold back the vomit. She took a few deep breaths, concentrating really hard on not letting the contents of her stomach make an appearance. When she got things under control, she was not happy to see Kahkay grinning at her like a schoolboy who had just gotten away with something big. Which he sort of was.

"What? Didn't you sign up to explore strange, new lifeforms?" asked Kahkay.

"Explore doesn't mean screw," said Grace.

"You have your definition, I have mine," said Kahkay, starting in on his eggs again. Grace didn't say anything else, a million thoughts going through her head. After a few seconds, Kahkay noticed and put his fork back down. "You trying to figure out how we..."

"No!" said Grace quickly, interrupting him. "OK, yes," she admitted. "But don't tell me. I don't want to hear it from you."

"Would you like me to radio them and see if I can get you a hookup?" asked Kahkay, smug as ever.

"God, no," said Grace. She had to admit, part of her was impressed. She would never have been able to get past how the Orso looked, and she actually thought better of Dick Kahkay for not being caught up purely in appearance. On the other hand, the thought of Orso appendages crawling across her body made her skin... well, crawl.

"Was it...fun?" asked Grace, in spite of herself.

"Like you wouldn't believe," said Kahkay victoriously. "Four bodies, twenty-four arms, one mind, you do the math."

"Ew, I'd rather not," said Grace. Her stomach was calming down and she was starting to get her appetite back. She reached across the table and grabbed Kahkay's half-empty plate, pulling it towards her. He crossed his arms and smiled again, doing nothing to stop her.

"I get why you like having me around now, Gracie," said Kahkay. "I do the things you don't have the courage to."

"It's not a matter of courage," said Grace. "You do the things I'm not stupid enough to do."

"That hurts," said Kahkay, not meaning it. They sat in comfortable silence for a few minutes. "Wait, aren't you on the bridge rotation this morning?"

"Shit," said Grace, sitting up quickly.

"If you're not feeling well, I'd be happy to cover for you," offered Kahkay.

"Not a chance," said Grace. She shoveled the last couple bites of his eggs, grabbed his orange juice and chugged it, then ran for the elevator, smoothing her wrinkled, yellow tunic as she went.

During her brief ride up to the command deck, she wondered if Dick was right. Was she more afraid of alien life than she was willing to admit? He always seemed to bring out the best in her, a motivating factor in school. Should she let him do the same for her in adult life?

Maybe, she thought as she slipped over to her station. (Roddenberry was in the command seat with his nose in a book and didn't notice her tardiness.) That could explain why she kept coming back to him and liked having him around as much as she did. His manners may annoy her, but there were positive things she got from her friendship with him, too.

If she had to be truly honest, she probably never would have slept with Karla, er, Lieutenant Trinity, without Dick's influence. Trinity had cornered her during her workout, and Grace's first instinct was to walk away. But she hadn't been with anyone in months, not since she'd left the Academy, and she had to admit that she found it flattering to have a senior officer take an interest in her. It hadn't been Kahkay's voice in her head telling her to go for it (that would have been a huge turn off), but it could have been the spirit he'd evoked in her, encouraging her to enjoy these missions they'd been on.

She had had a little trouble getting into the swing of space travel. She missed her family, and the last boyfriend she'd had, Keith, she'd dumped simply because she didn't want to long for him while she was gone. Most of the planets they explored were devoid of life, which was rather lonely.

Naturally, she'd gravitated towards Dick. He was her closest friend on the *Enterprise*, and they'd been partnered up often enough since their launch. Had that been his doing, or did the duty officer just think it wise to give newbies someone they were comfortable with? Either way, he'd been beside her, challenging her as he'd always done, and in part because of him, she'd gotten past those empty feelings and begun to enjoy herself.

Well, and the fact that she'd always wanted to explore new worlds helped, too. Kahkay didn't deserve all the credit; she signed up for the A.S.S. and fought hard for this assignment for a reason. He'd just given her that extra push when she needed it, and for that, she was grateful.

But she knew she'd never get pushed far enough to sleep with the Orso.

CHAPTER THREE
UNEXPLORED PLANET UNDOSTRES IV, 2424

"We've arrived, Mork and Mindy," said Garry, then immediately cringed. He knew he was nervous about the new ship and was unintentionally slipping back into his references to the other Garry Marshall, but he didn't know why the uneasiness remained. After all, Dick had greeted him warmly, like the old friends they were. Surely they were about to pick up where they'd left things.

"Where have we arrived, Garry?" asked Dick. Oh, yeah, Garry remembered. Kahkay had just given him a direction to go in, not a destination. Garry had stopped because they've driven near a planet, and instinct told him that must be where they were heading, his brain distracted by other things. He had no idea where they actually were.

"This is planet Undostres IV," said Lieutenant Commander M-, whom Garry was already finding to be a very annoying know-it-all. Plus, his voice sounded evil, so Garry immediately didn't trust the reptilian science office. "It is an uninhabited planet at the very edge of charted territory."

"Like, the very edge? Already? That was faster than I got the dress off that date at the fifth grade dance!" returned Dick with a laugh. Garry joined in the chuckle, though no one else on the bridge seemed to. In fact, the beautiful Lieutenant Tokaladie seemed quite perturbed, which made Garry lower his estimation of her. Who wanted a woman that couldn't take a joke?

"Wh-eh. The fleet has actually explored quite far from Earth in most directions, but not this one," said M-. Was that judgment Garry heard in M-'s tone? The A.S.S. had only launched their first starsheep eight years ago! How could they be expected to have explored in all directions already?

"That's strange," said Dick. "Is there a reason we shouldn't have gone this way?" Oh, crap. What had Garry done? Just driving the ship without thinking. What kind of XO and pilot did that make him? He'd only been back in Dick's presence for minutes, and he was already failing his pal.

"Hmm...," said M-. "Not that I can think of. I believe it's just what you humans refer to as a 'blind spot.' There are definitely no dangerous, non-corporeal, god-like beings down here that my people have known about and avoided for centuries."

"That's... oddly specific," said Dick, looking hard at M-.

"Is that a racist jibe, sir?" bristled M-. "I know my people may appear odd to your *human* sssssensibilities, but-"

'No, no, no, it wasn't!" interjected Dick quickly. "Not racist. Not racist." Garry frowned. He made a mental note to keep an eye on that M-.

"There are no life signs on the planet, Captain," reported Tokaladie from her station. How was it the communication chief's job to look for life signs, wondered Garry. What was she up to? Trying to suck up to the new boss on day one?

"Perfect," said Dick. "Let's go down there."

"Who?" asked M-.

"Us," said Dick wearily, answering the obvious.

"Who?" asked M- again. What was he getting at, wondered Garry.

"Us. You, me, and Garry," said Dick. Damn it. Garry's joy at being chosen for the mission with Dick was immediately dampened by hearing M- would be included. Though it made sense. When exploring a strange, new, alien planet, it was probably wise to bring along a science officer. But did it have to be this one?

"And Who?" asked M-. Oh, Garry finally understood. Dick clearly didn't, and Garry chalked that up to M- being intentionally obtuse in his query. What a tool.

"I don't see what you're getting at, Lieutenant Commander," said Kahkay testily.

"Don't go overboard, Captain," cut in Garry, wanting to end this before M- upset Dick further. "M- means Lieutenant Who Grappa, our security chief." There were no life signs that the *Thrifty* picked up, but what if there was a new kind of life or other, hidden dangers? It was a good idea to take Who.

"Oh. Nah. I think we're good," said Dick. "It's uninhabited, right? Who needs security on a desert planet?"

"I think Who would be more comfortable going along," said M-.

"Aw, too bad," said Dick, not sounding at all like he meant it.

"Actually, sir, regulation 314.2 C states that-," started M-, and Garry rolled his eyes.

Thankfully, Dick interrupted. "Screw the regulations. You coming, Meowmeowmeow?" Garry had to suppress a laugh. Messing up M-'s overly complicated name was sure to get under his hide, and that was something Garry was all for.

M- made an annoyed noise. "I have green, scaly skin. I resemble an Earth velociraptor far more than your common household feline." Ah, so he *did* know what his name sounded like to humans.

"Who's watching the kids?" asked Garry.

Dick nodded at him, thankful for the reminder, and Garry's heart soared. He could get the hang of this first officer thing. "Foley, you're in charge. Keep a channel open. You coming, Maleficent?"

This time Garry did let out a giggle, though M- was less than amused, answering with a deep sigh and a defeated, "Yessss."

Garry leapt from his seat and joined Dick, and a few seconds later, even though he sat closest to the door, an unenthusiastic M-. As they rode the elevator down to the shuttle dock, Garry couldn't help but beam at Dick's back. Buzz-killing dinosaur man or no, Garry was finally getting to explore the galaxy with his best friend!

Lieutenant Commander M- was having a bad day. It wasn't the first bad day he'd had since joining the Associated Starsheep Services, and he was sure it wouldn't be his last. He wondered if he hadn't made a mistake.

M- was the first, and so far only, member of his species to want to join Earth's exploration fleet. Most races in the known galaxy saw space travel as a necessity to get to popular vacation spots or professional conferences. The humans were the first ones to step forward with a plan and a mission for actually mapping out where everything was, bringing races together, accomplishing research.

When M- heard about the A.S.S. for the first time, he had almost literally leapt for joy. He had resigned himself to being stuck on his own planet, able to study only what he found there. He had no support among others of his people, who were overall very religious, and didn't regard science very highly. And the planets the vacation shuttles traveled to weren't exactly hubs of academia, either.

But then Earth, who had only made first contact with other species shortly before M-'s birth, had announced its intention to create the A.S.S., and opened up the application process to beings of all planets, attempting to build a coalition. Most of the residents of the various worlds in the vicinity had been amused by the attempt, and the humans found very little support among their brethren to help out. But a few non-humans, like M- and Lieutenant Who Grappa, outcasts among their own peoples, had applied and been gratefully accepted.

So far, the experience had not lived up to M-'s dreams.

"Ahhh. Smell that, boys?" asked Captain Kahkay with a big grin as he stepped out of the shuttle, M- and Commander Marshall following. The new commanding officer seemed liked an overgrown child to M-, who had expected more from the people who had undergone the same rigorous program he'd worked through.

M- sniffed gingerly, looking out over the mostly barren, yellow-brown rock-dotted landscape. "I detect a slight sulfurous odor..."

"No, I mean smell *it*! We're probably the first living beings to ever smell this place!" M- could appreciate the sentiment, but he found the captain's words more than a little ridiculous.

Then a loud sound came from Commander Garry Marshall's butt. "And now I've added my beans of Boston to the mix!" said the first officer.

Kahkay practically bent in two laughing. "Hohoho. Oh, darn it, Garry! Haha! I wanted to be the first one to fart on an alien world!"

"Sorry, Captain Mean Jeans," said the disrespectful Commander Marshall, who didn't sound apologetic at all, even to M-'s ears, which were only just beginning to pick up and understand human tones, very different from those of his own species.

"The sulfur content has increased noticeably," said M-, annoyed. Was he the only one that took the credo of the A.S.S. seriously? He pulled out a handheld scanner and began to take readings of the formations around them.

"Oh, it'll fade," said Captain Kahkay dismissively. "So where should we explore first? How about over there? Ooo, ooo, or, or, how about over there? Ooo, n-n-no, how 'bout maybe over there?" Yes, a total child.

"Anywhere is fine with me, Laverne and Shirley. I've got my flask. It'll all look the same in a few minutes," said Commander Marshall. M- did have trouble with some human slang, and though he felt he had learned a lot over the fifteen years he'd spent among humans, he noticed that Commander Marshall used a lot more unfamiliar phrases than most. Who were Laverne and Shirley, and what was a flask?

"Nice! You know, I wish I'd brought a flask," said Captain Kahkay wistfully. M- saw Commander Marshall pull out his small, metal container and take a swig, and suddenly M- understood.

"What?" asked M-, flustered. "Regulation 62F.32 states that no alcohol should ever-"

"Lighten up, Mukie-moo. It's just booze," interrupted Captain Kahkay. M- bristled. He knew humans couldn't get his name quite right, but at least most of them tried. M- couldn't imagine having to serve under this... man for long if Kahkay was going to continue to be so flippantly rude.

"OK, here's the plan," said Captain Kahkay. "We're going to split up. Lots to do. We'll meet back here in about, say, five minutes."

"That doesn't seem like enough time to really see anything," protested M-, who had been so eager to come down just a few short minutes ago when he realized he would be on a planet no one had attempted to learn anything about yet. He'd be the first. But if he were only to be given five minutes...

"Oh, look, nice! Those rocks over there look like boobs!" exclaimed the captain, ignoring M- completely.

"Ooo, I like the lights in that direction, like the twilight of the golds," said Commander Marshall. M- shook his head and moved away, with the first officer and captain walking in different directions.

Only a minute later, M- was examining a peculiarly shaped stone when he saw a bright flash out of the corner of his eye and heard a strange energy sound. Spinning quickly, he noticed Commander Marshall staggering, a slight glow emanating from his person. Confused, M- started to raise his scanner towards Marshall when Kahkay, running towards them, interrupted and inadvertently knocked the scanner from M-'s hands.

"OK, crew! Back to the ship. I should definitely have used the bathroom before flying down," said Captain Kahkay, who apparently hadn't noticed anything about Commander Marshall. M- let out an irritated sigh, picked up the dropped device, and began heading for the shuttle. Research would have to wait.

At the door of the small vessel, Captain Kahkay turned and looked back at Commander Marshall, who hadn't moved from his spot. "Garry, you comin'?"

Now M- could see there was definitely something wrong with the XO, though what, he couldn't tell. Garry was on his feet but swaying, eyes rolled up in his head. This was not normal human behavior that M- had observed before.

"Sir, Commander Marshall looks a little strange...," said M-.

"Oh, he's just a little drunk, Mewmew. Let's go," said Kahkay.

M- shrugged, suddenly seeing an unusual plant growth near the entrance to the shuttle. Pulling a glass container from his satchel, M- carefully scooped it up and climbed into the shuttle by the time Commander Marshall had joined them. M- quickly became way more interested in his sample than in the strange human.

Lieutenant Who Grappa liked humans a lot. In the nine years she had served the A.S.S., she had striven to copy many of their mannerisms and speech patterns in order to better fit in, and found them exotic and interesting. True, Who still spoke mostly in single syllables, like the rest of her species, but she was finally starting to feel like a full member of a crew, despite being one of only a handful of non-humans on the ship.

But her new captain was starting off on the wrong foot.

Who was not a stickler for rules. She believed that many were put in place by bureaucrats who knew little about the conditions the officers serving on starsheeps would realistically face. So when her previous captains or security chiefs would disregard some of the minor ones, Who thought nothing of it. But there was one guideline that Who firmly believed in, and that was that the security chief should protect her captain.

This applied doubly so now that Who had switched to security. Having joined the A.S.S. as a doctor, Who had grown frustrated at being left behind, away from the action, only coming in after to set the broken bones or stitch a cut. The chief medical officer sometimes got to beamer down to planets, but was almost never on the bridge or had any insight into ship's operations. Security seemed like a better way to get involved.

Yet, after a brief rotation as a security officer and as an assistant security chief (the field seemed to lose a lot of personnel, allowing for rapid advancement), Who had finally achieved the rank of chief of security, only to be left behind on the very first mission. Had Who been on the bridge when Captain Kahkay had put together the team, she would have objected. But Kahkay had been early arriving on board, and the *Thrifty* had left Earth hours before it was scheduled to. And so by the time Who got her department together and got up to the command center, it was too late.

This would not stand. If Who were going to be chief of security, she was going to act like it. That's why she impatiently waited now, standing beside Lieutenant Tokaladie, for Captain Kahkay to come back. Surprisingly, Who wouldn't be waiting long.

The doors to the bridge opened and Kahkay rushed past before Who could say a word, heading for the bridge bathroom. Unfortunately, Kahkay left the door ajar and subjected them all to the sound of his long piss. Disgusting. Who wondered why, if Kahkay had to go so bad, he hadn't just used the facilities on the shuttle or the shuttle bay upon docking instead of coming in here and doing this practically in front of them. Especially when the shuttle had docked in the bay below instead of using the bridge's port? There were easier ways to do things.

The toilet flushed and Kahkay emerged, not even bothering to wash his hands. Who grimaced.

"Sir, Who would like a word with you," said Chief Engineer Foley when Who failed to speak up herself. She was so busy being repulsed by the captain's behavior that she had forgotten her anger at being left behind. It quickly came rushing back.

"Who?" asked Kahkay.

"Yes," said Who, stepping forward toward the captain.

"Oh, you, Who," said Kahkay, unconcerned. Did he not notice her scowl?

"Captain. Security. Must. Go. Mission," said Who.

"Sorry, Who. It was just a quick look around a deserted planet. Nothing to worry about. Now, let's go back down..."

Why was Kahkay not intimidated by her? Who stood a full head taller than the decently tall captain, and with a build not unlike that of an Earth gorilla, most humans found Who pretty intimidating. Kahkay was barely sparing her a glance, though, already heading back towards the elevator.

Who opened her mouth to insist on accompanying the captain back to the planet, figuring she could lecture him on proper procedure in the shuttle ride down, where he would be a captive audience, but held her thought as the *Thrifty* suddenly lurched forward.

The captain spun back towards the bridge in surprise. "What- What's that? Are we moving?"

Lieutenant Commander M-, who along with Commander Marshall, had followed Kahkay in a couple minutes ago and resumed his station, was the first to answer. "Commander Marshall has just taken us to top speed, heading for the edge of the galaxy."

Brow furrowed, Kahkay looked at this XO, sitting at the pilot's station on the ship. "Well, Garry? What's the meaning of this?"

"I'm sorry, Captain. You are not in charge any more. Me and the chimp are," intoned Commander Marshall. Lieutenant Who had not yet met their first officer, but his voice did not sound like other humans' usually did. It was almost like he was in a trance or something. And she desperately hoped he wasn't referring to her when he said 'chimp,' as she looked much more like a gorilla than a chimp, and either would be an offensive label.

"The hell I'm not," said Kahkay, angry. "Turn this ship around, right this instant!"

"I'm afraid I can't do that, Captain," said Commander Marshall.

Who bunched her fists and looked to Kahkay for a sign that she should strike this insubordinate, possibly treasonous, officer. Kahkay looked more concerned than scared, and that surprised her. Who was this man to the captain?

Kahkay stared at Garry worriedly, his best friend having just taken control of his vessel. Kahkay admitted, their reconnection had been a little forced. Garry had seemed very happy to see him, and Kahkay was pleased, too. Admittedly, Kahkay hadn't been as good at keeping up their friendship as Garry had, but he still felt as close to the man as ever, even if they hadn't seen each other since the Academy. It was like they hadn't skipped a beat.

At first, Garry had acted the same as Kahkay felt, if perhaps a little overeager, which Kahkay had chalked up to just the way Garry was, the same as he had Garry's strange references that Kahkay wasn't getting. But now, deadly serious, hijacking the *Thrifty*, calling him 'Captain' instead of 'Dick,' Kahkay wondered if maybe he hadn't misjudged Garry, or had perhaps not given his XO the reunion Garry had hoped for.

Kahkay stepped up beside Garry at the pilot controls at the front of the bridge. Garry didn't turn to look at him, eyes on the big screen at the front, which showed stars streaking by. "Garry, it's me. Dick. What are you doing?" Kahkay tried appealing to that friendship they shared.

"Garry isn't here anymore, Captain Kahkay," intoned Garry flatly. Frankly, it was a bit scary. Kahkay had never, ever seen him act anything like this.

"You're freaking me out here, Gare. Are you feeling all right?" asked Kahkay with concern.

"This is the best I've ever felt, love American style," said Garry, in keeping with the new, weird speech pattern.

"That's not what the Remax women of Planet Beta would say, I'm sure! Heh," said Kahkay, hoping that bringing up a particularly erotic spring break they'd shared might nudge Garry out of this... whatever this was.

"Captain, the ship cannae take this speed for long!" said a panicked Chief Foley from the back of the bridge. Kahkay gave Foley a nod, but kept his focus on the immediate problem.

"Garry, did you eat mushrooms while we were down on the surface? Surely you must be smarter than to stick some strange things in your mouth," scolded Kahkay lightly, but when Garry didn't respond, Kahkay's stomach dropped. This wasn't the Garry he knew. Which meant either he didn't know his buddy at all any more, or something had happened and Garry wasn't in control of his own body. Kahkay desperately hoped for the second option.

"We're gonna break apart!" said Foley, and Kahkay finally turned to respond.

"Fine, fine. Foley, shut off the engine," said Kahkay. Immediately, the ship slowed, coming to a quick halt. Garry turned to look dangerously at Kahkay, and now Kahkay could see there was something weird with his eyes. In place of pupils were constantly pulsating yellow starbursts.

"Turn the engine back on, evil Roy Slade," said Garry in a voice that chilled Kahkay to the bone, though Kahkay was determined not to show any fear.

"I'm sorry, Garry. You don't give the orders. Who, toss him in a cell. He can sleep off his buzz." Kahkay knew this wasn't just a drug trip, but better not to panic the crew until he figured out what he was dealing with.

Lieutenant Who stepped forward, and Kahkay was momentarily distracted. Was there almost a spark between the ape-like security chief and himself? That was weird. Who definitely wasn't Kahkay's type. He had an equal opportunity policy for females and other, alien genders, but Kahkay almost never messed with males, which, going by appearances, Who surely was. Kahkay quickly shook it off, knowing this wasn't the time.

"Come. With. Who," intoned Who as he approached the pilot.

"No thank you, Sheriff Who," said Garry, facing forward again.

"Come. With. Who," repeated the security chief insistently. This time, Garry not only faced Who, but stood up. In one swift motion, before anyone else could react, Garry picked up Lieutenant Who and tossed him forward. Who flew several feet through the air, slamming into the wall next to the big screen and crumpling to the floor.

Kahkay was stunned. "Wow, Who is not a small guy! How did you throw him like that?"

"Turn the engines back on or else," said Garry.

"Or else what?" asked Kahkay with bravado he did not feel.

"Or else, make room for daddy, I begin killing the crew."

"Joke's on you. I haven't been here long enough to know any of them anyway," said Kahkay, trying desperately to keep the situation lighter than it was. He wondered if any of the rest of the bridge crew, all of whom seemed frozen at their stations, bought the flippant attitude? He certainly wasn't convincing himself. What a way to begin his captainship!

CHAPTER FOUR
UNEXPLORED PLANET
UNDOSTRES IV, 2424

Garry felt very strange. He could hear his voice and see the bridge around him, including his best friend, Dick, looking at him with a mixture of concern and anger, but he couldn't control his body or speech at all. It was like he was gazing through a Vaseline-smeared window, or peering up from the bottom of a swimming pool, or was just really, really drunk.

What really startled Garry, though, was when he threatened to start killing the crew. That's when he realized his body definitely didn't belong to him anymore. He didn't understand how that had happened. Well, it started when he got struck by that energy beam down on the planet. But his loss of self-determination had occurred slowly as they came back up to the ship, at first feeling like he was in a dream, and it was only now that he became aware of another consciousness within his brain.

Did Dick just say that he didn't care if any of the crew died? No, that wasn't the Dick Garry knew and loved. His Dick was compassionate, and Garry was sure that, as a captain, Dick would do anything for his crew. Garry thought the world of the man after all those nights they'd spent drinking together. Obviously he did, or Garry wouldn't have sent him all those shot glasses over the years.

The other being inside Garry grabbed the stray thought about the shot glasses and latched on, much to Garry's dismay.

"Then I will start smashing your shot glass collection," said Garry's mouth, though it wasn't Garry speaking.

"You wouldn't dare! You bought half the glasses in it!" exclaimed Dick, and Garry's heart soared. Dick did care about him, about their friendship! At that moment, Garry knew everything would be all right. Dick would save him, wouldn't let anything happen to his pal.

Smash! Garry heard faintly the sound of a shot glass in the cabin below burst into bits. Which was weird, because they shouldn't have been able to hear it through the floor. Someone had to be pumping an audio feed of Kahkay's apartment into the bridge.

"Uh, how are you doing that? My apartment is downstairs in the ship?" asked Dick, and Garry realized that the noise was actually the least of their concerns. The fact that this intruder was able to smash shot glasses he couldn't reach, in a room he wasn't in, was far more disturbing.

Two more shot glasses smashed. Garry didn't know how he knew, but he realized that the three broken were three of the oldest he'd sent Dick, and three of his favorites. Garry's heart broke, and he began to fight back. He had to get his body under his control again.

"Oh, all right, all right! Please, dear lord, stop!" said Dick.

"Are you going to turn the engines back on, Joey Bishop?" asked Garry's body. Garry didn't say that, of course, but he could feel a little of the control come back. The being tried to smash another shot glass, and Garry somehow managed to prevent it. He wasn't sure how, but his will did matter here, and the being who invaded his body wasn't all-powerful.

"Will you tell me where you're taking us?" asked Kahkay.

Garry felt himself slip, and another shot glass was smashed. He quickly pushed back, but it was like trying to grab hold of a slime-oid being, which were fun to sleep with because of their fluid-filled bodies, but incredibly hard to actually hold onto. Every time Garry thought he got purchase, it would slip away from him.

"All right! All right. Foley, turn the engines back on," said Dick. Garry tried to get his mouth back. He wanted to communicate with Dick, let his friend know he was fighting for him, but he just couldn't quite do it.

"I cannae do it, sir. After an emergency shut down, they need at least an hour to reboot," said Foley. Garry racked his brain. Was that true? He wasn't sure. Garry had never been all that good at engineering. The being within him seemed to accept it, though, and that was all that mattered.

"I cannot stay on this ship, barefoot in the park, for another hour," said the being.

"Garry... speak to me. What's happening?" asked Dick. Garry inwardly celebrated! Dick knew it wasn't him doing these things! For a second, the extra boost of elation this gave Garry allowed him to assert dominance, and his eyes cleared, returning to normal.

Garry saw Dick's face light with understanding, just before Garry was shoved back down again.

"I am not Garry," said the being through Garry's mouth. "I spy Zeusifer, a being you puny humans would consider a God. I hitched a ride off the planet and I've been trapped in this form you call 'Garry.'"

"Captain," said Lieutenant Tokaladie from her station. "I detect a large energy build up in this room."

It wasn't just in the room, it was in him. Garry could feel it in his own skin. Zeusifer was somehow growing bigger, but there wasn't room for him to expand much more. Things were already crowded in here. Garry felt himself being compacted into less and less space.

"Correct," said Zeusifer out loud. "This Gomer Pyle is not large enough to hold my true form for very long. I was just planning to stay in Garry long enough to get to Topleesia I." So Zeusifer was still making references to the other Garry Marshall's work. That meant he was still using Garry's brain. Could that be a hook Garry could use to wrest himself back?

"The party planet!" said Dick.

"Right, where I would leave this form like I left *The Lucy Show*. But I cannot wait an hour, so I guess you're all going to die now."

"Mee-na-ma," said Dick, and Garry could see how much effort he was making to stay calm in front of the crew, though he wasn't sure the others, who didn't know Dick as well, could see the panic inside their captain. "How far are we from the planet we just left by shuttle?"

"About fifty minutes, sir," said M-.

"Gare... Whatever your name was, can you hold it together until we get you back home?" asked Dick.

"Maybe," said Garry's body, and Garry wasn't sure if it was Zeusifer or himself that said it, still fighting the being that threatened to consume him from the inside out.

"Great. Garry and I are taking a shuttle back to the planet," said Dick. Yes! Garry knew Dick would rescue him! "Meenie, you're in charge. Follow us when you can get the engine started."

"Cap'n, I don't think that's wise...," said Foley.

"It'sss fine. Sounds like a plan," said M-, and Garry spared a brief flash of hate towards the science officer who would abandon Garry's best friend.

"But if the energy being erupts while trapped in the shuttle with you, Captain...," protested Foley, unwilling to finish his thought.

"...then I will be the shortest serving captain in history, and Mee-na-ma will be the first alien captain in the fleet," said Dick with just a hint of wryness.

"I would remind you how racist it is that there are no alien captains, or even that you're calling me an alien. But your logic seems sound," said M-. "Goodbye, Captain. It was an, uh... pleasure serving under you."

"You're going to come pick me and Garry up in an hour," said Dick.

"If you survive," said M-. "But if you don't, it was nice to meet you. Take care." Garry felt another flash of rage for the reptilian being, and it gave him strength to fight on against Zeusifer. If Dick was going to save Garry, then Garry was going to make sure he made it back to save Dick from that mutinous M-.

"You *will* pick us up," said Kahkay again, firmly.

"Sure, sure," said M-, unconvincingly.

"I'll make sure he does, Captain," said Foley.

"Thanks, Foley. Come on, Garry," said Dick. Zeusifer stood up from the station and followed Kahkay towards the shuttle dock, Garry fighting him the entire way.

Captain Richard S. Kahkay piloted the shuttle easily towards Undostres IV, every so often glancing over at the form of his best friend, Garry Marshall, slumped in the chair behind him. Garry's body had been still most of the trip, twitching every once in awhile, but other than that, remaining silent. The body didn't seem about to explode or anything.

Kahkay hoped Garry was all right. He knew that whatever was in control of this form right now wasn't Garry, but he could have sworn that he saw hints of his chum bubbling up to the surface periodically on the bridge. If Kahkay's suspicions were correct, Garry was fighting Zeusifer, trying to regain control. Kahkay hoped Garry could do it.

This was Kahkay's first mission as captain. He had worked very hard to get to this point, and in only eight years after graduation. Surely, whatever fates had allowed him to reach this pinnacle wouldn't also permit him to lose his closest amigo on his very first day, would they?

The shuttle landed gently on the planet, and Kahkay sighed, "Whew. We made it," more for Zeusifer / Garry's benefit than his own. Kahkay was beginning to doubt Zeusifer was correct about the impending death if it remained in Garry's body.

Garry's eyes snapped open, the golden bursts now filling the entire sockets, and Kahkay quickly realized how wrong he was. Zeusifer must have been silent because it was using all its willpower to hold things together. Now, moving again, the yellow light was shining through Garry's skin, out of every orifice, and was clearly contained by the thinnest of margins.

"Barely. Dominic's dream, I'm about to explode," said Zeusifer.

"Well, don't do it on me," said Kahkay, taking Garry by the arm and escorting him off the shuttle, back onto the barren, uninhabited world. They got about twenty feet away from the shuttle, then Kahkay stopped walking, stepping back just a bit. He braced himself for whatever came next, but nothing happened. Garry just stood in place, shaking and flashing.

"Wait, you're going to exit Garry now, right?" asked Kahkay.

"No," intoned Zeusifer, voice stronger and more powerful than it had ever been before.

"You can't leave his body?" asked Kahkay, confused. He was sure that once they got to this planet, Zeusifer would zip out, and then Kahkay and Garry could find a way to trick him and sneak back to the shuttle, returning to the *Thrifty* safe and sound.

"I can, I just don't want to," said Zeusifer. "If I did, there'd be someone left behind, the other sister if you will, to warn the crew that I'd taken over *your* body, and then I'd never get to Topleesia I."

"Wait, what?" asked Kahkay, totally confused now.

"You thought I'd just give up after one failed Wednesday night out?"

"Well... yeah," said Kahkay, which wasn't exactly true, but close enough. He didn't think Zeusifer would give up, he just assumed he'd be able to defeat it.

"This is why humans suck. Nothing in common. So... cocky," said Zeusifer.

"Yes?" asked Kahkay, confused as to why Zeusifer had said his name.

"Yes, you're cocky," said the being.

"No, it's pronounced Kahkay," said Kahkay helpfully.

"That's not what I... Dick?" The yellow bursts faded and Garry's gaze came through. Kahkay took a step towards him, but the yellow quickly returned. Then it disappeared again. Back and forth, Kahkay could finally truly see the war going on between the two consciousness in the frail form. It scared him more than he cared to admit.

"Never mind," said Zeusifer. "Come back," said Garry. "Runaway bride!" said Zeusifer. "Can't... take... more...," they screamed together, and then the last, clearly Garry again, "JOANIE... LOVES... CHACHI!"

The energy was no longer contained. Garry's body exploded in a burst of blood, guts, bile, and an assortment of other organ pieces and liquids. It shot up into the air, then rained back down, coating Kahkay and the ground around him.

"Garry, nooooooooooooooooooooooooo!" screamed Kahkay, dropping to his knees in grief, his mind struggling to comprehend what he had just witnessed. Then, in shock, his facade, the one that projected confidence and a sense of humor no matter the situation, took over.

"Oh, I have Garry guts on me, and in my mouth a little." He spit, expelling a bit of his friend that had made it inside. Staggering to his feet, he tried to wipe the gore off of himself. Too late, he noticed that where Garry had so recently stood floated a murky, yellowish energy cloud, and it moved towards him.

"Hey, energy... Oh, god, energy cloud, don't come over here. No, no, stay away! Stay away!" Kahkay danced quickly to put some distance between himself and Zeusifer's true form, but the cloud followed, reaching out with smoky tendrils to try to invade Kahkay's orifices. Moaning and groaning, Kahkay continued, "Get away from my butt. There you go. No, no, ah, ooo, ooo, yeah, right there, ohhh yea, oh, nope, nope. Take that cloud!"

It was no use. Kahkay was going to lose this game. Try as he might, he wasn't going to escape. There was a dark ball of color, a roiling mass of power, coming together at the center, and Kahkay expected it to surge out and zap him any moment, sentencing him to the same fate as Garry.

Color surrounded Kahkay and the tingle began. Everything went dark, briefly. When he opened his eyes, it was all different.

"Engines are back online, sir," reported Chief Engineer Foley.

"Excellent, Chief Foley. Set course for-," began Lieutenant Commander M- from the captain's chair.

"We're going back to get the captain now, right?" interrupted Foley, obviously on edge.

M- sighed. "Yes, we are."

"Good. I just wanted to make sure," said Foley. "Laying in course for Undostres IV now."

"Why do you doubt me, Chief Foley?" asked M-.

"Excuse me?" asked Chief Foley.

"You did not seem as if you trusted that I would go to the planet where Captain Kahkay was last known to be heading," said M-.

"Well, you said *if* he survives and all that. Didn't sound like you were hoping he would make it," said Chief Foley a bit sheepishly.

M- sighed again. "To human ears, my voice may sound evil, but I am *not* evil. Of course I will do my duty and retrieve our commanding officer, if it is not too late."

"All right," said Chief Foley, but M- could tell the engineer still didn't believe him. M- had been trying to understand humans for years, but clearly he still had a long way to go in learning how to communicate with them effectively.

"Lieutenant Tokaladie, please return to your station. Chief Foley, go," said M-. Lieutenant Tokaladie rose from where she knelt beside Lieutenant Who, still unconscious on the floor, and stiffly walked back towards her desk. Was she annoyed with M-, too? M- couldn't imagine why.

"We're here, sir," said Chief Foley.

"Lieutenant Tokaladie, please call the captain," ordered M-.

"Yes, sir," said Lieutenant Tokaladie. A ringing echoed throughout the bridge. M- reached down in the cushion of the captain's chair he was perched on and removed a phone. The screen showed that the *Thrifty* was calling.

"Oh," said Lieutenant Tokaladie in surprise, cancelling the call.

"We have to beamer down and get 'im!" said Chief Foley excitably.

"No," said M-.

"No?!" asked Chief Foley.

"No," echoed M-. "It is too dangerous to beamer down any more crew members."

"You're just gonna leave him down there, alone with that... thing?" asked Chief Foley. "You *are* evil!"

"I am *not* evil!" snapped M-. "Chief Foley, please lock onto Captain Kahkay to beamer him up."

"You good-for-noth-," began Chief Foley. "Oh. Right. Smart idea, sir. Locking onto the captain now."

"When you have a lock, beamer him up immediately," ordered M-.

"Aye, sir," said Chief Foley. A moment later, the form of Kahkay, covered in a red, chunky substance, his blue tunic torn, appeared on the bridge.

"Oooo. Whew! Thank god! That thing was trying to anally rape me! I think," said Captain Kahkay, heaving a huge sigh of relief. "Wait a second, we have... we have transporters? Why have we... why have we been using the shuttles instead?"

"Shuttles are cheaper, and we call them beamers, sir, not transporters. That term would be copyright infringement," said M-.

"I don't care what they're called. Get us out of here!" ordered Captain Kahkay.

"Aye, sir," said Chief Foley cheerily. The ship took off.

M- was less trusting, looking Captain Kahkay over carefully. He wasn't sure what had happened down on the planet, but he wasn't entirely sure this was their captain standing in front of them. "Wait. How do we know you're really Captain Kahkay and not Zeusifer in Captain Kahkay's body?" he asked suspiciously.

"Ummm, I don't know," said Captain Kahkay, taking the question seriously. "Ask me something that only I would know."

"I don't know you well enough for that, sir," said M-, still eyeing the human.

"Then I guess you'll just have to take my word for it," said Captain Kahkay.

Near the wall, Lieutenant Who groaned and sat up. Lieutenant Tokaladie looked like she wanted to rush from her station and help Lieutenant Who, but Lieutenant Commander M- was pleased to see that the communications head had the professional state of mind not to abandon her post.

"Is he all right?" asked Captain Kahkay, looking at Who.

For a moment, M- was confused. Lieutenant Who was very clearly female, but there was no one else Captain Kahkay could be referring to, so M- answered about the security chief. "I don't know yet," said M-. "We haven't picked up our doctor."

"Ah. Yes, OK, we should probably go do that," said Captain Kahkay. "And what planet is our doctor on?"

"Earth," said M-.

"Why didn't she just get on board the ship when I did?" asked Captain Kahkay.

"Well, she was about to, but you were in such a hurry to leave, we left her behind," said M-.

"Lord, man. Why didn't you say anything?" asked Captain Kahkay.

"I started to," said M-. "But you were so excited..."

"You know, an evil man might have purposely left without a doctor in the hopes that his captain would be injured and he could take command," said Captain Kahkay, eyeing M- suspiciously. M- found he did not like this kind of attention, and knew he must immediately clear his name.

"That is true, sir," M- answered honestly. "But as I've said, I'm *not* evil. Nor am I a man." M- finished triumphantly, sure he had proven his point.

"Riiiiight," said Captain Kahkay skeptically, confusing M-. What further evidence did the captain need to trust him?

"Shall I set a course for Earth, sir?" asked Foley gleefully, seemingly elated to have the captain back. M- opened his mouth to ask about Commander Marshall, but as Kahkay looked ahead with a steely gaze, the reptilian being knew that was a moot point.

"Yeah, Foley. Go!" ordered Kahkay. The ship shot forward, heading back towards Earth.

Kahkay shifted in his chair, staring absently at the screen in front of him. He knew it wasn't a true window, and the stars streaking by were from a live feed on the exterior of the ship, but it felt real to him. More real than this job, anyway.

Kahkay had assumed he was born for command. From a young age, he was a natural leader among his peers, on sports teams and in school. He had a joviality and charm that seemed to sit well with most people, at least superficially, and there was seldom a problem he could not talk his way out of.

When the A.S.S. was formed and it was announced they would be launching an entire fleet of starsheeps, well, that just seemed like the next thing for him to do. Kahkay had always been a little restless in his hometown in upstate New York, and he didn't really have a purpose until the A.S.S. advertised one he could buy into. It just felt right for him, and his fate was sealed.

So why, then, was this not working out the way everything else had? It was still his first day of command and he'd already blundered into an impossible situation, without a doctor no less, and lost Garry Marshall, not just his second-in-command, but one of the few people who knew and cared about him long after Kahkay left his orbit. That was a real blow.

Absent-mindedly, Kahkay flipped though Garry's psych profile on a portable computer pad. He suddenly felt the urge to know Garry the way that Garry had seemed to know him, something Kahkay had been neglectful of over the years, and now regretted. The more he skimmed, the more the words held his attention.

The man in this file was not the Garry Marshall Dick had gone to the Academy with. This record told of a broken man, a lonely man. He performed his duties just fine, most of the time, at least until he got close to his current rank. But he'd also become withdrawn, a loner, obsessed with an old Earth producer who shared his name. What had happened?

As Kahkay tried to dig further and further in the computer system, he felt more and more ashamed. Had he done this to Garry? Had he made Garry's young life so awesome that there was no living up to it after? The psych profilers seemed to think so, and clearly the only reason Garry had been assigned to the *Thirfty* was out of some misguided hope that being around Kahkay, whom Garry had mentioned frequently during his evaluations, would help him turn things around.

So not only had Kahkay screwed up Garry's past, he'd screwed up his future, too. He had been Garry's chance to get his life back on track, and he'd utterly blown it.

Just like Kahkay had blown his own life. He thought back to how he had achieved this command, and suddenly felt bad about it. He hadn't thought he'd done anything wrong, but Grace hadn't returned his calls in quite some time, and he had to assume that had something to do with his actions. The same kind of actions that were failing spectacularly the first time he got into this chair.

Was Richard D. Kahkay cut out to captain a starsheep? Had he just been getting by on luck and bravado his whole career, only to find himself lacking when the time came to actually perform? Had the lack of effort his life had required thus far poorly prepared him from the reality of being in charge of a ship and a crew of more than seven hundred individuals? Should he step aside now, before he did any more damage?

Kahkay glanced around the bridge. Tokaladie saw Kahkay's glance and quickly turned away, not willing to meet his eyes. The ensigns and lowly lieutenants on rotation wouldn't even give him that much. Only Foley caught his gaze and smiled, eager to serve and be Kahkay's friend. Kahkay didn't deserve him.

Taking a quick glance over the other Garry Marshall's resume, Kahkay finally knew what he wanted to say for his first log entry. He flipped the switch on his armrest to begin recording the words that would later be transcribed in paper form for him by his yeoman.

"Captain's Diary, or as Garry would say, *The Princess Diaries*. September 8th, 2424. I lost my best friend today, the man I trust and love most in this world." Kahkay could feel himself choking up, and also the eyes of the bridge crew looking at him. He wanted to be sincere, but he also didn't want to show weakness in front of the staff, so he quickly lightened the mood with a joke. "And also several of my favorite shot glasses, including the awesome one with the dancing naked Thrillians on it. Neither loss, though, will be easy to bear, but at least I think I have a brave crew under me now, and that helps."

Kahkay spared a quick glance around proudly, hoping he had inspired those who could hear him. Most looked back at least sympathetically. Mookiemoo, though, scowled at Kahkay. Kahkay narrowed his eyes back. That one was trouble.

"Except for Lieutenant Commander Mememe... whatever his name is. He's definitely evil. End diary." Mothman looked confused, but Kahkay allowed a small grin. Now the science officer knew Kahkay was onto him, if there had been any doubt before.

The grin faded as soon as Mothballs turned back to his work. Kahkay *would* keep an eye on Millie, but suddenly, the captain didn't feel confident that he was up to the task. Kahkay hoped Maltedmilk wouldn't be his undoing.

CHAPTER FIVE
UNKNOWN PLANET, DEEP SPACE, 2419

Lieutenant Grace Thomas turned from the communications station towards the captain's chair. Commander Larry Johnson, first officer of the *A.S.S. Enterprise*, was studying the planet on the big screen in front of them intently, as if he could see what was happening on the surface below.

"Sir," said Grace. "Captain Roberts is requesting assistance."

"Got it," said Johnson. "Have Lieutenant Kahkay and a team of security officers meet me in the beamer room." He rose from his chair and was halfway to the elevator before Grace could protest.

"I'm sorry, sir, but Captain Roberts specifically asked you to stay on the ship," said Grace.

"I know what my orders are." Johnson's voice was steely. He'd taken to the first officer position quite well, much better than his bookish predecessor, but he was beginning get restless. He wanted the responsibility of a captain, no longer content to sit on the sidelines when things got rough. Grace wondered how long the A.S.S. would make him wait for his own command.

"Of course, sir, it's just...," said Grace, trailing off.

"Yes?" asked Johnson, not angry, genuinely willing to let her have her say, just like a good commander should.

"Sir, if something's happened to Captain Roberts, then you..." Grace could have finished the sentence, but it would have been disrespectful. The bald man in the green uniform knew what she meant.

"Right. You're right, Lieutenant," said Johnson. "You meet Kahkay in the beamer room and lead the team."

"Me, sir?" asked Grace in surprise.

"You're command track, right?" asked Johnson, though of course he knew the answer.

"Yes, sir," said Grace, straightening in her chair.

"Show me your leadership skills," said Johnson, turning to stalk back to the chair from which he oversaw everything, but that also made him helpless to take part.

"Yes, sir," said Grace. She sent a quick message to the security department and strode into the elevator.

She wasn't surprised, upon arriving in the beamer room, to find Lieutenant Dick Kahkay standing smugly amid a squad of other security officers in the chamber. He probably hadn't come because of her message. He'd probably been waiting here for hours.

"What's the situation, Grace?" asked Dick, not looking at all surprised to see her instead of Commander Johnson.

"It's not good, *Lieutenant Kahkay*," returned Grace, emphasizing his rank and last name to get across that she did not appreciate his informality under the current circumstances. "Captain Roberts and his team are pinned down."

"So we're what, search and rescue?" asked Dick, pulling his laser gun from his holster.

"Essentially, yes. I'm in charge. Don't make a move until I say." Grace took her place beside Kahkay.

"Of course," said Dick, almost dismissively.

"I mean it," said Grace.

"I wouldn't dream of it. *Sir.*" The last word may have been borderline sarcastic, but at least she had gotten her point across. She hoped Dick would respect it.

He wasn't always the most obedient officer, especially since he'd been on his security rotation, which thankfully was almost up. She hoped she wouldn't be so cavalier during her own days in the department, which were fast approaching. She'd heard plenty about how the security men and women were a different breed, and she wasn't overly eager to join them. But part of being in the command track was a required number of hours served in each field.

Grace's musings ended abruptly as the beamer deposited her, Dick, and four armed soldiers on the outskirts of a major skirmish. The town before them was burning, smoke immediately rushing in to choke their lungs, people running amidst the chaos, screams and cries coming from somewhere within the flames.

Ducking low, Grace moved behind the closest wall, the others following, Dick near enough to practically touch her. She had to admit, she didn't mind his presence right now, her annoyance already gone and she was feeling much more secure with her closest friend by her side.

"Where's the captain?" asked Ensign Smith-Jones, peering through the haze.

Grace pulled out a portable computer pad and consulted it, searching for the captain's signal. It was only a few blocks away. She wished the beamer tech had put them down closer, given the situation, but assumed it was probably pretty hard to find a good spot in this mess.

"Stay low, be alert," said Grace, her own laser pistol in one hand, the pad in the other, mainly keeping her eyes off the screen as she ducked between shelters and shields, moving between the clay-and-wood structures of the village. Several times she paused to shoot a would-be attacker, as did the others in her group, but most of the inhabitants left them alone as soon as they glimpsed the orange and yellow tunics, their conflict not being with the A.S.S.

Considering the battle all around them, it didn't take long to reach Captain Roberts' position. His signal came from the basement of one of the taller structures, maybe a government building, towards the center of town.

There were no other A.S.S. signals in the area, which was troubling in of itself, since Roberts had beamed down with a full escort of his own. And they'd have to enter single file down a dark stair case that had several places for those hiding in wait to come down behind and cut off their retreat. Despite what very much felt like a trap, Grace knew that they needed to enter, their commanding officer's life quite likely at stake; Captain Roberts wouldn't have activated the emergency call if he didn't need them, and Grace would not let him down, at least not without confirming he was truly lost.

Motioning for the others to follow closely, Grace led the entry, flipping the flashlight option on her pad to light their way. As in most of the town, the power seemed to be out here. She moved as quietly as she could down the stone-hewn stairs, the sounds from outside fading as the last security officer closed the door to the exterior world, leaving them in musty darkness.

The staircase was longer than a standard Earth floor would require, long enough that the six of them were all more than halfway down before, as expected, several shadowy figures, definitely armed, came from landings and alcoves behind them to block the way they had come. Grace didn't immediately give the order to fire, wanting to get the full picture and the captain's status before doing so, so she ignored their stalkers and kept going. Thankfully, Dick and the others did the same.

At the bottom, a door was ajar, torchlight flickering through the crack. Stashing her pad back in her belt, Grace pushed the door open, and unfortunately, was not really surprised at what she saw. Her laser pistol went up as she stood firm in the doorway, determined not to lead the team in where they could be more easily grabbed.

Across the room, certainly a lure, sat Captain Gene Roberts bound to a chair, bloodied and bruised. His phone, from which the distress signal had gone out, was on a table next to him. Around Roberts were more than a dozen men with weapons, mostly spears, though a few primitive firearms were present.

Now that her hunch was confirmed, Grace took swift action. She hit a button on her own phone without pulling it out, her signal not a distress call. At the same time, she ordered "retreat!" to those behind, stepped back, and pulled the door closed. Using her laser pistol, she melted the knob and lock, hopefully sealing it well enough to give them time to fight their way back out of the building without allowing Roberts' captors to pin them from behind

Lasers shot upwards into the dark, shadowy figures falling. But their attackers were not defenseless, hurling a variety of weapons down at the A.S.S. security team. First Ensign Jovi fell, then Lieutenant Yeager. Grace confirmed both were dead as the remaining four moved past them and headed for the outside.

The problem was, there were *a lot* of enemy combatants pouring into the stairwell, and every hiding spot they'd filed out from on the way down seemed to be closed to the A.S.S. as they passed. The result was a confined corridor that kept the fighting contained and two-sided, but with escape firmly blocked by the bad guys, whose glowing red eyes made this scene feel like it was torn from a horror movie.

Grace stumbled as a projectile hit her leg and pain shot up her body. "Keep moving," she ordered, trying and failing to stand. Dick ignored her and picked her up, tossing her arm around his shoulder, leaving them each with only one free hand to continue defending themselves. Dick's available appendage was his left, not his dominant hand, but his shots still seemed to hit his targets far more often than not.

They made it a mere four stairs from the top, and lost one more crewwoman, Ensign Hattie, before Grace realized they were not going to get out this way, not now. The door they had come in from sprang open and at least a dozen more figures poured through. At the same time, the portal in the basement, upon which Roberts' assaulters had been banging for several minutes, popped open, and some of those ran up the stairs.

"Surrender. We surrender!" shouted Grace over the melee. She holstered her laser pistol, pulled herself away from Dick, and put her hands in the air. He gave her a brief look of disappointment, or so Grace thought; it was hard to tell in this lack-of-lighting, then followed suit, Ensign Smith-Jones doing the same.

These primitive people may not speak the same language as the A.S.S., but they understood when they had won. They stopped firing and throwing, instead swarming close and grabbing everything the three officers had from their belts. Then, without warning, Grace took a hard blow to the head and fell, passing out on the stairs.

Lieutenant Richard P. Kahkay regained consciousness slowly, not yet opening his eyes. His head hurt from where he had been struck, and it felt like there might be a bit of crusted-over blood near the spot. There was a rough wall on his back, and something heavy in his lap. One hand seemed trapped under a large, soft object, and a brief, familiar, welcome smell reached his nostrils despite the smoke and blood permeating the air.

Finally opening his lids, Kahkay looked down to where Grace Thomas laid, her head in his lap, on the dirt floor beside him. Carefully, Kahkay extracted his arm from under her, but as slow as he was, it was enough to wake Grace up.

Grace's eyes fluttered a few times, realized they were right in Kahkay's crotch, and she jerked back as if his penis (with was visibly erect through his pants) was a venomous snake. She did wince as she bumped her injured leg, but seemed happy to scoot away and put some distance between her and Kahkay.

Kahkay was almost offended. With everything else going on, he'd still gotten hard at the thought of her head so close to his manhood, and disgust was her reaction? What was wrong with her? He thought that they were closer than that, that a boner wouldn't offend, and while nothing physical had ever happened between them, Kahkay was still sure she'd give into his advances someday, hiding her attraction to him behind a mask of professionalism. Had he been so wrong?

Sadly, this wasn't the time to think about it. Kahkay glanced around the room to take stock of his surroundings, and saw Grace doing the same, not a word coming from her mouth about what had just happened, which Kahkay chose to take as a positive sign. Maybe it had been more surprise than disgust a moment ago.

Anyway, they were in a cell, bars on two sides, with thick, stone walls on the other two. A single bench sat along the wall Kahkay had not been leaning on, and Ensign Smith-Jones was asleep on it. Next to the bench, on the floor, sat Captain Roberts, head lolled, looking like Kahkay had the morning after he inadvertently insulted a couple of Rotarian bar wenches (Rotarians were not a small people) on Divia III. On the other side of the bench was a rusty bucket. Kahkay wondered what it was for, quickly realized the purpose, and couldn't contain a wave of disgust himself.

Other than that, there was nothing to see. Outside the bars was just bare hallway, a couple of torches providing flickering light, but no guards or furniture in sight.

"Ouch," muttered Grace. She had tried to stand, but her wounded leg hadn't cooperated and she sank back onto her behind. Kahkay rose and quickly moved to examine the injury, ignoring Grace waving him away.

"I'm fine," she muttered, sounding more angry than in pain.

"You will be," returned Kahkay. "As soon as I get this shard out."

"I don't need your help," she snapped.

"Come on, Gracie. Don't be like this," he said. Deftly, he pinched the barely-protruding metal fragment between two fingers and pulled it straight from the wound, which began bleeding. To her credit, Grace gritted her teeth and didn't make a sound as Kahkay ripped a strip of cloth from his shirt sleeve and began to fashion a crude bandage.

"Don't Gracie me," she said bitingly. "How do you expect me to be? We're captured and rotting in an alien prison." Her sharp retort was enough noise to cause both Roberts and Smith-Jones to stir. Kahkay turned to look towards them, and Grace made sure to scoot further away from him before anyone might see him being tender with her.

"Lieutenant Kahkay, Lieutenant Thomas," said Captain Roberts. "You received the distress signal I take it?" He sounded more unfazed than he had any right to be, and Kahkay admired that.

"Yes, sir," answered Grace before Kahkay could respond.

"I didn't send it," said Roberts.

"Yeah, we figured that out," said Kahkay.

"Where's the rest of your team?" asked Roberts.

"Dead," said Ensign Smith-Jones flatly as she sat up, her copper hair coming loose from her normally tight ponytail. Kahkay loved that ponytail. He liked how she enjoyed him tugging on it as they...

"Mine, too," said Roberts, interrupting Kahkay's thoughts about the comely, young security officer.

"I'll find a way to get us out of here," said Grace, managing to stand up. She swayed a little, but grabbing the bars for support, she made her way across one wall.

"It's no use," said Roberts. "I examined the cell when they put us in here, while you three were asleep."

"I'm sorry, sir," began Grace. "I–"

Roberts cut her off. "No apologies, Lieutenant. You did your duty and responded to the captain's distress call. You had no way of knowing you were walking into a trap."

"But I did, sir," returned Grace. "I knew it the moment I saw the building they had you in. I tried to be cautious, but they killed half our team and caught us just the same."

Roberts sighed. "Still not your fault, Lieutenant. Let's hope the next rescue team comes better armed."

"There won't be another rescue team," said Grace.

Kahkay looked at her confused. "What?"

"I got off a pre-recorded signal to the ship that this was a trap and we were lost," said Grace, looking down.

"Well, then, you have even less cause to apologize," said Roberts.

"Johnson won't leave us here," said Kahkay confidently. "Message or no, he'll come for us."

"Let's hope *Commander* Johnson does not," said Roberts. "There's no need to lose any more officers. Not for this place."

This place was Melania I, or so Kahkay had read prior to beaming down. The people here were relatively civilized, having built good-sized towns, but were still tribal in nature, and fought constantly. One tribe had advanced technologically enough to signal the *Enterprise* when it came into orbit, passing by on routine exploration, and instead of making awed first contact, as Captain Roberts had expected upon beamering down, he found a people who wanted to conquer the ship and use it and its equipment against their enemies.

Roberts had relayed all this back to the *Enterprise* before being captured. Rather than beamer back up and fly away immediately, though, he'd chosen to stay and try to broker peace between at least this village and their biggest rival, thinking if they were advanced enough to detect starsheeps in space and communicate with them, they were intelligent enough to be reasoned with. Clearly, Roberts had been wrong.

"OK, so we're on our own, but that doesn't mean we're lost," said Kahkay. "First, we need to find a way out of this cell."

"That's what I'm doing," snapped Grace.

"I'll help," said Smith-Jones, jumping up. Of all of them, she looked the healthiest, so it was probably a good idea. Not to be outdone, Kahkay quickly seconded the offer.

"We won't get out until they come for us," said Roberts. "They're going to torture us to try to get us to reveal how our equipment works, and to attempt to force us to take them to our ship."

"We won't break, sir," said Grace.

"No, I don't think you will," said Roberts. "Still, our best chance to fight them will be now, while we're still strong."

"All right. You stay back, Captain, and the three of us will jump them when they arrive," said Grace. Kahkay grimaced, and Roberts did not take the order well.

"I am at least as capable of fighting back as you are, *Lieutenant* Thomas. I do not need to hang back, nor take orders from a junior officer," he snapped.

"Sorry, sir. I didn't mean...," stammered Grace. "It's just, well, it looks like they've already..."

"I'm fine," said Roberts, who Kahkay could now see had a broken noise and two missing teeth, as well as a crooked leg and a mangled arm.

"Of course, sir," said Grace.

"Are any of the captors female?" asked Kahkay.

"Why does that matter?" asked Grace.

"I have a way with women of all species," said Kahkay. Grace glared at him, but Smith-Jones turned away shyly, her cheeks reddening slightly, and Kahkay grinned at her.

"I don't think you're going to be able to sleep your way out of this one, Kahkay," said Roberts. "The soldiers that move me have all been male, and while there are some female interrogators, they are very professional."

"I'll go gay if I have to. Leave this to me," said Kahkay. Roberts didn't look convinced, but Kahkay knew he could get them out of this situation. Grace would see, and then maybe this time, she'd finally reward him in the way he wanted. Sexually.

It was several hours before anyone came near their cell, but Kahkay was ready. As soon as he heard footsteps, he sprawled on the bench, shirt off, legs spread, lying on his side as seductively as possible. Although he couldn't see his fellow captors behind him, Kahkay could imagine their reactions. Grace would be scowling and trying not to look, Roberts would be watching the guards for anything he could use to his advantage, and Smith-Jones would probably be practically drooling, eyes glued to his rock-hard abs.

Five soldiers, each hooded with those eerie glowing, red eyes peeking out from underneath, entered. All bore sharp implements of some kind, from an axe, to a sword, to a machete, to a common butcher knife. None looked in the mood to play around, though one couldn't help him or herself from glancing continuously at Kahkay as another unlocked the cell.

Sensing an advantage, Kahkay winked and blew a kiss at the interested party, trying to determine if there were boob lumps showing in the nondescript robe. He was committed to going through with this either way, but he'd enjoy it a lot more if his quarry were female.

As the quintet entered, Kahkay motioned for his solider to come closer. He or she didn't, staring at Kahkay in what looked a bit, from the limited features he could see, like confusion. Their locked gaze lasted only a second, though, as another guard stepped in front of her (Kahkay was sure it was a her now) and punched the security officer in the stomach.

Doubled over, Kahkay rolled off the bench and landed on his knees. The guard kicked him in the gut, and Kahkay expelled whatever air was left in his lungs, struggling to catch his breath again.

Roberts didn't let the distraction go to waste. He rushed one of the other captors, grabbing for the knife and wrestling him to the ground. Grace and Smith-Jones were steps behind him, engaging with two others, leaving just the assaulter and the flirter with Kahkay.

The tussle might have gone in the A.S.S. officers' favor if three other guards hadn't immediately streamed in and joined the fray. In seconds, Kahkay, Roberts, Grace, and Smith-Jones were pinned against the wall, no better off than they had been before, sharp blades at their chests. One of the enemy's number lay dead on the cell floor, Kahkay didn't see which of his fellows had killed him, but other than that, they had achieved no victory.

For several minutes, the A.S.S.ers stared at the guards, and the guards stared back, no one saying anything. Kahkay grew impatient. Were they going to be taken away to be tortured? Were they going to be left alone? He didn't know, but he was tired of waiting to find out.

"Hey, honey," said Kahkay to the female, who now stood uneasily near the cell door, not among those holding a blade on them.

"Shut up," hissed Grace beside him.

"I got this, Gracie," said Kahkay confidently. He turned his attention back to the female guard. "How you doin'?" She didn't respond.

"Stop," hissed Grace.

"Like my pecs?" Kahkay asked the guard while flexing, pretending that they were the only two beings in the room, and a scimitar wasn't cutting slightly into his flesh. She still didn't answer. Kahkay opened his mouth to say something else, but stopped as another figure strode into the cell.

Clearly the same species as the guards, this new arrival had her hood down, and was definitely a she. Pointed ears, thin, long hair messily framing a bony, gray face, glowing red eyes above a tiny mouth with pointy teeth, she wasn't what Kahkay would call hot, but he'd had worse.

"Well, hello, beautiful," said Kahkay to the hoodless female. The woman pulled an A.S.S. pad from a pocket and spoke into it.

"I am Reetha," she said through the translator. "You will call your ship now."

"Oh, baby, there's no need to call anyone else. How about you and I go somewhere more... private, or at least less threatening, and talk?" asked Kahkay.

"I do not understand," said Reetha. "Are you the one in charge?"

"That would be me," said Captain Roberts.

"No, no, don't worry about him," said Kahkay as Reetha turned her attention to Roberts. "Look at me."

"Put a sock in it, Kahkay," said Roberts.

"I got this," said Kahkay. He reached up and casually pushed the blade away from himself so he could step towards Reetha. In less than a second the blade was back, and Reetha was glaring at the Lieutenant.

"Who are you?" asked Reetha.

"I'm Dick L. Kahkay, and I'd love to show you what the 'L' stands for with my dick," said Kahkay, flashing his trademark smile.

"You are in our control with a weapon at your throat. Are you not scared?" asked Reetha.

"I'm only scared you're not going to take me home with you tonight," said Kahkay.

"Why would I take you to my home?" asked Reetha.

"You want to go to my place instead?" asked Kahkay.

"Yes, you will take us to your vessel," said Reetha.

"How about I just take *you*?" asked Kahkay.

"That is not acceptable," said Reetha. "You will take myself and a contingent of my people to your vessel and hand over control to us."

"Oh, I like it when a woman takes control," said Kahkay.

"Knock it off," said Roberts.

"Who are you?" asked Reetha, turning her attention to the captain.

"I'm-," began Roberts before Kahkay cut him off again.

"He's not important. Look, Reeth, may I call you Reeth?"

"I do not like your words, but at least you are talking. Better than that one," said Reetha, pointing to Roberts. "Kill him."

"Wait, we can-" started Kahkay, but he sputtered to a stop as the guard with the machete neatly chopped Roberts' head right off. It rolled across the floor. Grace's face was pained, but she said nothing. Smith-Jones squeaked in terror.

"Oh my god! Why would you do that?" asked Kahkay, using every ounce of his will power to push down the panic that threatened to erupt at the surface. He struggled to maintain his bravado.

"He was not useful to me. Will you be useful to me?" asked Reetha, her eyes back on Kahkay's. He found it difficult to maintain the pupil-to-glowing-ember gaze, but forced himself to, trying not to vomit at the sight of Roberts' body.

"I can be very useful, in lots of ways, most of them sexual," said Kahkay, managing to summon up, with great effort, another signature grin.

"Radio your ship and have them prepare to surrender to us," said Reetha.

"Reeth, babe, that's just not gonna happen," said Kahkay.

"Cut off her leg," said Reetha, indicating Grace.

"Wait, stop!" said Kahkay, but it was too late. The blade sliced through the air and severed Grace's wounded leg just above the knee. She fell to the ground beside Roberts' body, letting out a scream that chilled Kahkay to the bone. Now he couldn't hold onto the façade. What had he done, provoking this woman?

"Will you radio your vessel?" asked Reetha with a sneer.

"Yes, yes! Can we help her first, though?" asked Kahkay desperately.

"She can return to your vessel with us to be medically treated. Hurry and radio your vessel," demanded Reetha.

"Of course. Give me my phone. I'll call right now!" said Kahkay.

Reetha nodded to one of her guards, and the phone was produced. Kahkay took it and immediately dialed the ship.

"Lieutenant Kahkay?" answered Lieutenant Ricart at communications.

"Prepare to beamer us up, party of...," Kahkay looked at Reetha, tears obscuring his field of vision. He kept glancing at Grace, writhing on the ground, blood pouring from the wound. She was bleeding out. Not Grace. Anyone but Grace. He couldn't lose Grace.

"Twenty-three," said Reetha as more armed guards poured into the small cell.

"Twenty-three to beamer up," said Kahkay. "Beamer Grace directly to the doctor's office. Hurry!"

Reetha gave Kahkay a satisfied smile as the world dissolved around them, everyone in the cell caught up in the beamer.

Grace saw nothing but white. A soft, white surface with no features whatsoever. It was peaceful. She craved peace, and wordlessly embraced it with all her soul.

"Gracie!" said Dick Kahkay happily, his face popping into her field of vision. He gave her a big hug. Grace let him for half a second, his being here almost as welcome as the peace of a moment ago.

"Get off her," snapped Doctor Grey, physically pushing Dick back. "She's healing."

"Sorry," said Dick to Doctor Grey, uncharacteristically sheepish, especially in the face of a beautiful woman, which Doctor Grey was. He looked at Grace and his expression changed. "And I'm sorry Grace. I don't know what I was thinking. I-"

"I know," said Grace with a calmness she didn't feel. It was all rushing back to her now, Captain Roberts, losing her leg, the tribal warriors...

"It's not all right," insisted Dick. "I was wrong. I thought I could-"

"Get out. Now!" demanded Doctor Grey, who, while only in her early thirties, already had the bedside manner of someone who had been a doctor a long time, and whom had grown desensitized to upset loved ones.

"Grace, I...," tried Dick again, and Grace's heart melted for him as he finally allowed himself to be shooed away by Doctor Grey. Grace had never seen Dick lose his cool, or show any vulnerability. This was a different man, a humbled man. A man who had realized he didn't have as much power over the world as he thought he did. This was the man Grace had always suspected lied under the surface of the blowhard, but had never glimpsed before. It almost made what they went through on the planet not so horrible.

No, it had been horrible. Seeing the captain beheaded right in front of her... She didn't blame Dick for it. Yes, if he hadn't run his mouth, it might not have happened. But then again, if Dick hadn't been an ass, they might still be down on the planet being tortured. Clearly, that hadn't been where things had ended.

Speaking of, how did she get back on the *Enterprise*? "Doctor Grey?" she asked.

"Yes?" said Doctor Grey, nose buried in a portable pad, not looking up.

"What happened?"

"I was able to reattach your leg and you're going to make a full recovery," said Doctor Grey absent-mindedly.

Oh, good. So the pain coming from under the blanket, which Grace felt too weak to lift up and look under, wasn't just the phantom kind. It was coming from her actual leg. That was a little bit of a relief.

"OK, but the mission. Did...?" began Grace, unsure what to ask.

"I have no idea, and frankly, I don't care. I'm busy," said Doctor Grey, striding out of view.

Grace laid on her pillow, staring at the ship's hospital ceiling, frustrated. She knew reattaching a leg was not a simple procedure, and one that probably wouldn't have been medically available a short time ago, so she needed to lay still for a while. But that didn't stop her from wanting to jump out of this bed and find out what she had missed.

Thankfully, less than an hour later, Commander Johnson stopped by to check on her. "Commander Johnson!" began Grace as soon as she saw him. In the less-than-an-hour, her brain had managed to formulate a few dozen questions to ask the next person she had the opportunity to talk to. Lucky Johnson. "What-"

"Shh, Lieutenant Thomas. It's all right," said Johnson reassuringly, gently. "How are you feeling?"

"I'm fine," said Grace, brushing off his query. "What happened?"

"Your message back was enough for us to figure out what was going on. I was weighing a few options when Lieutenant Kahkay called asking for a beamer up. It was easy enough to beamer the hostiles directly into our jail cells on the *Enterprise* and remove their weapons, and thankfully, the Lieutenant acted quickly enough for us to retrieve and reattach your leg."

"Of course," said Grace. Why hadn't she thought of the beamer trick? She could have just signaled the ship to hold tight until they were alone, and then they all could have been retrieved from the cell before...

Oh, god. This was all her fault. She hadn't needed to send a message telling the ship to give up on them. She should have just asked them to track her and her team's signals until they were with the captain, and then beamer them all back. How stupid could she be?

"I can tell what you're thinking, and forget it," said Johnson. "You're a Lieutenant with three years experience in the field. You can't possibly plan for every possibility. Hell, the whole A.S.S. starsheep program is only that old. We have Chief Engineer Garrett to thank for some quick-thinking ingenuity, and Lieutenant Kahkay for calling us before things got worse and prompting appropriate action."

"Yes, Dick is always lucky," said Grace with a twinge of bitterness. Lucky for himself, anyway. Not lucky enough to save Jovi, Yeager, Hattie, or Captain Roberts.

"Look, Thomas, what you went through was rough. Believe me, I've seen some action myself, lost some comrades," said Johnson. "What we do is dangerous, especially because we're doing it first. We all need to do our best to watch each other's backs. But we're going to lose friends along the way, and when we do, we must honor their memories by carrying on. That's what they'd want us to do."

"I-," began Grace.

"Don't say anything now," said Johnson. "It'll take a while to sink in. Just keep my words in mind when you're having trouble sleeping at night."

"Thank you, Commander," said Grace.

"You're welcome. And, by the way, it's Captain Johnson now," he said with a tight smile that told Grace this wasn't the way he had wanted the center chair, which only made her respect him more. "Admiral Jelly promoted me this morning."

"Congratulations, sir. Captain," said Grace.

"Thanks," said Johnson. "We all move on, Lieutenant Thomas. Or, if we don't, what's the point?"

CHAPTER SIX
EN ROUTE TO EARTH, 2424

Lieutenant Michelle Tokaladie snuck a glance at Captain Kahkay. How could he look so confident, so collected? Their first mission had been a disaster by any measure, starting with the fact that Kahkay had jumped the gun by leaving Earth too quickly, and ending with his best friend's death. How could the man appear so unaffected by it all?

Tokaladie had read Kahkay's record, of course. She knew he was the youngest captain in the fleet for good reason. But what didn't come through in the report was what kind of person that he was, what his morals were, how he slept at night after losing a colleague. To her, that was the kind of thing that made serving in the A.S.S. rough. Somehow, though, it seemed like Kahkay could compartmentalize and let things go. Or, at least that's how it appeared to her as he sat in the captain's chair and joked with his bridge staff.

"...and that's how I landed my 1,000[th] woman while at the academy," said Kahkay with a big smile.

"Goodness," said Foley, hero worship in his voice. Tokaladie did a double take. Why was Foley so sweaty? If anything, it was a little chilly on the bridge. Not for the first time this afternoon, she wished she'd worn a sweater instead of the skimpy orange skirt and short-sleeved top with the plunging neckline. She liked to look her best, but sometimes a girl just needed to cover up.

"So, Milkyway, why did you join the A.S.S. if you were evil?" asked Kahkay.

"I am *not* evil," hissed Lieutenant Commander M-, and Tokaladie's heart went out to the reptilian being. She hadn't seen any sign to indicate M- had anything but the starsheep's best interests at heart, and yet Kahkay continued to pick on him. Could their new captain possibly be a specist, or was this just his awkward way of ribbing crew members?

"Riiiiight," said Kahkay sarcastically.

"I am not!" insisted M-.

"I've read about your people. You can't fool me," said Kahkay.

"Yes, it isssss true, many of my sssspecies are evil," said M-, his s's growing longer as he became stressed, and his green scales turning a little brownish in frustration. "But I am not."

"Fool me once, shame on you," said Kahkay. "Fool me twice... you, uh, I can't get fooled again."

"That is not how the expression goes," said M-.

"Sure it is," said Kahkay.

"It is not," said M-, and something about the way he stood up to Kahkay with the undercurrent of hurt and nobility struck Tokaladie as very endearing, and dare she say it, attractive? She quickly pushed down that feeling, shaking her head. Seriously? She was going for scales now? Besides, she had a strict rule against dating co-workers. However, M- did have a certain exotic quality...

"Trust me. I'm from Earth, you're not. Which one of us would know an old Earth saying best?" asked Kahkay, with no hint that he was at all aware just how wrong he was at that moment. Tokaladie wasn't sure if she should admire his confidence, or just write him off as a total jerk, but she definitely took M-'s side in this exchange.

"Excuse me," said Foley, face green, rushing for the bridge's bathroom.

"What's with that guy?" asked Kahkay.

"Sick," said Who simply from the security station.

"Well, that's not good," said Kahkay. "It's his first day and all. Plus, he was the one driving the ship. Take the pilot controls, will you, Who?"

"Yes," said Who, who did not sound happy to do it, moving to Foley's abandoned station at the front of the room. Tokaladie could see Earth coming up quickly, and started. Had the engineer really almost let them crash into the planet? Thankfully, Who saw the same thing and swiftly hit the brakes.

No sooner did the ship slow than Tokaladie's panel beeped. Someone from Earth was calling them. She quickly turned her back on the captain to answer it.

"A.S.S. *Thrifty*," she said, just as regulations required. Communications was an odd position because she had lots of responsibility and needed much skill to perform the job, but sometimes she felt like a glorified secretary. She wished someone would segment answering duty out of her department.

"Where was I?" asked Kahkay rhetorically behind her. "Right. We were discussing how Menedict Arnold plans to betray us all."

"I do *not*-," started M-.

"Captain Kahkay," interrupted Tokaladie. "Admiral Jamieson is requesting that you meet him down on the surface."

"He- he's not coming up?" asked Kahkay with surprise.

"No, sir. He wants you to go to him," said Tokaladie.

"Geez. I mean, who does he think he is, in charge?" asked Kahkay. M- rolled his eyes, and Tokaladie met his gaze as it came back down. He gave her an encouraging look, and they shared a brief connection.

"Yes, sir. He does outrank you," said Tokaladie a little more casually than she intended, distracted as she was by the handsome lizard being.

"Well, on my ship, ranks be damned, I'm the boss," said Kahkay.

"Mmm, he's not on your ship. Perhaps that's why he wants you to go down?" panned M-, and Tokaladie couldn't help but grin stupidly at him, amused.

"Hmm, a power play, huh?" asked Kahkay rhetorically. "I respect that. Fine, fine. Who?"

"Admiral Jamieson, sir," said Tokaladie, confused.

"No, I mean Lieutenant Who, let's go," said Kahkay, rising from his chair looking like a kid who had just been told to go to the principal's office.

"No. Thanks," said Who, not looking up from the pilot's panel.

"Weren't you just saying that you need to accompany me on every away mission?" Kahkay asked the ape-like security officer.

"Not. Earth. Earth. Safe," said Who, who couldn't resist adding "-ish" a second later.

Tokaladie smiled again. Who struck her as the type who didn't take crap from anyone, no matter their rank. Tokaladie hadn't had much interaction with Who yet, but made a mental note to change that soon.

"OK, Marmalade, you're with me," said Kahkay.

"What? Why?" asked M-, sounding annoyed and a bit shocked. Tokaladie didn't blame him. She didn't know why the captain would take along the bridge officer he seemed to hate the most, either.

"Because I said so," said Kahkay.

"Do you need me to go to the potty with you, too, sir?" asked M-. This time, Tokaladie led out an audible laugh, which stopped as abruptly as it began. It hadn't been very loud, and she quickly turned away to hide her face, hoping no one had noticed.

"You're awfully close to insublordination, or whatever that word is, Lieutenant Commander," said Kahkay, the levity leaving his tone.

"Geez, what do you think you are, in charge?" asked M-.

Tokaladie's spine stiffened and she looked back at Kahkay for his reaction. True, M- and Who had said several things in their quick trip back to Earth that were maybe not entirely appropriate to say to a commanding officer, and Kahkay clearly tolerated, if not outright encouraged, it. This, though, seemed to cross the line to her and she braced for Kahkay's scolding.

Instead, though, a small smile flickered across his countenance. "I... Ooo, I get your point. Touché."

"What point?" asked M-, and Tokaladie couldn't tell if he was serious or not.

"Foley, you...," Kahkay started, then sighed. "Is Foley still in the bathroom?"

"Yes, sir," said Tokaladie, wondering how Kahkay even needed to ask. There was only one door out of the bridge bathroom, and it was right back into the command deck. Kahkay would have seen if Foley had left it.

"Lieutenant Tokaladie, when he finally finishes with his crap, will you let him know that he's in charge?" asked Kahkay.

"Of course, Captain," said Tokaladie.

"Hehheh. You see what I did there?" asked Kahkay. No one laughed. Tokaladie saw M- make an exasperated face behind Kahkay's back and she had to stifle another giggle, though not for the reason Kahkay wanted, which he realized as he turned around and caught M-'s facial expression.

"Yes, sir," said Tokaladie.

Kahkay shook his head. "This crew has no sense of humor. All right, let's go Mufasa."

"Fine," said M- with a sigh. The two stepped into the elevator and were gone.

"So, Who, until Foley gets out of the bathroom, am I in charge or are you?" asked Tokaladie.

"Go. For. It," said Who dryly.

Admiral Jamie Jamieson was having a day. He hadn't noticed when Kahkay left orbit suddenly this morning, but ever since then, it was one fire after another to put out. First, Doctor Boyce, who was supposed to be on the *Thrifty*, had called to angrily quit. Seems she didn't have any interest in serving under a man who recklessly flew away without his medical officer, and Jamieson couldn't say that he blamed her. Then, only hours later, the first report from the *Thrifty* arrived, stating that Commander Garry Marshall had been killed.

Jamieson had been at home when he got the news, having taken the afternoon off. His marriage hadn't been going very well lately, and he thought it might be good to spend some time with his wife. Unfortunately, he'd been wrong.

Ever since their only child had died four years ago in a tragic space battle, things had been tense between them. They grieved in very different ways. Janice was furious, while Jamie understood that it was more important for the A.S.S. to try to broker peace with the C'mons, the race that had killed their boy, to prevent more death, and embraced that position personally. Janice saw that as a betrayal of their son's memory.

At first, that had just meant some arguments between them, but lately it had been colder. Janice had been away from home a lot, and Jamie suspected that she might be cheating on him, though he'd yet to see any proof of it. Not that he'd looked very hard. He wasn't sure he wanted to know if she was being unfaithful.

Jamie did genuinely try to make her happy, though. He still loved her very deeply, his high school sweetheart, whom he'd been with for nearly three decades now. He hoped it helped that he was going to name her recommendation to be Commander Marshall's replacement on the *Thrifty* (she was very interested in Jamie's work, and often gave him advice, even with the recent chill between them), but he wasn't sure it made much difference to her.

Now, back in the office, Jamieson steeled himself to deal with Kahkay, whom he'd hoped to not see again for awhile. Granted, Kahkay was one of the captains whom Jamieson was assigned to oversee, but that would mainly involve relaying messages back and forth, not face-to-face meetings of the sort Jamieson was forced to conduct when Kahkay was local. Kahkay was already Jamieson's least favorite starsheep commander.

Jamieson heard the beamer right outside his office and straightened in his chair, all business. He needed to convey a strength with Kahkay if he was ever going to bring the unruly captain in line.

The door opened and Captain Kahkay strode in brashly, Lieutenant Commander M- following more respectfully behind. Jamieson was pleased to see that the two officers had hit it off so well, as M- would surely be a voice of reason on the *Thrifty*, and Jamieson could think of no other reason M- would accompany Kahkay down here other than because the being was well on his way to earning Kahkay's trust and affection.

"Thank you for coming down, Captain Kahkay, Lieutenant Commander M-," said Jamieson as the two took a seat across from his desk. M- sat stiffly, spine straight, while Kahkay lounged, leg sprawled across the chair's arm rest. Jamieson allowed himself a small frown at the man, who should be coming back here cowed and humble, not casually strutting. "We're having a little problem with your new chief medical officer."

"Oh, and what problem is that, Admiral Jamieson?" Kahkay asked, no sign of concern in his voice, bristling Jamieson even further.

"You don't have one," said Jamieson sharply, trying to convey with his tone that Kahkay was in trouble.

"I thought oh, uh, *Garry*, accidentally left without her. Yeah," said Kahkay, clearly pleased with his answer.

"You're really going to blame the mistake on your *dead* best friend?" asked Jamieson in disbelief.

"As Captain, I must place blame where blame is due. It is a vital quality of a starsheep officer to take responsibility for one's actions," said Kahkay. A bit of hope sparked within Jamieson for a second before Kahkay followed up with "Totally Garry's fault." Lieutenant Commander M- made noises of disapproval and Jamieson concurred, though not vocally.

"Well, anyway, the doctor we had assigned to you has requested a transfer," said Jamieson, moving on. The less time he had to spend with Kahkay, the better.

"Really? I mean, that's strange," said Kahkay. Was this man serious? Was he actually so obtuse that he didn't realize how incompetent he'd been today?

"It doesn't seem strange to me," said M-. At least there was one senior officer on the *Thrifty* in touch with reality.

"Well, you're strange," said Kahkay, sounding like a child.

"Yes," said Jamieson. "Her exact words were something along the lines of, 'I'm too old to put up with a commanding officer that is so careless that he leaves behind his department head and gets his best friend killed,' or something to that affect." Doctor Boyce hadn't actually heard about Garry, of course, but Jamieson couldn't resist the dig in another attempt to get through the seriousness of the situation.

"Well, this... this can't be right," said Kahkay in surprise.

"Yes, that sounds exactly right," said M-. "On a completely unrelated note, Admiral Jamieson, I would like to request a transfer."

"Ah ha!" shouted Kahkay to his science officer. "I knew you were evil!"

"How does requesting a transfer prove that I am evil?" asked a baffled M-.

"Only evil people betray their captain," said Kahkay smugly, as if that statement won the argument.

"I am not betraying you," protested M-. "I simply ask that if Admiral Jamieson has another position available, I be considered for it. I never mentioned you in my request."

"It was implied," said Kahkay.

"It was not!" said M- angrily, the captain getting under his skin.

"I-," began Kahkay, but Jamieson interrupted, not willing to let this go any further. He was clearly wrong about the relationship forming between these two, and as much as he sympathized with M-'s desire to get away from Kahkay, the exchange had only cemented Jamieson's resolve to keep M- on board, if for nothing other than as a check on the captain.

"Gentlemen, gentlemen, please. Transfer denied, Lieutenant Commander M-." Jamieson winced, sure he had mispronounced the officer's name; he'd never been that confident with saying the names of those of M-'s species, not really easy to do with a human tongue. "If you left the *A.S.S. Thrifty*, it would not meet its required quota of non-human officers."

"That's racist," said M-.

Jamieson hoped M- meant the last statement, and not the way he'd garbled M-'s name, and decided to proceed on that assumption. "It's kind of the opposite of racist, since the rule is in place to make sure that the crew remains diverse."

"And yet, it certainly feels racist." Jamieson tried not to take what M- said too personally. The science officer was probably just riled up because of Kahkay, which Jamieson couldn't blame him for.

"Now listen here, Mewlificent," said Kahkay, bungling the name far, far worse than Jamieson had. "If you really want t-"

"My name is not... what?" interrupted M-, equally shocked and offended. The lizard-man turned to Jamieson, the pleading clear even through alien eyes. "Admiral Jamieson, do you see what I have to put up with?"

"I do, Lieutenant Commander," said Jamieson with feeling. "But let's worry about replacing your chief medical officer before creating any additional holes in the roster." M- made an unhappy noise, but made no further argument. Jamieson appreciated the professionalism.

"What about a first officer? I- I need one of those, too," said Kahkay, almost whining, in stark contrast to M-'s decorum.

"That's taken care of. Commander Harry Dirt will meet you on the *Thrifty* in just a few hours," said Jamieson.

"Harry Dirt? That just cannot be a real name," said Kahkay.

"It is, indeed. Is that a problem, *Captain Kahkay*?" asked Jamieson, darkly serious, daring the captain to keep being flippant.

"Maybe," said Kahkay, ignoring the weight with which the response had been delivered. "I mean, we'll see. So, uh, who do you have lined up for the chief medical officer spot?"

"Well, there aren't that many qualified doctors in the fleet, but let me pull up my roster here..." Jamieson scanned the list of names quickly. They'd had a recent drought of accomplished medical professionals willing to ship out with the A.S.S. lately, and with as many new starsheeps as were being launched in recent months, only a handful of candidates weren't spoken for at the moment.

"It looks like Doctor Smokin is free," said Jamieson.

"Oh, haha, she's free all right," said Kahkay lustily and with familiarity. "But, eh, I slept with her and it didn't end well. Let's just say, uh, her last name has a triple meaning, OK? Haha. So that probably wouldn't be a good idea."

Jamieson opened his mouth to ask what Kahkay meant, but decided he didn't want to know, settling for an annoyed sigh instead. "Fair enough. Doctor Sawbones-"

"Yeah, he was married to Doctor Smokin when we had our, um, you know," said Kahkay, who then made squeaky noises that Jamieson assumed were supposed to be a reference to sex, though he wasn't sure how.

"Seriously?" asked Jamieson, disgusted.

"Oh yeah. I'm afraid so," said Kahkay, not sounding the least bit apologetic.

"Doctor Quinn?" asked Jamieson.

"Banged her," said Kahkay.

"Doctor Danvers?" asked Jamieson.

"Definitely did her," said Kahkay.

"Doctor Crusher?" asked Jamieson.

"Oh, yeah, that night was magical. Love me some red head."

"Doctor House," said Jamieson, glad to finally reach another male name on the list.

"Slept with him," said Kahkay casually, and Jamieson stopped in surprise, which Kahkay mistakenly took as an invitation for further explanation. "Look, it was spring break and there was a lot of alcohol involved."

"I really don't care," said Jamieson, who didn't. "Let's, uh, let's keep going and stop me when I get to someone you haven't slept with."

"Mmm, good luck with that," weighed in M-, not helping.

"Doctor Johns?" asked Jamieson.

"Yep, did her," said Kahkay.

"Doctor Grey?" asked Jamieson, getting discouraged by just how many of the few names left were female.

"Twice," said Kahkay.

"Doctor Yang?" asked Jamieson.

"Also twice, once being a threesome with Doctor Grey," overshared Kahkay.

"Doctor Tam?"

"Thought he was a she, but yep, did him, too," said Kahkay proudly. Jamieson almost had to begrudge Kahkay a little respect at how equal opportunity he was in his escapades, this list covering an extensive variety of individuals. Almost, if it hadn't been so gross.

"Doctor Who?"

"Actually, Admiral Jamieson," broke in M-. "Doctor Who Grappa switched fields and is now our security officer."

"Oh," said Jamieson, remembering. "I guess the doctor can't do double duty. Doctor McCoy?"

"Oh, he's a phony. Trust me," said Kahkay dismissively. "And he complains, like, *all* the time." He switched into a mocking impression that sounded nothing like McCoy, in

Jamieson's opinion. "'I'm a doctor, not a brick layer.' Like anyone's ever asked him to lay a single brick!"

"That leaves only one name left on this list," said Jamieson, already mentally penciling in Doctor McCoy, despite Kahkay's disinterest. "Doctor Awshucks."

Oh. Her. Jamieson remembered meeting Awshucks at an A.S.S. gathering last year. She had been very charming. Jamieson had been immediately drawn to her shapely figure and acerbic attitude. She had the presence of someone much older than she was, and yet, was also alluring. If Jamison hadn't been married, he'd have made a play for her. As it was, with the troubles he'd been having with Janice, he was tempted, but didn't end up doing anything about it.

"Doctor *Awshucks*?" asked Kahkay, thinking. "Hmm. Never heard of him."

"Finally!" said Jamieson, a little too triumphantly. "Uh, she's a her, and she's retired." That was weird. Why had she quit so young?

"Oh, a much older woman. Like fine wine," babbled Kahkay. "That's probably why I've never heard of her."

"From what I have heard, that's never stopped you before," said M-. Jamieson opened his mouth to scold M- for being insubordinate to his commanding officer, but stopped himself. He really couldn't blame the science head.

"So... call her back from retirement, Admiral, and send her right on up to us," said Kahkay, rising for his seat. "I mean, if that's all, Admiral Jamieson?"

"Actually, Captain Kahkay, you're going to have to talk to Doctor Awshucks yourself. She quit the A.S.S. last year when a starsheep rotation became required for all medical professionals," said Jamieson, reading on in her file. "She really hates technology, is deathly afraid of beamers, would rather avoid people altogether." It was starting to make sense now.

"Sounds like a peach," said Kahkay sarcastically.

"Interestingly, she does like peaches. Loves them, actually. Especially when it comes in a bottle...," said Jamieson trailing off, unable to stop himself from thinking about what might have been.

"That really seems like unnecessary information," said Kahkay, breaking Jamieson from his reverie.

"It won't be easy to convince her to rejoin the fleet. She's in West Virginia. Here's her address," said Jamieson, handing Kahkay the tablet computer with Awshuck's file displayed.

"Wait, you want *me* to go to *West* Virginia?" asked Kahkay, taken aback.

Jamieson shrugged, unapologetic. "Well, uh, you're the one that's slept with every other candidate in the A.S.S., so..."

"He really gives a whole new meaning to the organization's abbreviation, does he not?" asked M- drolly. Jamieson started in surprise. He had not expected the lizard being to make a joke, and that was a good one. Jamieson chuckled.

"He does indeed, Lieutenant Commander," said Jamieson.

"Are you two done?" asked Kahkay, unamused.

"Done with what, Captain Kahkay?" asked M- innocently. Jamieson smiled inwardly. M- had Kahkay's number. This only made the admiral more determined not to let the science officer transfer off ship.

"Heh, heh," said Kahkay dryly. "Let's go."

"What?" asked M- in surprise. "You want me to accompany you to this 'West Virginia?' It does not sound like a place that would be very hospitable to one of my ssspecies."

"Well, trust me, it's not very hospitable to anyone of any species," said Kahkay with resignation. Jamieson couldn't help but be curious as to what Kahkay had against the state, but refused to ask a question that he knew he'd regret hearing answered.

"I wish I had stayed on the *Thrifty*," said M-.

"I'm sure they're having a lot more fun without you," said Kahkay, steering M- out of the office. Jamieson was not sorry to see them go.

Lieutenant Who Grappa slouched at her security station on the bridge of the *Thrifty*, tapping impatiently on the side of the panel. In orbit around Earth, there wasn't much for her to do up here, but she didn't intend to leave the bridge until Foley re-emerged from the bathroom and took command. Until that time, it was her responsibility to oversee the rest of the crew up here.

Or maybe it was Lieutenant Tokaladie's. That wasn't clear. They were both the same rank. Who had been a lieutenant longer, but switching fields had set her back a little, the lateral shift slowing her advancement up the chain of command. Which was just fine with Who, who had no desire to command a starsheep whatsoever, and was in no hurry to be promoted to a headquarters position.

But Who barely knew Tokaladie, and had no idea what her ambitions were. She seemed like a smart individual, though a little mild-mannered for Who's taste, Tokaladie not having asserted herself to the captain, despite disagreeing with his disregard for protocol. Or, at least, that was the assumption that Who made in their brief time together. Who didn't like to jump to conclusions, but that was the only one she could figure based on her limited exposure so far. Maybe she should get to know the communications chief a little and see if that opinion changed.

"Who. Bored," said Who, as an attempt at casual small talk.

"Me, too, Lieutenant Who," said Tokaladie.

They sat in silence for several more minutes, Who wondering if Tokaladie would return the favor and try to engage in conversation with her. It took a little bit of time, but Tokaladie finally spoke again. "Just how long do you think Foley is going to be in the bathroom?"

"Who. Not. Know," said Who, disgusted. She had no desire to think about what Foley, clearly ill, was doing in the small room just off the bridge.

"He really should have used the one in engineering," said Tokaladie, sounding slightly amused amid her own revulsion.

Who suddenly decided that she didn't need to converse with Tokaladie, and that Tokaladie could handle the bridge just fine. If Tokaladie was interested in potty humor, they probably didn't have much in common. Besides, there was a whole security team below decks Who should probably check on and get into shape.

"Stink. Y. Who. Go," said Who, passing the bathroom on the way to the elevator and wrinkling her nose at the odor.

"No, Who! Please don't leave me alone with this!" begged Tokaladie, the amusement gone from her tone. Who took pity and paused.

"Sor. Ry," said Who.

"I'm sorry, too. I don't know why I started talking about what Foley is doing. I'm just a little nervous. This is my first bridge assignment. Is this how starsheeps usually run?" asked Tokaladie.

"No," said Who bluntly. Kahkay was not turning out to be a captain she could see herself serving under long-term, and that was just after one day.

"We haven't formally met," said Tokaladie. "I'm Michelle."

"Me. Who," said Who.

"Right. I heard you were called Lieutenant Who Grappa, and then Lieutenant Who. Is Who your family name?" asked Tokaladie with curiosity.

"No. Family. Name. In. Who's. Spec. Ies," replied Who. She was thoroughly confused at the human system of first and last names. In fact, among her own people, Who was known only as Who. She'd added the Grappa part herself to better integrate into the A.S.S. with the earthlings, but Lieutenant Grappa just sounded so foreign to her that she'd asked to be addressed as Lieutenant Who, which was apparently not how it worked with humans.

"Interesting," said Tokaladie warmly. "Why did you join the A.S.S., Who?"

"Who's. Plan. Et. Small. Mind. Ed," said Who. "Who. Did. Not. Fit. In."

"I understand," said Tokaladie. "I come from a small town. People didn't get me, either. They thought I was a dork."

"What. Dork?" asked Who.

"A nerd? A geek?" Who looked at Tokaladie in confusion. "Someone who likes weird things that no one else likes," said Tokaladie.

"Ah," said Who. "A. Plenx."

"Sure. A plenx," said Tokaladie, trying out the word. "I guess I just wasn't in sync with what my peers were into. At first, I was pretty enough that boys overlooked it and I got plenty of dates. As soon as I started talking to them, though, they lost interest. But I just wasn't willing to pretend to be someone that I'm not just to fit in."

"Smart," said Who, not seeing how Tokaladie would be considered pretty, human standards of beauty were as confusing as their naming structure, but respecting that Tokaladie chose to be herself. That was a rare thing among Who's people, and part of why Who never fit in there. The species tended to follow trends and try to be like one another more than any other Who had encountered since leaving the orb.

"Thank you, Who," said Tokaladie with a smile.

Who tried to return it, probably not successfully. Her face wasn't suited to the expressions that her fellow officers from Earth seemed accustomed to. But Tokaladie's grin didn't waver. She was someone Who could definitely be friends with. This was why Who liked to get to know people. First impressions could be wrong.

Though Who doubted that would prove to be as interesting or as deep as his communications chief.

Richard U. Kahkay trekked up the steep dirt road in the middle of the mountains. Trees surrounded them on all sides, and Kahkay liked trees about as much as he liked walking: not at all. Especially uphill, which was where he was heading.

Sure, Kahkay and M- could have beamered straight to this Doctor Awshucks' house. But Kahkay needed some time to think about his next move in private, away from the *Thrifty*, and so he had opted to walk a mile or two instead.

Beside him, M- made several unhappy noises, swatting away insects. His green scales were looking yellowish, a sign of his discomfort. Inwardly, Kahkay allowed himself a small smile, happy to have anything annoy M-. Kahkay stood by his assertion that the science officer was evil; he just had to be, with that voice and smarmy attitude. If Kahkay could make him miserable enough to quit, that would be great.

Though, Kahkay wasn't even sure how long he'd stay on the *Thrifty* at this point. He'd been so excited this morning to take command of the starsheep. Now, as evening approached, he reflected on just how horribly his day had gone. Every decision he'd made, from recklessly leaving early, to beamering down to the unknown planet without taking enough precaution, nagged at him. It was Kahkay's fault that Garry was dead.

Poor Garry. Kahkay knew Garry had desperately wanted to rekindle their friendship, and Kahkay had looked forward to that during the couple of hours they'd served together.

Kahkay had allowed himself to get busy with his career and he'd neglected Garry, even as Garry stood by him all these years. Garry deserved someone better than Richard E. Kahkay to bear witness to his passing.

Kahkay forced a big grin on his face. "Isn't this great, Moocey? The trees, the birds, the fresh air?"

"No, ssssir," hissed back M-. "I find this climate most unpleasant."

"I don't know what I was thinking when I said West Virginia wasn't hospitable. This is great! I should build a vacation cabin here to return to when we come back to Earth," said Kahkay.

"You do that," snapped M-. "I will not be visiting you at this 'vacation cabin.'"

"Well, I wouldn't invite you," said Kahkay, wondering why M- needed to stress the words 'vacation cabin' and say them so weirdly.

Walking on, Kahkay fell silent. He felt the need to needle his science office periodically because it maintained the illusion that Kahkay was comfortable in his role as captain and that everything was going well. This seemed especially important to do today, when so much had gone wrong. Appearances must be kept up. If the crew lost confidence in him, he'd be toast.

Kahkay wouldn't blame them for losing confidence, though. He'd certainly lost it in himself, if he'd ever had it. At the beginning of his career, he remembered that he had felt sure of himself. That had been wiped away long ago, though. If it hadn't been for Grace...

Not for the first time, Kahkay's thoughts returned to Grace Thomas. He knew she was mad at him, and deservedly so. He'd never say that to her, of course; she didn't need any bigger ego than she already had. But she'd seen what he'd done as using her, and maybe he had. He hadn't tried to steal a promotion from her, but he could see why she thought that he had, and he felt horrible about it.

If it had been anyone but Grace, Kahkay thought he wouldn't worry about it. But her of all people, someone who had proven a true friend over the years, had stuck by Kahkay through everything, who helped make him what he was...

And now, he was squandering his chance. He was thumbing his nose at what Grace had done. She had helped him achieve his goal of being the youngest captain in the A.S.S., and in return, he'd failed her miserably, not living up to the commanding officer he wanted to be.

How could Kahkay turn this around? How could he make up for his wrong? How could he be worthy of her, a standard of measurement he yearned to achieve more, even, than being an A.S.S. captain?

Surely, though, this wasn't all his fault. How could Jamieson have given him command with so little direction? Why hadn't any of his senior officers advised him better? What kind of luck did Kahkay have to have to encounter such a powerful, hostile being on his first mission? Yes, this was just a run of misfortune, Kahkay told himself. This didn't mean he sucked as a captain. They were a couple of minor setbacks. Lots of people had rough first days, and turned out just fine.

They came around a bend and Kahkay saw their destination to be closer than he had expected. He steeled himself. The first step towards rebounding was to secure a senior crew, and this Doctor Awshucks was his best chance of filling an important hole. Hehe. Kahkay was determined to accomplish this small goal, do something right on his first day and prove that what had happened to Garry wasn't his fault and wouldn't define his legacy.

CHAPTER SEVEN
WEST VIRGINIA, EARTH, 2424

Doctor Prudence Awshucks sat on the porch of her quaint cottage, staring at the horizon. She had a beautiful view from here down into the valley below, all the splendor that Mother Nature had intended on display, isolated from people, for the most part. Her nearest neighbor was at least a mile away. She wondered why others hadn't moved to this eden ages ago, filling up the mountain with their dwellings, but then decided she didn't care, as long as they weren't here.

To be fair, the view was a bit blurrier than it should have been. That was likely due to the large quantity of peach schnapps Awshucks had consumed today. Which reminded her, her throat was a bit parched. She reached for the cool glass on the small table beside her rocking chair and raised it to her lips, imbibing some more of the sweet beverage.

Awshucks didn't have a drinking problem, she just enjoyed the drink. It was the one thing that gave her comfort, and kept away the nagging doubts about her future.

Prudence Awshucks was a brilliant surgeon and general practitioner. Graduating at the top of her class, she'd taken a job with the A.S.S. because that's what people in her position did. The A.S.S. was among the most sought-after employers. They had lots of resources, and would grant her access to the most brilliant minds in the universe, on Earth and beyond. If she wanted to be the best, it was the logical step to take.

But Awshucks had never fit in fully with the A.S.S. For one thing, she didn't much care for people, let alone aliens, and the A.S.S. was full of both. She was constantly besieged by those who wanted her attention, and she'd been forced to learn the anatomy of dozens of species. That wasn't how she wanted to spend her days.

When the announcement had come down that all A.S.S. physicians had to accept a tour on a starsheep, that had been the last straw for her. She knew that the A.S.S. was building its fleet as fast as it could, and its medical branch had been too picky in its hiring practices, leaving them without enough senior doctors to go around. But that was their fault, not hers, and she didn't think she should have to pay for it.

Awshucks had no desire to go into space. As far as she was concerned, it was just a big, cold, empty death trap. She didn't trust machines, and starsheeps were filled with mechanical contraptions, as well as being one themselves. That ridiculous name, starsheep, not a real word, only reinforced her beliefs. Why should she entrust her life to such things, especially when Earth had been launching them for less than a decade? They couldn't have gotten the bugs worked out yet. That there had been few major incidents only reinforced that belief.

The doctor thought back to the first contact the A.S.S. had with the C'mons. Doctor Lawrence Taylor had been the senior medical officer on the *A.S.S. Avis*, and he'd also been her closest friend. When he'd signed up to go off planet, she'd called him a fool. After a few months of service, with frequent calls from him, he seemed happy and satisfied, and she had started thinking that she might have been wrong to be so against space travel. Then the C'mons had blown up the *Avis* and everyone on board, including Doctor Taylor, and Awshucks knew she was right. She was never leaving Earth.

But now what? She didn't dare apply for another medical job. She'd had two interviews right after her resignation, both with very prestigious universities, and both interviewers had been completely blown away that she was voluntarily walking away from the A.S.S. One had been sure she was there to engage in corporate espionage, spy on their facility for the A.S.S., and the other just told her she was far too overqualified to come work for them, a hospital that only dealt with humans. Neither believed that she had made the right decision in quitting, if they believed her story at all.

And so, Awshucks had decided moving to the remote wilderness and being drunk all the time, something she had rarely done before resigning from the fleet, was much easier than dealing with the constant judgment and the disappointment. Not that she much cared what anyone else thought of her, she just didn't want it rubbed in her face that they looked down upon her.

Yet, there were nagging doubts about her decision. Not because this wasn't the life she wanted; it absolutely was. But to be thirty-four and retired wasn't exactly a smart option. Her pension checks were very small, and while her bills were low, too, she was going to run out of booze sooner or later. Her tolerance was building, and she'd almost run through her supply.

Awshucks didn't think she could stand to be sober any more. When she was drunk, she was happy. She could forget about the decisions she'd made, the people she'd driven away. Like her fiancé who accused her of being too wrapped up in her work. Admittedly, she'd unintentionally left him at the altar while engaged in research, but still… Or her family, who were as judgmental about her walking away from her career as everyone else, and whom she hadn't been able to face since then.

With time running out on this sabbatical, Awshucks was going to have to do something soon. She'd either have to return to civilization and find a new line of work, or find a way to be alone with her thoughts in the middle of nowhere. Neither sounded like a viable option to her.

This was the mindset she was in, tipsy and full of regrets, when she saw the two figures, drenched in sweat, stagger up the dirt road towards her house. At first, she assumed she was imagining them. Sadly, she was not.

"Well, hello, pretty lady! Is your mother home? Ha!" laughed Kahkay, and beside him, Lieutenant Com M- grimaced. Bad enough that the captain had forced M- to climb a mountain, or a small version of one, in this muggy weather. Now M- had to stand here beside him, as if he were supporting the idiocy coming out of Kahkay's mouth.

This was not what M- had signed up for. M- had heard wonderful things about humans, and had been looking forward very much to working alongside them. Temperamentally, he considered himself much more like the Earth beings than his own people.

But the reality of serving under Captain Richard W. Kahkay was proving to be far less than expected. Kahkay wasn't a curious explorer, he was an ass who made M- feel small. If M- wanted to feel small, he could go home. He wanted to be among esteemed colleagues, part of something larger than himself, working together for the greater good. One day under Kahkay's command and M- didn't see that happening any time soon.

The *Thrifty* was M-'s first starsheep post, coming with a promotion in rank. He had graduated from the academy already a lieutenant, his experience on his home world and unique race, M- being the only one of his species currently serving, earning him a bit of privilege. His classmates resented him for that, as did the scientists he'd worked alongside at headquarters. M- had been glad to get away from that, figuring he would have a fresh start on a starsheep, his goal post when joining the Associated Starsheep Services, anyway. How wrong he'd been.

Now, M- had to pretend that he approved of Kahkay's actions, which reflected poorly on the entire crew, and stand beside the jerk while he wooed a doctor to come out of retirement and join them. M- had a hard time doing that when he didn't respect Kahkay one iota, and was already plotting to transfer off the *Thrifty* at the first opportunity.

"Lord have mercy, who wants to know?" said the woman in the rocking chair, clearly inebriated as indicated by her wild and erratic rocking. M- disliked her instantly, the picture of sloppiness and unprofessionalism. Given his low first impression of the human, M- was unsurprised that Kahkay had the opposite reaction.

"I'm Captain Richard G. Kahkay of the *A.S.S. Thrifty*. The 'G' stands for gorgeous, just like you are," said Kahkay, far too full of himself. How could this man be so cavalier after the disaster of a first mission he'd just led?

"Flattery will get you nowhere, son," said Awshucks, earning M-'s respect momentarily until she followed it up with, "I have no use for the A.S.S."

"Son? Uh, it looks like we're the same age," said Kahkay. M- looked back and forth between them, but couldn't tell. Most humans looked the same to him, though he was recently able to ascertain the difference between females and males fairly easily, something that had stumped him the first few years he spent on Earth.

"Mmmhmm," said M- in amusement at seeing Kahkay thrown for a loop. "Pardon the Captain. I'm Lieutenant Commander M-. We're looking for Doctor Awshucks."

"That's me all right, Scaly Skin," said Awshucks. "At least, I think I heard my name in that gobedy gook you call a language. Whatta ya want with me?"

M- made an insulted sound, his scales starting to tinge brown. The nerve of this woman! Had she no decorum? She was supposed to be an A.S.S. officer. M- assumed Kahkay was insensitive because he was dumb, but this woman seemed not to care who she insulted. Yes, M- knew he was probably a little too touchy about his differences sometimes, but this was just obviously so far beyond the rules of polite society that he was sure anyone in his position would feel the same.

"You?" asked Kahkay in surprise. "You're retired?" Of course he wouldn't rise to M-'s defense. M- expected no better of him, and yet, was still hurt that his commanding officer ignored Awshucks' awful comments.

"An *early* retirement," said Awshucks.

"Ah, oh, OK, OK," said Kahkay quickly, thrown off balance again, which was the one comfort M- got from this exchange. "Well, uh, Miss Awshucks…"

"*Doctor* Awshucks," she corrected him haughtily, though M- couldn't blame her for this one. An earned title should be used with respect.

"OK, Doctor Awshucks," said Kahkay dismissively. "We've come to bring you out of retirement to serve as the chief medical officer on the best ship in the fleet." Kahkay made it sound like such an honor, which M- had thought it would be. Too bad reality fell so short of expectation.

"What happened to Doctor Bashir?" asked Awshucks with concern.

"Who?" asked Kahkay with confusion.

"Doctor Bashir, the chief medical officer of the *A.S.S. Dream*, the best ship in the fleet! Did that rascal get himself killed?" asked Awshucks. M- bristled. True, the *Dream* was a fine vessel, but M- agreed with Kahkay that the *Thrifty* was now taking over that title. It may have been a biased opinion, but M- was nothing if not loyal. Until he felt disrespected, anyway, and the starsheep itself hadn't insulted him.

"Uh, no?" said Kahkay. "Now, hold on... I'm the best captain of the fleet. I'm the captain of the *A.S.S. Thrifty.*"

"Oh. *That* one," said Awshucks scornfully. "I thought you said the *best* ship."

M- made a noise of deep offense taken. The *Thrifty* had had some rough test runs, but M- had been part of a team that oversaw those early days and fixed the issues. And the tests certainly hadn't gone any worse than many of the others for new ships. The *Dream* itself had had an unusually uneven start. What facts could she possibly be basing her opinion of inferiority on?

"Well, it is the best!" proclaimed Kahkay defensively, and for the first time today, M- felt a kinship to him, believing the same. That camaraderie was erased as soon as Kahkay said, "Well, help me out here, Mugo. I mean, what's...?"

"Why? You seem to be doing just fine on your own," said M-. If Kahkay couldn't even bother to get M-'s name right, there was no way M- was going to help him out now. M- was loyal to the A.S.S., but not to this bumbling imbecile.

"Evil prick," muttered Kahkay under his breath, which stung M-, even though he tried not to care. "All right, Doctor Awshucks, we need you to join our crew."

"And why would I want to do something stupid like risk my life flying around on a flimsy hunk o' metal, inches away from death in the cold jaws of outer space, when I can sit on my porch enjoying the beautiful view and this nice, cool peach schnapps?"

"Peach schnapps?" asked Kahkay. "Yeah, yeah, we have all the peach schnapps on the ship. All the peach schnapps you could want."

"Free?" asked Awshucks.

"Yes," said Kahkay.

"Uh, it actually comes from the ship's operating budget, so-," began M-. Beverages fell under the science department's purview, as chemistry was often needed to mix drinks on the fly, the *Thrifty* not having room to take unlimited quantities of everything with it. If Kahkay promised this woman unlimited drinks, given how much she seemed eager to consume copious amounts, M- would have to cut back in other areas. That was unacceptable. M- had budgeted only for normal levels of consumption.

"So it's free to you," interrupting Kahkay. "Will you join us?"

M- looked at her, willing her to say no. Surely she would refuse. Answering to Kahkay was bad enough. He couldn't imagine serving alongside someone like this... woman.

"Well, I am down to my last barrel of the stuff, and retirement doesn't pay that much at my age. I reckon if I were drunk all the time, I might forget where I was," mused Awshucks out loud, clearly talking it through instead of thinking it through. M- detested individuals who did that. "Assumin' we're not goin' very far from Earth and the crew promises not to need me sober."

M- opened his mouth to say with faux apology that that would not be the case at all, but Kahkay was quicker. "Well, I am the captain, so I'm sure there will be very few injuries."

"Technically, I believe you to be correct...," stated M-.

"I know I am," said Kahkay smugly.

"...since we're more likely to die than be hurt under your command," finished M-, amusing himself with his wit. Normally, he wouldn't dare speak to a senior officer this way, but Kahkay needed to be reminded of what happened earlier. His attitude was really getting on M-'s nerves. Besides, Kahkay didn't seem to get angry about the barbs, which made M- a bit bolder about tossing them.

"Shut up, Manclap," said Kahkay, disappointingly unfazed by M-'s zinger.

"I cannot understand a word this lizard man says! Where's your ride?" asked Awshucks. M- shuddered. There would now be two of this type of person on the starsheep? The thought chilled him.

"Kahkay to *Thrifty*," said Kahkay into the air.

"Yes, Captain Kahkay?" came back Lieutenant Tokaladie's response.

"Three to bring up, Lieutenant Tokaladie," said Kahkay.

"Aye, sir," said Tokaladie.

"B-beamers?" asked Awshucks in panic. "You didn't say I'd have to-."

The noise of the beamer cut her off, and M- allowed himself a modicum of satisfaction at her discomfort. He may have to serve with this woman, but he didn't have to like it.

Chief Engineer Foley peered warily out of the bathroom onto the bridge. This was so embarrassing. His first day on the job and he couldn't hold himself together. What would the captain think?

Thankfully, Kahkay was nowhere in sight. Only Lieutenant Tokaladie and a smattering of ensigns manned the various stations. Foley saw one of his engineers at his bridge post, and knowing he wasn't needed, decided to try to slip as unobtrusively as possible downstairs.

"Feeling OK, Chief?" asked Tokaladie as soon as Foley emerged. Several of the ensigns look his way and Foley's face turned red. He should have known he couldn't get to the elevator unnoticed. It was just too small a bridge.

"Fine. Just a wee bug, I think," he replied. "I'm gonna lie down for a spell."

"Feel better," said Tokaladie encouragingly, and Foley managed a small smile of gratitude. She was a good lass, smart and accomplished, and a kind heart to boot. He made it into the privacy of the elevator without further incident.

Unlike most of the senior staff, who lived close to the bridge, Foley's apartment was on the lower decks, near the engine room. Thankfully, it wasn't time for a shift change, and so he made the ride and the sprint down his hallway without encountering another soul, a rare feat on a ship of more than seven hundred. Though, dozens of them hadn't yet come on board, like the good Doctor Boyce.

Foley ducked through the door to his home gratefully. A woman was waiting for him, tapping her foot impatiently.

"Colm, dear, how are ya?" she asked. "The bridge called down to me and told me you were comin'."

"They shouldna done that," said Foley wearily.

"Aye, they should have. I have a right to know," she said.

"Ah, Fitzy," said Foley, sinking into their couch. "I've been better."

"Have ye now?" asked Fitzgerald Fitzsimmons, Foley's beloved wife and assistant chief engineer, moving behind him and feeling his forehead.

Normally, spouses would not be permitted to serve so closely together, but the A.S.S. had made an exception for them because they'd accomplished much together professionally and had more than proven how well they worked together before such rules had been put in place.

Interestingly, they'd actually grown up only a few miles from one another in Ireland, but school district boundaries being what they were, hadn't met until the academy.

"Ya feel clammy," she said, running her hands around his face.

"Aye, I am," said Foley, appreciative of her tender touch.

"On your first day, too!" said Fitzy with sympathy. "That's horrible."

"Aye, love," agreed Foley.

"How was he?" she asked.

"How was who?" asked Foley, stomach calming down. Nearly two hours in the bridge bathroom with stuff coming out both ends, he desperately hoped he was through the worst of it.

"Don't pretend with me, Colm. I know ye better than ye know yourself, and I know why we took this assignment," she said with a bit of reproach.

"We took this assignment because the *Thrifty* could be the best ship in the fleet, with our help," said Foley defensively.

"And because its captain is Richard K. Kahkay," said Fitzy.

"That's mad," said Foley.

"Tell me I'm wrong," said Fitzy, knowing Foley wouldn't outright lie to her.

"There might be some small, very wee bit of truth to that," admitted Foley. "But I stand by that we're going to make this starsheep the best."

"Of course we will, darlin'," said Fitzy. "I have no doubt about that."

"Captain Kahkay is..." Foley searched for the right word. He wanted to convey the impressive air about their new commanding officer without being overly gushy. "He's grand."

"I'm glad for ye and yer new boyfriend," said Fitzy.

"Oh, stop it," said Foley.

"What about the mission? We're headin' back to Earth awfully soon."

"Aye, it didn't go well. It weren't the captain's fault, though. We ran into a spot of bad circumstance," said Foley.

"We left without four of our engineers," said Fitzy.

"And?" asked Foley.

"And what?" asked Fitzy innocently.

"What are ye implyin'?" asked Foley.

"I'm not implyin' nothin'," said Fitzy.

"Don't try foolin' me lass. There was judgment in yer tone," said Foley.

"So what if there were?" asked Fitzy. "Can the Captain Kahkay of your dreams be so great he can't ever make a mistake?"

"Of course he can," said Foley.

"Will I not be allowed to question him in my own home? Not cast aspersions when they're warranted?" asked Fitzy.

"Now, lass, I said nothin' of the sort," said Foley.

"Darn right you didn't," said Fitzy, softening. "I was just sayin', things didn't seem to go all that swimmingly."

"I couldn't say for sure," said Foley. "I admit, I mighta been a bit distracted with this ailment."

"Poor Colm," said Fitzy tenderly. "Can I make ya a bit a soup?"

"That would be lovely," said Foley. He felt bile rising in his throat again and dashed for their own bathroom. "Later."

Kahkay strode back onto the bridge, triumphant. Looking around, he was disappointed to see both Chief Engineer Foley and Lieutenant Who were not at their duty stations. What good was triumph when it was just in front of a bunch of ensigns? Though, that pretty Lieutenant Tokaladie was here to witness it.

"I did it. I got us a new doctor," said Kahkay proudly. Lieutenant Commander M- made some noises Kahkay didn't like as he retook the science panel. "How awesome was I, Mallamar?"

"You did a satisfactory job," said M-, barely sounding like he meant it.

Oh, well. M- could sulk all he wanted. The *Thrifty* needed a new chief medical officer, and Kahkay got it a new chief medical officer. M- couldn't ruin that. Besides, what did Kahkay care what an evil being thought of him?

"Good job, sir," said Tokaladie brightly, though was there a hint of patronizing in her tone?

Kahkay waved it away. Probably just his imagination. Surely, she looked up to him the way all the junior officers did, and this was the right way to end his first day on the job. Sure, it started a little rough, but here he was at the end, sitting in the center chair, getting things done. Like a boss.

"Captain's Diary," said Kahkay, flipping the recording switch on his chair. "I got a Captain's Log when I saw Doctor Awshucks, if you know what I mean, hoho, and you do because you're me; no one else is allowed to read this diary.

"Anyway, she's not my usual type... Ah, who am I kidding? All women are my type." He paused briefly to toss a wink at Tokaladie, but she was facing away from him. Ah, well. Plenty of time for that later.

"She might prove a challenging nut to crack, but get a couple of drinks in me, I'd still do her. Might not even need the drinks." Kahkay spared a glance around the bridge. No one was looking at him. Hmm. He thought recording the diary on the bridge, giving the lower-ranked crewmen and women a peek into how command works, would be met with more awe. He had always wondered why no captain he served under had done it. It seemed to him like a great way to set a tone and style.

"Today was a long day, but as I end with this great accomplishment, I can't help but look forward to all we're going to accomplish on the *Thrifty*, surely the best ship in the fleet, with the best crew." That was for them. He hadn't worked with anyone enough yet to know how good they were, except Garry, who was dead, and M-, who was almost definitely evil. But he assumed the rest were really good. Still, no one was giving him an encouraging smile or proud thumbs up. Weird.

"Now, our good deeds done, I retire to my bed. Looking forward to another great day tomorrow. Captain out."

Kahkay thumbed off the recording and stood, stretching in an overexaggerated way. "I don't know about you guys, but I'm beat. Get some rest. We've got another big day tomorrow."

"Do we, sir?" asked M-. "I was under the impression we had not yet received our orders."

"Well, not yet, but I'm sure they'll be great," said Kahkay. M- made a noise that did not sound like agreement, but Kahkay decided to let it slide. He was feeling magnanimous, ending on such a high note.

"Lieutenant Tokaladie? Care to join me for a drink?" he asked.

"Sorry, sir. I'm working late," she said.

"You know, I'm the captain," said Kahkay.

"Yes, sir," she said.

"That means I can decide who has to work late and who doesn't."

"Yes, sir," she replied, still no emotion in it.

"So what I'm saying is, you don't have to work late tonight," said Kahkay.

"Sorry, sir. Still getting my department set up," she said, not even turning to look at him.

"All right. Totally get it," said Kahkay, not expecting the brush off, but certainly not going to push it further and draw attention to it.

"I, too, will be working late this evening, so cannot join you," said M-.

"I didn't invite you, Malia," said Kahkay. "Catch you guys on the flipside." He strode confidently off the bridge and into the elevator, waiting for the doors to close before slumping.

The doors opened again almost immediately. Right, his apartment was right below the bridge. He'd forgotten. Thankfully, the doors opened into his private quarters for him (the back doors would have opened to the hallway for anyone else) and he didn't have to walk past any crewman.

Kahkay was satisfied with the brave front he put on. It had been an act, but a necessary one. A captain couldn't show weakness, and after a day like today, he needed to go out on a good note. He privately patted himself on the back for making that happen. Mission accomplished. He took off his uniform and allowed himself a few celebratory whoops around his head in celebration.

A throat clearing sound made him freeze. He spun around to see a very young man standing there in a red tunic and firmly pressed slacks. Since Kahkay had chosen to wear the skirt version of the uniform, and he was a firm believer in going commando, he was fully exposed. Kahkay made no attempt to cover himself up. After all, he was in his own apartment.

"Who are you?" asked Kahkay in surprise.

"Cliff, sir. The captain's yeoman," said the officer with a slightly squeaky voice.

"OK... I thought I requested a female yeoman?" said Kahkay, head tilted to the side. Cliff very purposefully did not look at Kahkay's enormous package, fully on display.

"I, ah, don't know about that, sir," said Yeoman Cliff. "Admiral Jamieson personally gave me this assignment."

"Figures," muttered Kahkay.

"I'm sorry, sir?" asked Cliff.

"Nothing," said Kahkay.

"Very good. I've turned down your bed and your dinner is on the table. Anything else I can do for you tonight, sir?" asked Cliff, the picture of decorum and politeness.

"No, thanks, Cliff. Good job," said Kahkay. Cliff nodded, then left the apartment just a little more quickly than normal.

This was Kahkay's captain's yeoman? Well, that was disappointing.

CHAPTER EIGHT
CETI BETA SYSTEM, 2420

Lieutenant Commander Grace Thomas, security chief, stepped off the elevator onto the bridge of the *A.S.S. Advantage*. Captain Jamie Jamieson turned from the big screen and smiled at her.

"Congratulations on the promotion, Lieutenant Commander Thomas," said Captain Jamieson.

"Thank you, sir," said Grace a bit shyly, glancing around the bridge and seeing all eyes on her, most offering warm encouragement, a few of the younger ones being a bit awed. It had been hard work to get to this rank, but she felt like the years had been worth it. After this, the goal was to become a first officer, and then a captain. She was well on her way.

She spared a quick thought of her best friend, Dick Kahkay, whom she hadn't spoken with in weeks, but who, of course, had sent a note of congratulations.

Dick had hit Lieutenant Commander more than a year ago, not long after the incident in which they'd lost Captain Roberts. While Grace did receive a commendation for bravery, she had lost a leg and blacked out, while Dick had technically saved the landing party. Grace sometimes thought Roberts may have survived, too, if Dick had just kept his mouth shut, but A.S.S. Command had disagreed, and really, they'd never know if she was right or not, especially as it was an opinion she'd kept to herself.

Truly, she didn't begrudge Dick anything he'd gotten. Their rivalry had just been going on for so long that it was hard not to analyze every decision or action either of them made or took, wondering if she could have done or said something different to outpace him. He was also on track to be a captain, and Grace thought she still had a chance at beating him, behind as she was.

"We've arrived at Ceti Beta VI," reported the pilot and XO, Commander Justman.

"Thank you, Commander," said Captain Jamieson. "Lieutenant Commander Thomas, don't settle into that security station just yet. You and I are beamering down. Have your team meet us in the beamer room."

"Aye, sir," said Grace. She knew things would be tense down on the surface. Ceti Beta VI boasted a small, undeveloped indigenous population that had recently been conquered by a band of outlaws, little more than space pirates. The *Advantage* was here to free the locals and bring the thugs to justice. Grace already had three squads at the ready to assist with that.

As she joined Jamieson in the elevator, Grace hoped she was up to the task. It wouldn't do to disappoint her captain in her first day as head of the security department.

Lieutenant Commander Richard J. Kahkay sat listlessly at his bridge station on the *A.S.S. Cruise*. Communications was a topic Kahkay had mastered years ago, and had long grown bored with. Which meant it was the perfect place to hide out.

What had happened with Captain Roberts had affected Kahkay greatly. He had been on top of the world, er, worlds, before that; thought he had everything figured out. His bravado and his swagger were his greatest assets, and they'd always gotten the job done. Until they hadn't, and had cost Kahkay's commanding officer his head.

How had he allowed it to happen? Why had he not been good enough? The whole thing had really made Kahkay take a long, hard look at his personality and command style, and he kept coming up short. Perhaps he wasn't cut out to captain a starsheep after all.

Which is why he was now serving as the head of a department he didn't have anything left to learn from, or at least nothing he wanted to learn, getting by without having to try too hard.

Hearing about Grace's recent promotion had brightened his day a little. While Kahkay now doubted that he himself was meant to be a leader, Grace certainly was. That woman had worked hard from day one, always trying more than Kahkay had, and the only surprise, in his mind, is that their superiors hadn't noticed earlier. She had more than earned everything she got, unlike him.

The communications console beeped. Kahkay lazily put the ear piece into his canal, sure it was another routine report from A.S.S. Command back on Earth. He bolted up right as soon as he realized it wasn't.

"Lieutenant Commander Kahkay?" asked Captain Fontana from the center chair, her attention having been caught from the corner of her eye by his rapid movement.

"One moment, Captain," said Kahkay, playing the message again. It had to be wrong. It just had to be.

"Lieutenant Commander?" asked Fontana impatiently.

"Distress call from the *A.S.S. Advantage*. They're asking for immediate assistance," said Kahkay, his stomach on the floor, his blood cold. That was Grace's ship.

"How close are we?" Fontana asked her XO, Commander Coon.

"Not far. A couple of hours at maximum speed," said Coon as he consulted his readings.

"Let's get there then," said Fontana.

"Aye, sir," said Coon.

"What was the nature of the *Advantage*'s mission?" Fontana asked. Kahkay stared back at her blankly for several seconds. Fontana's eyes narrowed. Kahkay knew that Fontana knew that he was just skating by, and she didn't approve. This wasn't the first time her look of judgment had been cast upon him, and he wondered how much time he had left before she asked for him to be transferred from the *Cruise*.

"Well?" she asked after several moments, during which Kahkay didn't even turn back to his station.

"Oh. Right," said Kahkay, consulting his panel. "Space pirates have conquered a small tribe of people on Ceti Beta VI, and the *Advantage* was sent to free the indigenous population."

"All right, the pirates must have proven more dangerous than we predicted," said Fontana thoughtfully. "Lieutenant Smith-Jones, ready multiple squadrons to beamer down to the planet's surface as soon as we get there. Arm them with assault-grade rifles."

"Aye, sir," said the security chief, whom Kahkay realized had been looking at him, too, but whom was more professional and now focused on her job.

Smith-Jones was another part of Kahkay's comfort. They weren't dating, but Kahkay knew she requested the post on the *Cruise* because of him. She'd been trying to tie him into a relationship since the Roberts incident, seeing Kahkay as some sort of hero. He usually avoided her, only giving into the occasional sloppy hookup while heavily intoxicated. Kahkay wondered how soon before Smith-Jones realized he was a fraud and gave up on him, too. Probably not much longer.

As the *Cruise* rocketed towards Ceti Beta VI, Kahkay tried to stay busy, hailing the *Advantage* repeatedly to no avail. Even the distress signal stopped. Nothing was coming from the planet but silence.

Kahkay tried not to think of what he would do if Grace Thomas was dead. She was the one person Kahkay cared most about in this universe, and without knowing she was out there doing great things, he wasn't sure he wanted to go on. He lived for their video calls, usually once every couple of weeks, and without them, he didn't think he'd have the heart to even pretend for the A.S.S. any more.

The hours that it took them to reach Ceti Beta VI were a blur that Kahkay didn't remember immediately after, so distraught was he. He didn't even notice when Captain Fontana and Lieutenant Smith-Jones left the bridge to beamer down. He would remain at his post and do nothing other than wait until he heard definitive proof, one way or the other, that Grace Thomas was still alive.

Ducking a laser pistol blast, Lieutenant Commander Grace Thomas dove behind the barrier. Captain Jamieson gave her a relieved look. "What's going on out there, Lieutenant Commander?"

"Not looking good, sir," said Grace, pushing a loose strand of hair from her face, her hand adding a smudge of dirt to an already blackened countenance. "We haven't broken through to the weapons center or the communications center they've set up."

"I still can't raise the *Advantage*," said Jamieson with a frown.

Another figure darted behind the barrier beside them, the blasts from various pirates missing him, too.

"Report, Ensign Flufy," said Jamieson.

"I managed to overhear a conversation between a couple of the pirates," said the security officer seriously. Though, Grace reflected, Flufy was always serious. "It sounds like they took out weapons, shields, and communications on the *Advantage*."

"Damn," said Jamieson. "We had no idea they had such sophisticated defensive capabilities. Our starsheep wasn't prepared for an attack from the ground."

"That's what they were counting on, sir," said Grace. Jamieson nodded, considering their options. He didn't berate himself for not predicting this outcome, and she admired that. Instead, he was focused on the situation at hand.

"All right, we have to assume that the *Advantage* wasn't able to call for help before they were disabled, so we're on our own. How many security officers do we have left?"

Grace looked at Flufy for confirmation, and the Native American shook his head. She knew that meant he was the only survivor from his squad. "Sixteen, sir," said Grace. "Out of forty-three."

"OK, that'll have to be enough," said Jamieson. "I've identified where the lead pirate is holed up on my last reconnaissance sweep. He's vulnerable if we leave the settlement and come back in from behind."

"How can we do that without them knowing that's what we're doing?" asked Grace. "The second we stop engaging them on this front, they're going to realize that they need to watch their backs."

"Good point," said Jamieson. "Thomas, you stay here with Flufy and two others and keep them engaged. I'll take the rest straight out of town and go the long way around. If you can hold out for a couple of hours, I think this'll work."

"Fine, but you take Flufy," said Grace. "He's my best."

"All right," said Jamieson. "How soon can you get the rest to me?"

"Five minutes, maybe ten," said Grace, thinking through the signals she'd need to send and the moves she'd have to make to get word to the others. It would be tricky to do without getting shot in the process, but considering they'd be retreating, not charging, that would make the task considerably easier.

"OK, I'm heading straight out now. Good luck, Lieutenant Commander," said Jamieson, grabbing her arm and looking her dead in the eyes in a display of confidence and respect.

"You, too, sir," said Grace, returning the gaze. Then he was gone along with Flufy, and she was left alone in the middle of a war zone.

"Kahkay," said Commander Coon testily, and Kahkay started in his chair, realizing that this was at least the fourth time in a row that the XO had said his name, the first couple having been more patient and including his rank.

"Sorry. Uh, yes, sir?" asked Kahkay.

"I asked if you'd been able to reach the *Advantage* yet. It would sure help to know if the A.S.S. still held that ship, and what its landing party's plans were on the surface."

"Um, no, sir," said Kahkay, trying to call them again and failing. "The line is dead. Can't even get their voicemail."

"There's got to be another way," said Coon, thinking and staring at the big screen hard. The other ship floated in space in front of them, getting closer as the *Cruise* neared orbit. It was mostly dark and unresponsive, though a few lights showed signs of life over there.

"Wait, is that window blinking?" asked Coon.

"Which window, sir?" asked Kahkay.

"The bathroom off the bridge."

"Oh, yes, sir. Irregular pattern. Must be electrical failure," said Kahkay.

"No, it's repeating. I think it's Morse code," said Coon.

"Hmm. Maybe you're right," said Kahkay.

"Well?" asked Coon impatiently after a minute.

"Yes, sir?" asked Kahkay.

"You're the chief of communications. Can you read Morse code?" asked Coon, clearly unhappy at being stuck with such an incompetent officer, probably wondering how Kahkay had ever risen to this position in the first place.

"I'm a bit rusty, but I've got a translator here," said Kahkay, turning back to his station. At least this would give him something to do other than stare blankly. "Looks like they're saying... 'Systems off, attack from surface.'"

"Shields up!" shouted Coon urgently, and thankfully, Smith-Jones' replacement at the security panel was more alert than Kahkay. The *Cruise* was just sliding into orbit, and no sooner were the shields raised than powerful beams from the surface struck the starsheep, knocking it sideways.

"We're being fired upon from the surface!" said the lieutenant at security, an older, plump woman whose name Kahkay didn't know, even though they'd served together for an entire year.

"So I see, Lieutenant. Can our shields withstand their barrage?" asked Coon.

"For a few minutes, sir, but it looks like they have limited range. We can pull back just a little and still be in beamer and call range of the surface."

"Great. Pulling us back now," said Coon. "Kahkay, call down to engineering and tell Chief Engineer Okuda to assemble a repair team and beamer over to the *Advantage*. Let's get them back up and running, too."

"Aye, sir," said Kahkay, his mind still barely on his job. Grace was down there somewhere, down where those energy beams came from. The fact that the weapons hadn't been taken out yet wasn't a good sign. He felt sick to his stomach.

Grace crouched behind a piece of masonry, lungs burning, gasping for breath. It was just her now, the other three security officers she'd kept behind lying dead amid the destruction. The loss of her team here was staggering, but she tried hard to stay focused. Captain Jamieson was counting on her, and god damn it, she was not going to let that man down.

Grace popped up and fired off a couple of shots from her own laser gun. They were wild and probably didn't hit anything, but at least she was engaging. Hopefully, they'd believe she wasn't alone, or that they'd taken out the rest of her men and women, which they mostly had. Jamieson had to be almost around back by now.

Movement caught her eye. She saw a couple of the space pirates circling the ruins, of what last week had been a small village, towards her. They looked angry, and she didn't blame them. She'd killed many of their friends in the two days she'd been down on the surface of Ceti Beta VI. They probably wanted revenge.

As Grace scurried backwards, she spared a quick glance over her shoulder and saw a couple more pirates coming from the other way. Both were effectively behind her barrier, and though they were far enough off to the sides that she had some cover, that was temporary. They were surrounding her, and she was done. She steeled herself, preparing for her own impending demise.

Interestingly, her thoughts went to Dick Kahkay. She wasn't convinced he'd ever make a good romantic partner; she'd certainly had no sign that he'd slowed his womanizing ways since the academy. Yet, somehow, she had always assumed in the back of her mind that they'd end up together. Maybe not until retirement, when they were both done with their A.S.S. careers, or perhaps as fellow admirals at headquarters after long tenures as captains, but some day. She was surprised to admit this to herself, and regretted it would never happen. She hoped he'd settle down with someone else and be happy, eventually seeing and giving up the error of his ways.

The pirates were getting close now, but she didn't have a good angle to fire on any of them. Grace hoped she'd get a chance to pick off at least one or two before they took her down. She was prepared for the end, but she wasn't going out without a fight. With luck, her sacrifice would give Jamieson the opening he needed.

Then, suddenly, laser beams shot at the pirates from multiple directions and all four fell before her eyes. Before she could even register what had happened, a small group of women and men in A.S.S. uniforms came around the corner. She didn't recognize them, but she could tell from the tunic color of the grey-haired woman in front of her that Grace was looking at a captain.

"I'm Captain Doro Fontana," said the severe-looking woman. "Report."

"Lieutenant Commander Grace Thomas, security chief *A.S.S. Advantage*," said Grace. "Most of my team is down."

"So I see. Are you all alone, Lieutenant?" asked Fontana as the others around her spread out, getting the lay of the land.

"No, sir," said Grace. "Captain Jamieson is leading an assault as we speak."

"Jamieson, huh?" asked Fontana. "Fine man."

"Thank you, Captain Fontana. I feel the same about you," said a familiar voice. Grace stood up, exposing herself to the enemy too quickly, she'd scold herself later, but instead of pirates, she saw Jamieson, Flufy, and a couple of her fellow *Advantage* crewmates coming towards her.

"Glad to see you're all right, Jamieson," said Fontana.

"I am, Fontana, and the situation is well in hand now," said Jamieson.

"Of course it is," said Fontana. "Let me guess, you were outnumbered three to one..."

"Five to one, actually," said Jamieson.

"And you still won the day. I suspect you'll make Admiral after this," said Fontana. "If you want it, that is. I'm sure Janice would love to have you safe and sound back on Earth."

"Perhaps," allowed Jamieson, though there was pain in his eyes. Grace knew he'd lost his only son last year in the incident with the C'mons, and while Jamieson never talked about his personal life, it had to be taking a toll on his marriage.

"*Advantage* to Jamieson," chirped the phone on the captain's belt.

"Excuse me," said Jamieson to Fontana, flipping open the device. "Jamieson here."

"Captain! Glad to hear your voice," said Commander Justman. "Thanks to some help from the *Cruise*, systems have been restored. Do you need back up?'

"Not anymore," said Jamieson. "We've got this."

Kahkay made it into his apartment on shaky legs and slid down the wall wearily. He couldn't believe the day he'd had, worried sick from morning 'til night. Not until the communications officer on the *Advantage* had acknowledged that Grace was alive and unhurt did Kahkay allow himself to breathe normally or leave his station, though his shift had ended hours ago. Thankfully, that was the case, as he'd finally learned.

Kahkay put his head in his hands and wept. He wept with joy at Grace surviving the assault that so many of her team did not. He wept in sorrow at what he had become, a man he didn't recognize, certainly not the promising young star he'd been less than two years before. He wept because he was exhausted and he had to let it out.

No one would ever know this, not even Grace. Kahkay could talk to her about almost anything, but he refused to tell her the joke his career had become. He was too ashamed. He'd never be able to bear the look of pity she'd give him. That would be worse than anything.

Kahkay briefly considered calling Lieutenant Smith-Jones for comfort, but abandoned the idea as quickly as it came. He was not willing to be emotionally raw with her, not least because she was sure to take it the wrong way, and the thought of sex right now didn't appeal to him.

That was the first time in his life Kahkay had admitted that. In truth, he'd been feeling it for a while now, but this was the first time he'd truly owned up to it. The constant string of bedmates just hadn't been the same after Captain Roberts. When Kahkay had lost his mojo, he'd lost his libido, too. Mostly.

So where would he go from here? Could he really just continue to go through the motions? Do a job that his heart wasn't in? Or was there something he could do to turn things around? Honestly, that wasn't even something he wanted to consider right now. For today, it was enough that Grace was alive. Anything else was less important and could wait.

Kahkay's personal computer buzzed a notification. That was strange. Anyone on the *Cruise* would have just tapped into his apartment intercom, and he wasn't expecting to hear from anyone else. Unless it was Garry Marshall. Was today some birthday or holiday Kahkay had forgotten?

Standing on shaky legs, he made his way to his desk, figuring he'd just press ignore or Garry would keep ringing him. To his surprise, though, the call wasn't from Garry; it was from Grace.

Kahkay sat in his chair a little straighter, wiping his eyes and smoothing his hair. He spared a quick glance at the mirror across the room, and while he wasn't perfect, a big, forced smile made him look at least somewhat convincing. Hopefully, after all Grace had just been through, she wouldn't notice. He hit the button to answer her call.

"Gracie!" he said with a cheeriness he didn't feel. "What's happening?"

"Hi, Dick," she said warmly. "How are you?"

"Oh, I'm fine. How about you? Anything interesting happen lately?" He flashed his trademark grin that worked on nearly all females save the one he was talking to now.

Grace laughed. That was strange; she never laughed at his lame jokes. "You could say that."

"I was glad to hear you were OK," said Kahkay, allowing a small amount of sincerity to creep in.

"Me, too," said Grace, her eyes looking haunted. "We lost a lot of people down there."

"Not you, though," said Kahkay. "Pirates can't take out my Gracie."

"They could have," she admitted. "They took out a lot of men and women they shouldn't have. I survived mostly by luck."

The sincerity was too much for Kahkay. He didn't want to see her like this, or worse, her to see him like this. He had to lighten the mood, quickly. "Well, all's well that ends well, right?" he asked.

"I guess so," said Grace distantly. He was losing her. He just had her for the first time with that laugh, and now he was losing her. A sense of desperation rose within him.

"You gonna get a few days off?" he asked.

"What?" she asked confused.

"I just thought that, after everything down on Ceti Beta VI, they might give you a little vacation time," said Kahkay.

"Oh! Probably. I didn't even think about that," said Grace. "Do you have any leave coming up?"

"No," said Kahkay sadly. Why had he even asked about hers if he couldn't reciprocate? "We were heading to deep space when we diverted here. Gonna be off the grid for a couple of months."

"That's too bad," said Grace. "I guess our timing has never been great."

Did she just say what he thought she said? That almost sounded like... No, Kahkay quickly brushed away the thought. He was imagining things, and even if he wasn't, which he knew he was, he wasn't in any shape for her right now. She could do so much better.

"Speak for yourself. My timing is always perfect," he said smugly, then kicked himself mentally. How cheesy could he be?

She smiled wryly, though the bemusement didn't reach her eyes. "I guess it is," she said.

"So why are you calling?" Kahkay asked. D'oh. Even worse.

"I... I just wanted to say hi," she said, and he knew that whatever chance she might have possibly been giving him a moment ago was gone. He'd blown it, just like he'd blown everything else lately. "We were so close, you know, physically, and didn't get to see one another, so I thought I'd call."

"I'm glad you did," said Kahkay with feeling. "It's always nice to hear from you."

It was too little, too late. She didn't meet his eyes. "Well, I guess I have reports to file, need to make calls to the loved ones of the team members I lost."

"I'm sorry, Grace," said Kahkay. "Truly. And I'm really glad you're OK."

"Thanks, Dick. That means a lot," said Grace. "Talk to you later."

The screen went dark and Kahkay leaned back in his seat, feeling as lost as he'd ever felt.

CHAPTER NINE
A.S.S. STATION BP4, 2424

Lieutenant Commander M- eyed the first officer at the pilot station warily. He had only met Commander Dirt this morning, just before Admiral Jamieson had ordered the *Thrifty* to the space station at the edge of C'mon territory, but he couldn't shake the feeling that Dirt was up to no good.

Having been raised around a race of duplicitous beings, M- considered himself skilled at spotting that quality in others. While he himself was rarely, if ever, evil, most of his family and school chums absolutely were. M- was an oddity for his species, and part of why he had joined the A.S.S. was to get away from such beings. That one was now serving alongside him on the bridge was troubling.

M- couldn't prove his suspicions yet, but the reasons for them were numerous. For one thing, Dirt kept looking around in wonder, seemingly unaccustomed to being on a starsheep. Also, Dirt asked a lot of questions about the *Thrifty* that he should already know the answers to, including what the controls at his station did. That didn't feel right.

In the early days of the A.S.S., officers may not have had experience in such vessels before shipping out, but now, made necessary by numerous personalities unable to handle the rigors of the job, it was required that all captains and first officers spend some time in starsheep service prior to taking command. Other senior officers could slide by on occasion, but not an XO. At least not to the best of M-'s knowledge. He supposed an Admiral could make an exception in appointing an officer, but he didn't see any compelling reason Dirt should be the beneficiary of that.

Speaking of sliding by, M- didn't much care for Doctor Awshucks, either. It wasn't that she was hiding some sinister, ulterior motive; quite the contrary. If anything, Awshucks spoke her mind too much. Normally, M- could overlook that, and even the insults she hurled at him, as M- did with the captain. But her intoxication while on duty made him bristle.

Not for the first time in the three days since the *Thrifty* had begun its mission, M- wondered if he had made a mistake by enlisting. This experience wasn't what he had expected, and if he had to keep putting up with constant incompetence, it might not be worth the risk to his life to continue to serve here.

"Dirt?" asked Kahkay from the chair at the center of the room.

"Yes?" asked Commander Dirt, turning around and abandoning his controls completely to look at his commanding officer.

"Is that space station BP4 on the big screen?" asked Kahkay. Dirt looked at Kahkay quizzically, as if confused by the question, then spun back around to consult his panel.

"Yes, sir, it is. We've arrived," said Dirt, slowing down the starship as it neared the outpost.

"I thought so," said Kahkay. "OK, Dirt, Foley, you're with me."

"Mmmay I accompany you as well, Captain Kahkay?" asked M-.

"No, I need you to run the ship, Meemow," said Kahkay, getting his closest correct approximation of M-'s name to date. Maybe he was merely a slow learner and was finally coming around? Which made pushing the captain right at this moment a difficult decision for M-, though duty won out over the desire to be accepted.

"Ssssir, I really think-," started M-.

"Not in front of the children, Mo," said Kahkay.

M- bristled. How could he serve a man that didn't trust him? Why did Kahkay make this so difficult? "Can I speak to you in your office for a moment?" M- asked.

"Fine," said Kahkay, eyeing him cautiously. "I'll be right back. Chief Engineer Foley, you have the bridge."

Kahkay rose from his chair and strode through the door between Tokaladie's station and the bathroom that led to his private work space, not bothering to see if M- would follow. M- did, of course, entering the small, surprisingly tastefully decorated, room before the automatic doors could start to slide close.

Kahkay strode behind his desk, then turned to look at the science officer, not bothering to sit down, a frown on his face. "What is it Mannymow?"

"Captain, I have ssssuspicions about Commander Dirt," said M-, his 's's elongating more often than usual because he was stressed. "He seems to be, as you say, 'casing the joint.'" M- was pleased to use the phrase he had recently learned, though he worried that he had pronounced it wrong. He'd have to double-check with the ship's library.

"Nonsense, Meme-too," said Kahkay flippantly. "He's new here; he's just figuring out where everything is."

M- sighed, frustrated that he had to spell things out. Could Kahkay possibly be so dense and unobservant?. "A.S.S. Academy training should familiarize crewmen with the controls before they ever set foot on a starsheep, and before one becomes XO, one must serve on other starsheeps with identical control panels. The questions he is asking are not appropriate for a man who has risen to the rank of Commander. Additionally, he seems far too interested in the individuals that make up the crew."

"Relax, Mewcaroni. If anyone is evil around here, it's you, not Commander Dirt."

M- bristled. He was trying to help, had done nothing but try to help, and his loyalty was constantly rewarded with more insults. "As I have told you before, Captain Kahkay, my voice is perfectly normal for my species, and does not belie any ulterior motives."

"Riiiiight," said Kahkay, still obviously not believing M-. "OK, I've got my eye on you, Mimi."

M- sighed again, heavier this time. "If you will not allow me to accompany you, will you at least take Who with you?"

"Who?" asked Kahkay.

"Ahhh, Security Chief Who Grappa, the officer that is supposed to protect you on all away missions," said M-. This was something Kahkay knew and should have been aware of. The captain was sounding like Dirt, completely obtuse about operations. Maybe this was a common quality in human leaders M- had just not encountered until now?

"You mean that gorilla guy?" asked Kahkay casually.

M-'s scales flashed yellow as he became flustered. "Who is not a 'gorilla guy.' Why must you insist on applying human animal names to describe alien species? Who is a trained A.S.S. officer."

"Yeah, I'm good. It's just a space station," said Kahkay, waving M- away.

"Protocol-," started M-, refusing to give up. He knew he was in the right, and the regulations would back him up.

"No need to start quoting the rules to me," said Kahkay. "I know them. And none compare to rule number one: captain's prerogative."

M- quickly ran through the regulations in his head again. There was no such thing. Did Kahkay really think he could just make it up? "That is not a real rule."

"Sure it is. Only rule I've ever needed to live by," said Kahkay, far too casually for M-'s taste.

"But ssssir...," said M-.

"That's enough, Moutymee," said Kahkay, striding past the science officer back to his office door to indicate M- should leave. "I'm taking Dirt and Foley and that's final. You have the bridge."

M- had never felt more helpless, and more ignored. "Do not say I did not warn you," he said.

"Well, I won't," said Kahkay.

"Well... good," said M-, unable to summon a more biting comeback.

"Yes, good," said Kahkay.

"Fine," said M-. He wasn't letting this oaf get the last word just by repeating him.

"Fine," said Kahkay.

M- tensed. Where was the line between insubordination and voicing legitimate concerns? He hesitated a moment, trying to decide if he should speak again. After a few seconds, he couldn't help but toss out another "Good."

"OK, I'm done with this," said Kahkay, thumbing the button that opened the office door, the automatic opening only working from the bridge side and when the office was vacant to allow greater privacy.

Mustering as much dignity as he could, M- squared his shoulders, or tried to anyway, as his shoulders were low, round, and barely existent, then marched past Kahkay back to his station. Actually, it really wasn't a march, either, as M-'s physiology was more apt to glide than march. But he tried to imitate the human version of such a move and thought Kahkay had to have gotten the picture.

Colm Foley was excited to be picked to go over to BP4. He had thought he'd blown his first impression with Kahkay, but if the captain chose him for this trip, he must not have. There was no good, logical reason to take an engineer along, and they were going to a bar. Kahkay must see him as friend potential, which was exactly what Foley was hoping for.

Thankfully, Foley's stomach flu had turned out to be only the twenty-four-hour variety, and was completely gone now.

As they entered the bar, Kahkay masterfully slid onto a stool at the bar, somehow making it look cooler than it had a right to be. Foley tried to grab the one next to him, but Dirt was quicker and Foley had to settle for the other side of Dirt. No matter. At least Foley was here.

"Now, Dirt, if you're going to be my XO, the most important job you have is to drink with me," said Kahkay. "Bartender, two Thrillian Thumblasters please."

"Absolutely, Captain!" said Dirt enthusiastically. Foley liked the new XO's style. "What are your top three favorite liquors, in order?"

"Mine's Scotch," chimed in Foley, wanting to be part of the conversation.

"Really?" asked Dirt, turning to the engineer in surprise. "I thought you were Irish."

"I am. Scotch-Irish. Meaning, I'm an Irishman who likes his Scotch," said Foley, dropping his well-rehearsed line. He thought it would kill, no matter what Fitzy had said. To Foley's delight, Kahkay smiled, though Dirt only nodded, taking in the information as if it were serious.

Kahkay opened his mouth to reply, but before he could, a C'mon approached him from the other side. There had been a janitor sitting on the stool next to Kahkay, opposite Dirt, but at the sight of the imposing figure whose race was known to be hostile, the janitor fled. Kahkay didn't seem to notice until the newcomer spoke.

"Well, if it isn't Captain Richard. F. Kahkay!" said the C'mon broadly. Foley recognized the rank insignia of a captain.

"Uh, do I know you?" asked Kahkay, eyeing the being warily.

"I hope so," said the pleasantly deep voice. Foley liked him instantly. He didn't seem overly violent or offensive, as Foley had been led to believe all C'mons were. "I know you. You're the youngest, most handsome captain in the fleet."

That was exactly the right way to greet Kahkay, who smiled back broadly. This C'mon was smooth. "Oh, fo-sha, c'mon!" said Kahkay with very fake humility.

"Yes, human, I *am* a C'mon. Captain Yeez. Have you heard of me?"

"Umm... yeah, of course I've heard of you. The best... uh, hairline in the fleet," said Kahkay, and Foley could tell Kahkay was making it up on the spot. Poor guy. Yeez had done his research and Kahkay hadn't. Foley's commander was overmatched.

"Thank you! Yes, that's me!" said Yeez.

Foley tilted his head in disbelief. Could Kahkay be a really excellent guesser, or was Yeez just being polite? Though, Foley had to admit, Yeez *did* have an exceedingly handsome hairline, not a feature usually paid attention to, but in this case, Foley couldn't help it. It rose exactly the way a hairline should, not too far back, but curving away from the center tastefully. Below it, Yeez's bushy, black eyebrows perfectly matched the angles of the brow. Though the purple eye shadow below them looked a little out of place.

Dirt said something under his breath, but Foley, mesmerized at studying Yeez's follicles, didn't catch it.

"So what are you doing on this space station, Captain Yeez?" asked Kahkay, won over by the C'mon's broad grin and warm demeanor.

"On shore leave," said Yeez casually, as if it was the most normal thing in the world to take a holiday on a utilitarian space station run by a rival planet. Relations between the A.S.S. and C'mons had been nothing but tense since their first encounter, four years earlier, during which a few C'mons and many A.S.S.ers lost their lives.

"Certainly there are better places to go for vacation than a musty old hunk of junk like this?" asked Kahkay, gesturing at the room. Even the bar they were in had rusty walls, paint chipping away, and an unpleasant odor. And this was where the space station crew spent their leisure time. Foley had to admit, it wasn't a cheery place, even for someone who liked dive bars as much as he did.

"Ah, Captain Kahkay, there are, but this is the only bar I can go to with chocolate liquor, and that is my favorite alcohol," said Yeez, his smile still in place, though Foley was now beginning to wonder if the sincerity was fake. Chocolate liquor made an all right mixer in the pinch, but it couldn't possibly be anyone's favorite.

"C'mon! Really?" asked Kahkay, echoing Foley's thoughts.

"Absolutely. It has been banned all across C'mon territory, but this station, being A.S.S. run, I can get it here," said Yeez.

Foley searched Yeez's face for any sign of dishonesty. The engineer didn't see any, but that couldn't possibly be true. Why would anyone ban chocolate liquor?

"Are you sure you being here has nothing to do with the cargo on board?" asked Kahkay. Right. Jamieson had sent them to BP4 because he thought the C'mons might try to steal the food supply running through the station. Foley had forgotten.

"What... cargo, Captain?" asked Yeez.

"C'mon, Yeez. You know what I'm talking about," said Kahkay. "The broccolilite."

Yeez made a face. "I *hate* broccolilite." Foley had to hand it to him. Yeez did sound convincing.

"C'mon, you expect me to believe that?" asked Kahkay incredulously. "Broccolilite may be vegetable's scapegoat, but everyone likes it. At least with cheese."

"Captain Kahkay, I have never heard of this 'cheese' you speak of," said Yeez seriously.

"C'mon!" exclaimed Foley, unable to keep silent any longer. Yeez *had* to be trying to pull one over on them. Claiming he had never heard of cheese was the most outrageous thing the enemy officer had said yet. "It's made from cow's milk."

"Cow? The Earth bovine? Y-you consume that which comes out of their teets? Yuck!" said Yeez, sticking his tongue out with disgust.

"You really should try it with your chocolate liquor and some vodka. Delicious," said Foley.

Yeez made a noise to indicate he didn't believe him. "I will take your word for it."

"So you're just here for the drinks then, Captain Yeez?" asked Kahkay, measured.

"Yes, Captain Kahkay. I am only here for the drinks," insisted Yeez.

"Fine," said Kahkay in a tone that was at odds with the word. "But I've got my eye on you."

Foley was about to echo Kahkay's warning, but they were interrupted by Lieutenant Who. Foley had a hard time reading certain non-human faces, and with all the fur around Who's visage, his expression was harder to interrupt than most. But his pointed stride made it impossible to think he was anything but furious.

"Captain. Who. Need. Word," said Who loudly.

"Not now, Who. I'm having a drink," said Kahkay.

"Now. Captain," said Who.

"Well, excuse me, Captain Yeez. I have to take this," said Kahkay wearily, rising from his stool. The two moved out of Foley's ear shot.

Lieutenant Tokaladie stared longingly at the big screen. Space station BP4 hung in the void, an ugly chunk of metal in the vacuum of space, circling a mostly barren rock. The station was a trading post, situated along a supply run to some outer colonies, and also serving as a warning buoy for the C'mons, though that was not its original design, it having been built more than a decade before the A.S.S. was even aware of the other power's existence, before even the starsheep fleet launched.

Still, as mundane and uninteresting as the station itself looked, Tokaladie could not help but wish she were asked to go with Kahkay. She got tired of sitting on the bridge. Yes, it had only been a few days since they left Earth, but Tokaladie had purposely chosen starsheep duty in order to explore the galaxy. She yearned to be included in the adventure. Otherwise, she'd be the head of a lab on Earth instead of just a department chief on the *Thrifty*.

The bad side of if she had been included was that Tokaladie didn't want to spend any more time than she had to with the captain. She found his manners atrocious. If anyone other than her commanding officer spoke to her the way that Kahkay did, making unwanted overtures, cutting her off, she would have spoken up by now. But he was her boss, so she had been trying very hard to let it go, assuming this was just part of the learning curve of breaking in a new captain.

Was it possible that Kahkay was a sexist? The thought hadn't occurred to her until just now. After all, sexism had not been a part of Tokaladie's life. It had been wiped out on Earth centuries ago as mankind had become more enlightened, so while it was something she'd heard about in school, like slavery, Nazis, and man-made climate change destroying the planet, it was something she'd only been away of in a very abstract way.

But that was the most likely explanation. Somehow, Kahkay was a sexist. She knew he was from Buffalo, so it couldn't have been part of his upbringing. Was it possible that if gender equality were to be taken for granted, and no examples, positive or negative, were at hand to caution against it, it could return to the world?

This bore further study, and Tokaladie made a mental note to look into it later. While she mainly concentrated on the technical aspects of communications professionally, she did have an interest in interpersonal relationships and cultural dynamics, as well. Accomplished in research and published studies, Kahkay might make a great subject for her next paper.

Tokaladie wouldn't pursue this tonight, though. She was far too sleepy. Which was odd, because it was only early afternoon, and she was usually quite alert at this time of day. Why was she yawning? Maybe some coffee...

"Lieutenant!" she heard M- yell as she fell off her chair and hit the floor of the bridge, hard. Blackness threatened to take over as her consciousness faded. She was aware of M- barking orders and crewmen running towards her, and then nothing else.

Tokaladie awoke to the reek of peaches and liquor. Doctor Awshucks crouched over her, scanner in hand. "Easy. You're all right," said Awshucks, grabbing her elbow and helping her sit up.

"What happened?" asked Tokaladie.

"Life support was turned off," hissed M-, furious.

"How was life support turned off?" asked Tokaladie, confused.

"The switch on Commander Dirt's station was flipped," said M-, pacing near the pilot's board. "I didn't realize what was happening until you pitched over. It looks like the starsheep's alert system that would warn us of such an eventuality was turned off as well."

"Why would Dirt do that?" asked Tokaladie, head still a little fuzzy. It wasn't making sense.

"Maybe he was drunk," said Doctor Awshucks, hiccupping.

"You're drunk, Doctor," said M-. "Is Lieutenant Tokaladie going to be all right?" Was there a tenderness in his voice as he asked the question, or was she just imagining things?

"She'll be fine. Just a little oxygen deprivation," said Awshucks, standing. "Where does Kahkay keep the good stuff?" She began opening cabinets.

"If the alert was off, how did you know?" Tokaladie asked M-.

"An educated guess. I have observed that Commander Dirt has not been behaving like a typical first officer," said M-. Smart *and* compassionate. Maybe Tokaladie was too hasty in creating her policy not to date co-workers. It could be the lack of air to her brain, but Tokaladie thought M- looked handsome and brave standing next to the captain's chair.

"Good work," she said.

"Thank you," said M-. "Do you require relief?"

"Relief?" asked Tokaladie.

"From your station? Shall I summon a member of your team to take over for you?"

"No, thank you M-. I'm fine." She blushed. She had forgotten to use his rank. That was unprofessional, especially considering he was above her in the hierarchy. If he noticed, he didn't mention it, which she was grateful for, and only made her hold him in higher esteem.

"Excellent. Please call Captain Kahkay," said M-.

"Yes, sir," said Tokaladie, rising slowly to her chair and flipping the toggle at her station. M- came and stood beside her. She was very aware of his presence, his scaly arm hovering mere inches from her breast. She nodded to him when the line was open.

"Go for Captain Kahkay," came the captain's voice through Tokaladie's speaker.

"Captain, you're needed back on the *A.S.S. Thrifty*," said M-.

"Ah, now, Memothra? I haven't even ordered my second round yet," complained Kahkay, wholly unfairly Tokaladie thought. She felt a kinship with M-, knowing she wasn't the only one Kahkay was rude to.

"I'm ssssorry, Captain," said M- gracefully, nobly not letting on that he had been insulted. "I'm afraid it's quite urgent."

"Ugh. Fine, fine," said Kahkay before cutting the connection.

Lieutenant Who Grappa watched Kahkay go, furious. Three days into the *Thrifty*'s mission, the starsheep had seen two landing parties leave the ship, and Who had not been included in either of them. Perhaps she should have been on the bridge more, but in her first leadership role over a department, she thought it important to get her own team in order before leaving them alone for extended periods of time.

With a sigh, Who decided that, while she was in the bar, she could use a shot. Yes, she was on duty, but if Kahkay didn't have to follow the rules, then neither did she. Just one to take the edge off. This was already turning out to be a tense day.

"So, you're Captain Yeez, huh? Big fan, big fan," the new XO was saying to the C'mon at the bar as Who approached them. "So, tell me, just how many C'mons do you have on space station BP4 at this moment, and how often do they rotate shifts?"

"Uh, that's classified," said Yeez uneasily.

"No problem. I'll just go around the room and count," said Dirt.

"Don't do that," said Yeez, perplexed.

"OK, what steps will you take to stop me?" asked Dirt. "Please be specific."

"Um, I will tell you not to do it," said Yeez, shooting a pleading glance at Who. Who stared back at the C'mon impassively.

"And then...?" asked Dirt.

Who tensed, ready for trouble, but Yeez just sighed, figuring out he wasn't getting any help from the security chief. "And then, nothing."

Interesting. Who had no reason to trust the C'mons. Her own race had had no contact with them prior to the A.S.S.'s first encounter, nor since for that matter. Her only frame of reference were the official A.S.S. reports, which were surely biased. But Who had expected the C'mons to be more prickly than this.

"Great! See you later!" said Dirt, who began wandering around counting C'mons. Who didn't blame the commander for being suspicious of the aliens, but it occurred to Who that Dirt had seemed equally curious about the *Thrifty,* and that didn't sit right with the security chief.

Who looked at Foley. "Who. Not. Like. Dirt. Who. Follow," she said to the engineer.

"Go ahead, Lieutenant Who. I'll stay here with the good captain," said Foley, raising a shot glass to Yeez. Yeez returned the gesture pleasantly. Clearly, Who wasn't needed here. The C'mons weren't going to cause trouble.

Dirt had left the bar now, so Who moved to follow. She caught just a brief glimpse of Dirt disappearing around the corner down the hall, and started following. When she reached the bend, he was gone, the passageway completely deserted.

Wandering further, Who heard a ding from up ahead. Coming around the corner, she saw an elevator had just departed and was heading down. That was strange. There hadn't been signs of any crew about, so she had to assume that Dirt was the one taking the ride, but there was no reason for Dirt to go downstairs. It was all cargo holds and shuttle docks below, neither of which Dirt needed.

Unless Dirt wasn't who he said he was, a distinct possibility. Who hit the button for the next elevator, and noting what floor Dirt's transport stopped on, followed.

The doors opened on the lowermost deck, which appeared to be deserted to Who. It was just one big, empty room, save for a few transports. As Who walked slowly down the row, she looked around each ship, which represented a variety of species and constructs. Who guessed these were mostly rentals or salvaged vessels, as visitors would dock higher up on the station.

The hold to the last ship on the deck was open. Who peered in cautiously and saw boxes labeled broccolilite. This was the cargo the *Thrifty* was here to make sure the C'mons didn't steal. Who knew from the official documents that it should be several floors up, on a barge that was getting ready to leave. What was it doing down here?

Who felt a sharp pain on the back of her head. Someone had just smacked her with something large, heavy, and metallic. She reached for her laser pistol and began to spin around, hoping there weren't too many C'mons. She didn't think she'd have time to call for help.

Just before Who turned, though, she was conked again. This time, she dropped to her knees, the laser pistol clattering away. A third clonk knocked her out, and Who wasn't aware of what happened next.

"I told you, Captain Kahkayyyyyy," hissed Lieutenant Commander M-. Kahkay was getting a headache from this lizard-man stretching out letters.

"Yes, yes, Mitochondria," said Kahkay dismissively. "You did tell me that Dirt is evil. But how do you know that it wasn't just an accident?"

"If it was an accident, the ship's systems would have informed us of what was happening," said M-. "Turning off the notifications indicates that this was a deliberate act of sabotage."

"Ah, but how do you know Dirt was the one who shut off the life support to the *Thrifty*?" asked Kahkay.

"The switch was flipped on hisssss station."

"And no one else had access to his station?" asked Kahkay skeptically.

"Well...," admitted M-.

"Tokaladie? Could you have walked over to Dirt's station and flipped off the life support switch?" asked Kahkay, turning on the pretty communications chief. She looked startled, not expecting to be brought into the argument between the captain and his science officer, gingerly holding an ice pack on her forehead, a bruise forming where it had hit the floor.

"Yes, sir. But-," began Tokaladie.

Kahkay cut her off. "How about you, Ensign Gertie?" asked Kahkay of the relief officer currently at Dirt's control panel.

"Absolutely sir," said the smart, young woman sharply.

"And I know you had access, Midal, because you were on the bridge the entire time, right?" asked Kahkay, swinging back to M-.

"That is true, ssssir," said M-. "But as I have already told you numerous times, I am not evil."

"Your voice sounds evil," said Kahkay.

"Yes, sir, but I am *not* evil," insisted M-. "Besides, I do not currently possess the computer skills necessary to stop the warning notification from alerting us that our oxygen was depleted."

"I'm sure dozens of officers would know how to do that!" said Kahkay.

"Correct, ssssir," said M-. "Engineers, communications chiefs, those in the command track..."

"Exactly," said Kahkay. "We don't know who did this."

"However we do know that *someone* acted maliciously against the crew," pointed out M-.

"Potato, potato," said Kahkay.

"What?" asked M-, confused.

"Never mind," said Kahkay. "It's back on now. No harm, no foul. Hehe. I rhymed."

"Captain Kahkay-," started in M-.

"I don't want to hear any more about it, Muckious," interrupted Kahkay.

Intellectually, Kahkay knew M- was right. Someone had to have purposely threatened the lives of his crew, and that was something that couldn't stand. He had to find the culprit before any lasting harm was caused. Tokaladie's gorgeous face would heal, but if anyone else died under his watch so soon after taking command...

For a moment, Kahkay had considered agreeing with M-, but several things held him back. One was ego. Kahkay had already screwed up multiple times in the last couple of days in big ways, and he couldn't bear to face another glaring error so early in his captaincy. The crew would lose faith in him, and without that faith, he could not effectively lead them.

Secondly, knowing there was a saboteur on board but not knowing who it was would cause panic. Even trained A.S.S. officers could melt down if they all suspected one another of having done something wrong. Considering Jamieson had chosen Dirt personally, and Jamieson was a well-respected admiral, Kahkay thought there was a good chance Dirt wasn't really the culprit, and Kahkay wasn't about to condemn an innocent man. Though, M- was right in that Dirt had been acting a bit abnormal...

Third, in Kahkay's opinion there was a very real chance M- was the villain here. The lizard-like being *sounded* evil, and his species had a reputation for being untrustworthy. Kahkay wasn't sure what game M- was playing, pointing out the devious act, if he had intended to mess up his own vessel. But M- was clearly smart, and Kahkay would not play his game.

All of which meant that, although Kahkay conceded it very likely there was a traitor on board, he was not yet ready to announce it to the crew. That could wait until he had a better handle on the situation.

"Captain?" asked Lieutenant Tokaladie from her station.

"Yes, Lieutenant Tokaladie?" said Kahkay.

"Security on space station BP4 is calling us," she reported.

"Tell them I'm on my way back over right now and I can talk to them in person," said Kahkay.

"Actually, sir, they are suspending our visitation privileges." She had a hard look on her face, like she couldn't believe what she was saying any more than he could.

"What? Why?" asked Kahkay. "Don't they know who we are?"

"Yes, sir," said Tokaladie. "But they say there's been a fight."

"A fight?" asked Kahkay. What in the hell was going on now?

CHAPTER TEN
A.S.S. STATION BP4, 2424

The ride in the elevator from the beamer room to the bridge was a long one for Chief Engineer Colm Foley. He oh so wanted to be buddies with Captain Richard C. Kahkay, but he kept self-sabotaging. First, there was the stomach bug that kept him in the bathroom, and now he let his temper get the better of him. He had assaulted Captain Yeez, a superior officer of a race for whom things were tense enough with the A.S.S. What had he been thinking?

The doors slid open and Foley hesitated just outside them, the portal almost slicing his back as it closed behind him. Kahkay turned and glared at the engineer. Foley tried to shrink himself as Kahkay rose from the center seat and stalked towards the Irishman. Foley couldn't help but notice that, while most of the crew didn't react, pointedly ignoring what was about to happen, Lieutenant Commander M- was staring openly, the cold-blooded git.

"Foley," said Kahkay coldly, by way of greeting.

"Captain," replied Foley with a gulp.

Kahkay looked hard at him, then sighed with the air of a disappointed father. He also asked questions he already knew the answers to like one. "OK, who started the fight?"

"Sir?" asked Foley, feigning ignorance. "Who wasn't even there! He was followin' Dirt around."

"You know what I mean, Foley! I'm not talking about Lieutenant Who. *Who* threw the first punch?" At Kahkay's anger, Foley regretted trying his cheeky response a moment ago. He decided to take a different tact and fess up.

"I did, sir, but it wanna like that. He goaded me into," said Foley, hoping desperately Kahkay would understand. He looked like the type of guy that socked someone in the jaw occasionally.

"Oh?" asked Kahkay quizzically. "I'd just left. What did he say to make you react so quickly?"

"Well, sir, first he asked if you were ineffectual...," said Foley.

Immediately, Kahkay loosened up, the tension dropping from his shoulders. "Ah, good job, then, Chief Foley. Way to defend your commanding officer."

"No, Captain," protested M-. "That is still against protocol 156-"

"Shove in, Munit," said Kahkay. "Foley was just sticking up for me. That's called being a good and loyal officer." Foley glared at the science officer. What business was it of M-'s?

Foley was about to duck back into the elevator, but something stopped him. He was off the hook, but he just couldn't lie to Kahkay like this. Not if he ever wanted to be his true friend. So, although he thought he might regret it, Foley spoke up again. "Actually... sir, I cannot lie. That's not when I punched him."

"Ugh, really?" asked Kahkay, clearly wishing Foley had just let it rest, unhappy to have to continue dealing with this. "I mean, what did he say after that?"

"He insulted the ship. Called her a 'bucket of bones,'" said Foley, who had been deeply offended by that remark, and made sure the captain knew it with his tone.

Kahkay sighed. "Well, I don't approve of your actions, Foley, but I guess I can see how an engineer has to defend the equipment he devotes his life to."

"Aye, sir, but that wasn't... that wasn't when I punched him, neither," admitted Foley, wishing he *had* punched Yeez then.

"Oh god sakes," said Kahkay perplexed. "What did he say that started the fight?"

"He didn't like the White Russian I bought him," said Foley a little more defiantly than he intended. If there was anything Foley was protective of in this world, besides his wife and his work, it was his booze.

Kahkay looked at Foley incredulously. "OK, you bought him a White Russian *after* he established he found the idea of consuming cow products repulsive?"

"I just thought he had t' try it first, sir," said Foley, who was still having trouble wrapping his head around how someone could possibly not like a White Russian. It just didn't make sense. He had been prepared to gloat when Yeez enjoyed the drink, but having the opposite reaction had infuriated Foley even more.

"Goddamn it, Foley," said Kahkay. "I can't believe you-"

"Captain Kahkay?" interrupted Lieutenant Tokaladie, spinning around in her chair. Foley was relieved at the interruption.

"Yes?" asked Kahkay.

"I'm receiving a distress call from the space station," she reported.

"Has the broccolilite freighter, uh, loaded up and left yet?" asked the captain.

"It has, sir," said Tokaladie. "But the station commander reports finding the pilot stripped of his uniform and left in a custodial closet. The shipment has been stolen."

Kahkay smiled triumphantly, vindicated. "*The C'mons*! I knew they were up to no good!"

"Sir, the C'mons are radioing us to see if we want them to help us chase the ship down," said Tokaladie. That was odd. Why would they steal the cargo, and then offer to help retrieve it, wondered Foley.

"What?" asked Kahkay, equally surprised. "If it wasn't the C'mons, then who?"

M- spoke up smugly, the stuck-up twat. "Might I point out, Commander Dirt has not reported back to the ship, ssssir. This, combined with the fact that I had to call you back here because he turned off the ship's life support at his station..."

"All right now, Muriah," said Kahkay, plainly continuing an argument from earlier. "You don't know he did that on purpose. And the next time, just turn it back on without calling me. You're a big boy... lizard... thingy... creature."

"I am not a lizard creature!" said M- angrily, making some displeased noises.

"Lieutenant Tokaladie, call Commander Dirt," ordered Kahkay. Foley took the opportunity to slide over to the engineering station on the bridge, glad for the change of subject.

"Aye, sir," said Tokaladie. Then, after a moment. "He's not picking up, sir."

The ride in the elevator from the beamer room to the bridge was a long one for security chief Lieutenant Who Grappa. She had only been head of security for a brief tenure, three days to be exact, and already she had failed miserably.

Had Who made a mistake switching fields from medical to security? She didn't know, but the early signs weren't good. Who thought she had decent instincts, having sensed Dirt was up to no good and following him. But she let him get the drop on her, or at least, she assumed it was Dirt that knocked her out. She had been following him, after all.

Who was nothing if not dedicated, though, and she would face whatever consequences Captain Kahkay decided to bring to bear. If that meant she would have to give up her post, so be it. She owed her crewmates and her honor nothing less.

The elevator doors opened to much activity. Who saw M- and Tokaladie both working furiously at their stations, and Foley looked tense, on the edge of his seat. Kahkay alone bore a cheerful expression, turning to look at Who as she entered the room.

"Lieutenant Who, what happened to you? You look like poo! I rhymed," said Kahkay. He grinned at his own bit, but Who was too ashamed to be amused.

"Who. Follow. Dirt. Dirt. Circle. Round. Attack. Who. From. Behind. Coward," Who couldn't resist tossing the insult in, though she was more angry at herself right now than at the rogue first officer. Watching the security tape on the station had revealed she had been attacked by her crewmate, not the C'mons after all.

"Lieutenant Who, I must say, I'm surprised you let Commander Dirt, or whoever he is, get the better of you," said Kahkay, though he didn't sound all that concerned as he quickly spun away from his security chief. "Foley, take the wheel, raise shields, and arm weapons. Tokaladie, tell Captain Yeez we appreciate the offer, but we have this."

"Aye, sir," said Tokaladie.

What was going on? The crew must have realized Dirt was fooling them, but Who had no idea why the *Thrifty* was speeding away from BP4. What had happened? And why were the C'mons offering their help?

Who was a little offended that Kahkay asked Foley to arm the weapons systems instead of her, but she understood, after her blunder today. Foley could run the lasers from his desk just as well as she could. But even without an assignment, she quickly took her station next to Tokaladie, ready to assist. Tokaladie, with a couple of quick whispers, filled Who in on the situation, which Who was grateful for.

"All right, go!" Kahkay was saying, the crew following his orders.

"Ah, there it is, sir, on the big screen," said M-. Who looked at the image, which was of a standard cargo vessel.

"Good, it didn't get very far," said Kahkay. "Tokaladie, hail the cargo vessel."

"Putting video call on screen, sir," said Tokaladie.

Who watched as the image of the ship was replaced by the familiar and despicable face of Commander Dirt. At least Who's instincts hadn't been off about him, which was some small comfort. The next time, if she didn't lose her position, Who would be sure to take along back up when confronting a possible evildoer.

"Captain Kahkay!" said Dirt warmly, as if greeting an old friend. "A pleasure to see you. OK, completely unrelated, just out of curiosity, what frequency are your shields on again?"

"What are you doing, Dirt?" asked Kahkay accusingly.

"Admiral Jamieson asked me to escort this ship to its destination, just to make sure the C'mons didn't get it," said Dirt.

"Right. They found the pilot, Dirt. We know you stole it. Turn around right now and surrender or your name is mud," said Kahkay.

Dirt looked down and muttered, "Well, crap. I thought I'd have more time to escape." Then, as if everyone on the bridge hadn't just heard him, which they most assuredly did, he looked up all smiles again. "Sure, sure, Captain. Uh, lower your shields and I'll dock."

Who opened her mouth to protest, but before she could, M- urgently interjected. "Captain Kahkay, I'm reading an energy buildup on the freighter. It's getting ready to fire on us." Fire what, Who wondered. Cargo vessels were not equipped with much in the way of weaponry, certainly nothing that would pose much of a danger to an A.S.S. starsheep.

"Foley, shoot the bastard!" ordered Kahkay. "Target weapons only. We don't wanna hurt the cargo." Who reflexively flexed her fingers over the laser controls, but refrained from doing anything to get in Foley's way.

Bright blue rays of light shot out from the front of the *Thrifty*, surgically striking the other ship at critical junctures. Who watched in astonishment as the cargo barge exploded, a brilliant flash of orange, red, and yellow light, debris strewn in all directions.

"Foley!" exclaimed Kahkay in alarm. "I said to just disarm him, not blow him up!"

"But I did, sir!" protested Foley. "He musta rigged the weapons into the engines. A ship like that wouldn't typically have very powerful guns, but if he rerouted power to the engines, well, it woulda packed a punch... but it's a dangerous mistake to make."

"Well, hmm. I thought, despite everything, Dirt was smart. Guess I was wrong," said Kahkay. He turned towards Who and she braced herself for the paused dress down to continue.

Instead, though, Kahkay kept turning until his eyes landed on Foley. "Chief, you have the bridge." Then the captain strode into the elevator, and Who sighed in relief. She was glad she hadn't lost her job.

The ride in the elevator up to his apartment in an expensive residential complex was a long one for Admiral Jamie Jamieson. He was frustrated with Kahkay for turning out to be such a poor captain, though it wasn't Jamieson's call to give him the promotion in the first place. He was frustrated with the A.S.S. for saddling him with Kahkay, and at the higher ups who wouldn't allow him to fire the captain. He was frustrated with himself for not properly vetting Commander Dirt before assigning him to the *Thrifty* when he had a perfectly good computer expert, Lieutenant Commander Buzz, on staff who could find Jamieson all the dirt he might desire on anyone.

But mostly Jamieson was frustrated with his wife, Janice, for convincing him that Dirt was a good candidate in the first place. What had she been thinking, and why had he allowed his spouse to make that kind of professional decision for him?

In truth, Jamieson relied on Janice a lot, and always had. Getting together so young, she'd been intimately involved in his early career decisions, and he'd come to rely on her as a sounding board and advisor. This wasn't the first time he'd listened to her about such a choice. It was just the first time she's screwed him so badly with it.

Or was it? The past four years had been really rough, and it had been that long since Jamieson had felt like he was connecting with her. Listening to her when she suggested Dirt for Kahkay's XO position had been the latest in a long line of peace offerings he made towards her, but she continuously rejected him anyway, and made no such advances towards him.

Jamieson still loved Janice more than anything. He just wished he knew how to get back what they had. When could they start being Janice and Jamie again, or would they ever? Had losing their son also stolen their union? What if they couldn't come back from this?

The elevator stopped at floor twenty-three and Jamie got off. This high rise was in a district known as Bexley, and was older than most of the surrounding buildings. Known for being an historic part of Columbus, many of the higher ranking A.S.S. officers chose to set their home here, or at least the ones who couldn't live closer to downtown did. Jamieson could probably afford some slightly more central digs, but he liked the community he still felt in this portion of the metropolis, which was pretty close to the middle, though on the opposite side of the city center than Command was.

His door was the third one down, and as he opened it, he was greeted with the very bare, early twenty-first century décor that Janice had chosen. Before, he'd always seen it as an extension of her eccentric personality. A bit artsy, she loved this period that was called "modern" four hundred years ago.

Now, though, to Jamieson, it seemed impersonal. The lack of many intimate belongings and photographs, save one family portrait on the mantle, made him feel like this wasn't his home. Anyone who entered wasn't likely to know who lived here unless they were invited in by the owners. It made him sad, especially when there was so little to remind him of his boy.

Jamieson hadn't gotten five steps in when Janice strode down the hall to start in on him. "Jamie!" she screeched.

"Not now, Janice," said Jamieson tiredly, stacking some portable tablets on the dining room table, work he had brought home. "I've had a long day."

"So have I," said Janice without a hint of sympathy.

"Would you like to tell me about it?" he offered.

"No, I would not!" declared Janice. "I'm going out for a drink. Make your own dinner."

"I always do," said Jamieson.

"What's that supposed to mean?" asked Janice, whirling. Jamieson had never noticed how grating and shrill her voice could be until it was turned on him, and the tones he used to find comforting now set him on edge.

"It means you don't cook any more," said Jamieson simply, quietly, not looking to provoke a fight, but feeling the need to answer her factually.

"Well, neither do you!" she accused.

"I do on the weekends, when I'm home," said Jamieson.

"I'm never here on the weekends," said Janice.

"I know," said Jamieson.

"You knew when you married me that I had to keep busy, to travel. I was never the housewife who would just sit at home," said Janice angrily.

"I know," said Jamieson again, in the same mild tone of voice.

"Do you suddenly have a problem with that?" asked Janice.

"No," said Jamieson.

"Do you suddenly have a problem with me?" asked Janice.

"Actually, I do have one problem with you," said Jamieson, finding his last bit of will to fight back, tired of just taking it from her.

"Don't hold back!" demanded Janice.

"Why did you tell me to choose Harry Dirt as Kahkay's XO?" asked Jamieson.

"I thought they'd get along," said Janice. "Why? What has that idiot Kahkay done now?"

"Nothing, unfortunately," said Jamieson, not willing to get into explaining those mistakes to Janice. "But Harry Dirt turned out to be a traitor and an imposter. He wasn't a real A.S.S. officer."

"What?" asked Janice in surprise.

"Yes. His files were faked. He'd spent months, maybe years, building a cover story," said Jamieson. It shouldn't have taken Lieutenant Commander Buzz to tell Jamieson that Dirt's files were fake, but as Buzz admitted, they were very good fakes.

"To what purpose?" asked Janice.

"I don't know. He's dead," said Jamieson flatly. "Whatever his goal was, it doesn't seem like he was able to complete it."

"Well, I never!" said Janice. "How did you not realize that before you put him on a starsheep?"

"Me?" asked Jamieson, starting to match her anger. "You recommended him!"

"I recommended him because I'd chatted with him around the A.S.S. offices and he seemed like a lovely man. I don't do background checks," said Janice haughtily.

"I thought I didn't need to look into a man my wife recommended," said Jamieson.

"Poor Harry," said Janice.

"Poor Harry?" asked Jamieson incredulously.

"Yes, you said he was dead."

"So?" asked Jamieson. "I thought you didn't know him very well?"

"I didn't," said Janice, breaking just slightly.

"Were you having an affair with him?" asked Jamieson, anger replaced by deadly calm as he stared her right in the eyes.

"I never!" said Janice, seemingly shocked, though Jamieson wasn't sure he bought it. "How dare you accuse me of cheating on you!"

"It would make sense," admitted Jamieson, as much to himself as to her. "The long weekend trips you take, the calls you leave the room to answer, your distance towards me..."

"I am not distant towards you!" said Janice. "I am your wife."

"It doesn't feel like it," said Jamieson.

"How *dare* you!" said Janice. "Twenty-nine years we've been together, and you don't feel close to me?"

"I did," said Jamieson. "I don't any more. Ever since..."

"Don't you say his name," said Janice, fury in her eyes.

"Why not?" asked Jamieson, confused.

"You don't deserve to say his name. The hell I've been through since we lost him, and your total lack of feeling. You're the one who's distant, not me."

"I care, Janice," said Jamieson with sincerity. It was too late, though. He knew he'd already lost her. She'd shut down and she was done engaging him.

"Like I said, I am going out. Don't wait up," said Janice, grabbing her purse and storming out.

Silently, Jamieson watched her go. Then he crossed to the bar and poured himself a whiskey. He didn't indulge in alcohol very often, but today, he needed it.

Two hours and six whiskeys later, he scrolled through vacation spots on a tablet, dreaming of getting away. He needed a break from here, from her. He needed to find joy again, by himself, before he could try to interject it into their marriage. Before he could try to win back Janice, who, the more he thought about it, the more he realized she was definitely cheating on him and had been for awhile, likely with multiple partners. It was the only explanation for her activities that made sense. But he could get past that, if he could just put himself in order first.

An advertisement for Topleesia I popped up on the screen as he surfed for deals on a booking website. Jamieson had never actually been to Topleesia I, but knew it was famous in the galaxy for being a party planet full of booze, debauchery, and naked breasts. While he normally would have never even considered such a destination, in the moment, with a fuzzy head, it suddenly seemed perfect.

Jamieson had a few assignments that needed to be completed, roster holes to plug, but in a few weeks, he could carve out some time. Smiling a small, sad smile, he went ahead and made a hotel reservation. This jaunt might be just what the doctor ordered.

The ride in the elevator from the beamer room to the bridge was a long one for Captain Richard H. Kahkay. OK, it was only one floor, but after the day he'd had, it felt like a long one. Slightly.

Kahkay settled into his seat on the bridge, looking over his crew. He wondered if any of them guessed why he had fled the bridge so quickly after Dirt's ship blew up. None met his eyes as he surveyed the various stations, so he supposed not.

Or, more disturbing, they were doubting him but not voicing those opinions, which not only made them poor A.S.S. officers, but also people he couldn't trust.

In truth, the reason Kahkay had fled was because he didn't want anyone to see him have an emotional reaction. In the moment, the weight of everything that had happened so far, losing not one, but two XOs, bungling two missions in three days, was just too much for him to bear.

Kahkay had been in the depths of despair before, doubting his abilities and his life choices. Then, Grace Thomas had been there to pull him out of it. She was his rock, his steady, the one person in the world he could count on to only judge him in constructive ways, and to encourage him back onto the right track.

He had tried to call Grace from his apartment as soon as he composed himself. She didn't answer. He didn't know why he was surprised. Ever since his promotion to captain, she didn't return his calls. He knew why, but there was nothing he could do about it now. Why didn't she just pick up and chew him out so they could move on?

Kahkay didn't have any other option. He would have to find his leadership skills within himself. He was in charge of the *Thrifty*, and as long as A.S.S. Command deigned to leave him out here, he was determined not to give up. But he was having a damned hard time of it right now.

How could Kahkay not have seen though Harry Dirt? In retrospect, it had been obvious from the get-go that Dirt wasn't on the up and up. M- and Who had voiced their suspicions, and were even now filing reports outlining what they did about it. Kahkay had ignored them, ignored his own senses, convinced there was no way he had a crooked right-hand man so soon after losing his first, best one.

Garry's death weighed heavily on him. More than anything else, that was what was bringing Kahkay down, impairing his judgment, threatening to reveal a crack in front of his crew. He couldn't allow that to happen. He had to find a way to get past it. That's what Garry would want.

Kahkay's instinct in the face of death, or really, any adversity, was to make a joke. It didn't have to be a funny joke, and no one but himself needed to laugh at it. It was the attitude he displayed, the confidence he exuded, that was important. He couldn't return to the bridge and face his senior staff until the façade was back in place. It was now.

As he looked out over his crew, he smiled broadly, disguising the pain and fear welling up from within. In the privacy of his room, he could scream and cry. Quietly, since his apartment was just below the bridge and the ceiling was mostly, but not entirely, sound proof. But still, he could allow an emotional display, especially when it was into a pillow. Now that he was back up here, he couldn't afford to show such humanity.

Swallowing a sob, Kahkay flipped the recording switch on his chair. He needed to make a diary entry anyway, and surely that would keep him focused, help him maintain control.

"Captain's Diary, September 11th, 2424. Well, Memamoma was right and our new XO was a traitor. All the broccolilite was destroyed, and now the people of Hunguy III have only meat and potatoes for dinner, no greens. This is probably the worst thing to ever happen on this date in all of history. September 11th will live forever in infamy now, at least for the residents of Hunguy III. Such a shame."

Kahkay made a quick survey around the bridge. Tokaladie blanched a little, but no one else reacted. Had they gotten his reference to the terrorist attack on New York City in 2001? That was comic gold; tragedy plus time and all that. But no, other than the sickened expression from his communications chief, no one else showed any signs of understanding the reference. Tough crowd.

Flipping the diary off, he turned to Tokaladie. "Lieutenant, any orders from HQ?"

"No, sir," reported Tokaladie.

"Are you going to check?" asked Kahkay.

"I did, sir," said Tokaladie.

"No you didn't," said Kahkay. "I can see your hands. They weren't anywhere near the button to open our Inbox."

"Any communication from command pops up an immediate alert, and I report it to you right away," said Tokaladie, a little edge in her voice at having her capabilities called into question. Kahkay decided he'd better back off. Women could be so touchy!

"Fine, fine," said Kahkay. "We need a new XO, though. Admiral Jamieson should be calling to tell us where to pick one up."

"Yes, sir," agreed Tokaladie.

"You'll let me know the minute he does, right?" asked Kahkay.

Tokaladie sighed. "Of course, sir."

"Good, good," said Kahkay. She was annoyed with him, but annoyance was better than despising him. So all in all, he probably salvaged the day.

Why had Jamieson not called, though? Was he even now making preparations to relieve Kahkay of command? Kahkay wouldn't blame Jamieson if he did, but Kahkay also thought he could still be a great captain. Maybe. Or at least a decent one. As long as he could hold things together.

CHAPTER ELEVEN
2422, SPACE STATION EL9

"Lieutenant Commander Kahkay," said Commander Winters, making the rank sound like an insult "Winters to Kahkay? Are you with me?"

"Huh?" asked Kahkay fuzzily, breaking his staring contest with the metal wall. It won; it always did.

"Lieutenant Commander, do you have your reports done?" asked Winters, glaring down at Kahkay, who sat at his station in the command center at the top of the space station.

"Reports?" asked Kahkay in confusion.

"Yes, the reports on all of the vessels that have docked and undocked from here last month? The ones due to A.S.S. command more than a week ago?" asked Winters testily.

Kahkay couldn't blame Winters for his attitude. Kahkay hadn't been much of a good right-hand man to the older officer, who ran the station. Not that Winters deserved a solid XO, himself banished to this backwater outpost, away from any action. Winters was a mediocre officer at his best, though next to Kahkay, Winters looked like Captain of the Year. Still, Kahkay could be doing better.

"No, sir," said Kahkay. "I'll have them for you tomorrow."

"*Today,*" commanded Winters. "Don't go off duty until they're on my desk."

"Of course, sir," said Kahkay without feeling. Winters walked off, seemingly satisfied, though far from happy with the answer.

Kahkay supposed he belonged with Winters. Once a promising, rising star, he'd become lackluster on his good days. For more than two years now, Kahkay had just been skating by, doing the bare minimum for his job, and not always even that, as evidenced by the reports that were weeks late.

Not that the reports were all that important. What did A.S.S. Command care about some routine freighter shipments out on the fringes of space? Still, he supposed that filing the reports was his duty, and so he had better get on that, lest Winters ask for a replacement.

Kahkay wouldn't be surprised if Winters did request someone else as first officer. It wouldn't be the first time Kahkay was forced out of a position. Three starsheep captains in the past fifteen months had found him not up to their standards, and so he was bounced around until ending up on this station, a major step down from starsheep service, even with the title of XO, which was often a lower rank in a place like this.

Where would he go if he couldn't hack it on EL9? This was probably Kahkay's last chance. If he didn't make it here, it would probably be back to Earth for him, forced into an early retirement. At this point, Kahkay wasn't so sure that was a bad thing.

It seemed so long ago that Kahkay had been on the command track. Technically, he still was, hence why he was allowed to be XO of EL9. However, most starsheep captains never took a turn on a space station. It wasn't a stepping stone to greater things.

Hours later, Kahkay finally did get the reports together and stumbled wearily into Winters' office, which overlooked the rest of the command deck. Kahkay always found the placement unsettling. He much preferred the floorplan of a starsheep, where the captain's office was just an unobtrusive door off of the bridge. Why would Winters need to look down from above like this? It reminded Kahkay of an old factory, the office a nest for a foreman who justifiably didn't trust his crew.

As Kahkay set the tablet of info down on the large, cold metal desk, he was surprised to see Winters sitting behind it, sipping a scotch. During the walk across the room, Kahkay hadn't noticed anyone there, though he had probably been distracted by daydreams of what once was, his usual state these days.

Disturbingly, Winters was smiling a broad smile. Kahkay had never seen him happy before, and the look did not suit Winters, who resembled a vulture preparing to feast.

"Here are the cargo reports, sir," said Kahkay uneasily, backing up towards the exit.

"Want a scotch?" asked Winters.

"Sir?" asked Kahkay.

"I asked if you'd like a scotch," repeated Winters.

"Um, all right," said Kahkay, since Winters' words didn't really sound like a question. He tentatively took a few steps forward and accepted the crystal tumbler of rich, amber liquid Winters poured him.

"We're celebrating," said Winters.

"What are we celebrating?" asked Kahkay, taking a sip. The burning beverage was comforting, much better than the swill Kahkay sipped most nights in the space station bar.

"Your last day," said Winters. "You ship out tomorrow."

"Sir?" asked Kahkay in confusion. "Did I do something wrong?"

"Pretty much everything, from what I can tell," said Winters.

"I can improve, sir," said Kahkay, a bit of desperation in his voice. Faced with the imminent end of his career, the thought of being sent home now more than just an abstract musing, Kahkay suddenly didn't want things to end. Maybe he could convince Winters to let him stay, work harder, work at all, start turning things around...

"No, Kahkay, I don't think you can," said Winters. "If you could have, you would have before I became the fourth boss in a row to fire you."

"I'm fired?" asked Kahkay.

"I requested you be transferred out of here almost as soon as you arrived. About time the orders came through," said Winters, almost sounding proud of what he'd done.

"Sir, I-," began Kahkay.

"No," said Winters, raising a hand. "I don't want to hear it. Finish your scotch, go back to your apartment, and pack your bags. I'm done with you."

Kahkay said nothing, but tilted the glass back and swallowed the rest in one shot. He was embarrassed that he flinched following the gulp, this particular alcohol not made to go down so quickly. But he mustered as much dignity as he could, set the glass down upside down on Winters' desk, then turned on his heel and strode out of the office.

Getting into the elevator that would take him away from the command deck for the final time, Kahkay wasn't sure which emotion he felt more strongly: dread or relief.

Commander Grace Thomas steered the *A.S.S. Redspot* into dock. Butterflies danced in her stomach. She was finally the XO of a starsheep, and as such, only one step away from her ultimate goal to become a captain.

"We've arrived," she said over her shoulder to Captain Robert Yates, or Bob, as he preferred to be called. She didn't turn around, but she could see his knowing nod in her mind's eye. A month of serving together, and she was already in sync with her commanding officer, though she didn't much care for his informality.

"Great!" said Bob enthusiastically. "Let's go meet our new logistics officer, Grace."

"Yes, sir," said Grace, rising to join Bob in the elevator.

Bob waited until the doors closed on them to speak. "Please," said Bob wincing. "How many times do I have to ask you to call me Bob?"

"I'm sorry, sir, er, Bob," said Grace. "It's just taking a little getting used to."

"It's all right, Grace. So, tell me honestly, do you think the new guy's going to work out?"

"Absolutely. If you're concerned because I recommended him..."

"Not concerned, exactly," said Bob frowning.

"With respect, he is not the first crewman or woman I've recommended," said Grace a bit more defensively than she intended.

"I know, but this one didn't come with the glowing resume that Lieutenant Flufy did. I have my concerns," said Bob.

"Trust me, sir," said Grace firmly. "I know him, and he'll be good. It may take a little bit of time and effort, but I can whip him into shape."

"Elevator, pause," said Bob, just in time as they were almost at the beamer room level. Bob sighed and turned to Grace. "Do you and he have a history?"

"We have been friends since the academy, but we also served together on previous assignments," said Grace.

"Just friends? Never anything more?" There was a tone in Bob's voice that indicated he believed this to not really be a question, having already decided Grace was keeping something from him. And while she was, sort of, she also was telling the truth. She was offended by his implication otherwise.

"Sir-"

"Bob," he interrupted.

"Bob," she continued, without missing a beat. "I know Dick Kahkay. He's been through a rough patch, but I've seen what he can do. I believe I can reawaken his spirit, and he'll be a great officer when I do."

"Good. Because the position of logistics officer is a senior one, and very important," said Bob, as if she needed to be reminded of that.

"Yes, and he'll be reporting directly to me, so I can ensure he does the job I know he's capable of," said Grace.

"If you don't mind me asking, what happened?" asked Bob.

"Did you not read his file?" asked Grace, confused.

"Yes, yes," said Bob, waving his hand dismissively. "Of course I did. It shows a brilliant officer who rose fast, and then in the past couple of years, a complete 180. A total burn out."

"That's not the whole story, Bob," said Grace, his name sounding foreign on her tongue.

"All right, I don't need to know the story," said Bob, giving up. "As long as you do, and you have no concerns..."

"None," said Grace confidently.

"Then we'll go with your boy. But I do need to see progress right away. We have a starsheep to run here. Personal favors are acceptable in limited amounts, but not at the expense of our crew."

"Understood," said Grace, wondering if perhaps she and Bob weren't as copasetic as she had thought. If he felt the need to question her judgment this way, even after already giving in to her recommendation, that was concerning. She'd just have to prove to him that he could trust her.

The elevator began moving again at Bob's order, and seconds later, the doors opened onto the beamer room. Ensign Miles was standing smartly behind the control board, and nodded to them as they entered.

"Go ahead, Miles," said Bob. Well, reflected Grace, at least he didn't call everyone by their first name.

The dancing colors appeared over the platform, and the form of Dick Kahkay took shape. He looked bedraggled, worn out, bags under his eyes, his clothing unkempt. He had stubble that was a bit past regulation length on his face, and he was slouched, his bad posture matching everything else. Grace could see, out of the corner of her eye, Bob was not impressed.

It took only a split second for the Dick she remembered to emerge, though. It happened as soon as he saw her face, and a mixture of surprise and joy washed over his features.

"Gracie?" asked Dick, immediately moving towards her.

"Hello, Lieutenant Commander Kahkay," she said stiffly, not wanting to appear soft in front of Bob.

"Why didn't you tell me you were the one escorting me to Earth, Commander Thomas?" asked Kahkay.

"Earth?" asked Bob, confused. "No, son, you're not going to Earth."

"I'm not?" asked Kahkay, equally uncertain, looking back and forth between Grace and Bob.

"No. Didn't Commander Winters give you your assignment?" asked Bob.

"Not exactly. He just said to be at the beamer room at 0900 hours sharp," said Kahkay.

"Well, you're our new logistics officer. I'm Robert Yates, the captain. Call me Bob," said Bob. "Grace can show you to your apartment and get you up to speed." Shaking his head a little, Bob, got back on the elevator and sped off, clearly not impressed with the new crewman.

"Logistics officer?" asked Dick, cocking an eyebrow as he looked at Grace. Ensign Miles, for his part, stood at attention, staring straight in front, ignoring them completely. Grace was grateful, but still wouldn't be comfortable discussing this until they got somewhere private. She tapped her foot impatiently as she waited for the elevator to return, and Dick took the hint.

Once they were away, though, Dick turned to her, chuckling now. "Logistics officer?"

"Didn't you still need that position in your command rotation before you make captain?" asked Grace.

"Gracie...," said Dick, not meeting her eyes.

"Don't call me Gracie," she said, annoyed.

"I can call the captain Bob, but I can't call you Gracie?" asked Dick.

"Yes," she said.

"All right. Commander Thomas..."

"Oh, stop," she said. "Just Grace is fine and you know it."

"All right, Grace. Answer me this. Why am I here?"

He looked her right in the eyes, and she could see how far he'd been lost in a way she never had realized through their subspace communications. He put on a good front on the screen, but now she saw his vulnerability laid bare, and for the first time, she wondered if she hadn't made a mistake by bringing him here.

Grace let the silence linger between them a moment, then squared her shoulders and returned his gaze. "Because you're Dick freakin' Kahkay, and you're going to be the best damn logistics officer Bob has ever seen. Or else."

The elevator doors opened and she escorted him to his apartment. The door opened automatically, but he lingered in the door way. "I'll try, but no promises," he said, and then he was gone, the door sliding shut behind him.

Shit, thought Grace. She'd definitely made a mistake.

Lieutenant Commander Richard Q. Kahkay glanced over at the security officer next to him. Then he glanced up. Lieutenant Flufy was not a small dude. Kahkay hadn't actually worked with him before, but Grace seemed to like him for some reason. Kahkay wondered if he should be jealous.

Not that Kahkay had any right to be jealous, nor had he given Grace any reason to choose him over Flufy or anyone else. If she was even interested in Flufy, which he had no confirmation on, just a suspicion given he'd heard they were friends, which was really a pretty flimsy connection. Besides, Flufy was way taller than Grace, herself being a tall woman, and Kahkay thought she'd probably want someone more her own height.

Flufy noticed Kahkay's glance had turned into a stare and returned it with a frown. Embarrassed, Kahkay quickly looked away. Thankfully, Flufy chose not to comment on it.

"...and so I think this is a perfectly fair, and dare I say, generous deal being offered to you by the A.S.S.," said Bob, standing in front of Kahkay and Flufy. Bob was looking down at a small woman, barely waist high to the captain, who was a man of average height for a human. The woman was not human, with elongated vertical eyes, a flat nose, and pale, green skin. Somehow, though her visage was completely alien, Kahkay knew she wasn't pleased.

A series of clicks were the woman's response, and even before the translator kicked in, Kahkay saw Bob tense, not liking the response. "You are arrogant, human, if you think we will make any deal with you."

"Please reconsider," said Bob. "You are very near C'mon space and-"

"We can protect ourselves," interrupted the woman, premier of the planet Halogen I, which they were currently on. The several dozen guards near her bristled, looking menacingly at the small, three-member landing party from the *A.S.S. Redspot*. Kahkay grew nervous. "We know the C'mons and they have not threatened us before. But if they do, we will be ready."

"Respectfully, Premier Yani," said Bob, or at least the name sounded like Yani, with an extra vowel sound in there somewhere. Kahkay wasn't quite sure, so he mentally named her Yani. "The A.S.S. has more advanced weapons and vessels."

"You are a filthy mobster," spat Yani. "We do not need to pay you protection money."

"We are not asking for payment," said Bob.

"Yes you are if you want any A.S.S. personnel to set foot on my planet," said Yani.

"Well, we'd have to set up a base of operations so that we would know if there is a danger here, and to radio for assistance as needed," said Bob. "A small contingent only."

"Not acceptable," said Yani.

"Look, Dick here can show you our plans. It's really rather simple," said Bob. He motioned to Kahkay, who obediently pulled out a tablet computer with the proposal he'd worked up. Kahkay was rather proud of it, probably the thing he'd put the most effort into in years.

Grace had that effect on him. He'd been on the *Redspot* for five weeks, and he'd already noticed a change within himself. He stood a little straighter, he shaved a little more regularly, and he actually did his work. Well, the work that interested him, anyway. Some of the duties of a logistics officer were plain boring, and Dick just couldn't work up the motivation to do all of those. A few, sure, but not all of them.

Admittedly, part of Dick's slacking at present might not be because of the same laziness or apathy that had set in previously. Now, he had a reason not to do his work. Every time he missed filing a report, or was even a few minutes late with an assignment, Grace was down in his face to talk to him about it. Kahkay didn't necessarily want to make her mad, but he relished any opportunity to see her, and she was very sexy when she was flustered...

Kahkay's focus snapped back to the present as Yani grabbed the tablet from his hand and threw it at him, hard. Kahkay winced as it bounced off his chest, but thankfully A.S.S. equipment was made of sterner stuff than that which would shatter easily.

In an instant, Flufy was in front of Kahkay, and Kahkay stumbled back a bit. He knew Flufy was a security officer, and so it was his job to protect the crew, but did the big man need to be this aggressive? Kahkay could handle a tablet being thrown at him; this certainly wasn't the first time.

Unfortunately, Flufy's quick movements unsettled more than just Kahkay. The closest several of Yani's guards rushed Flufy and grabbed the Native American's weapon from his grasp. This didn't sit well with Flufy, and soon the security officer was wrestling with several of Yani's tiny people, kicking a few away, but before long, tackled to the ground by lots of small bodies.

Kahkay watched, almost amused. He would have helped out, but Flufy almost looked like he was having fun, and Kahkay would not enjoy being buried under a pile of aliens wearing as many clothes as these aliens did. Besides, there was the whole thing of suspecting Grace might be attracted to Flufy, for reasons Kahkay couldn't fathom, and he looked forward to telling Grace how her man had been laid low. A small grin touched his lips at the thought of the conversation.

Bob was far less amused. "Stop this at once! Flufy, stand down!" Kahkay didn't know why Bob was ordering Flufy to stand down. Flufy wasn't standing at all.

"Take all three into custody!" ordered Yani, furious.

"Now hold on," started Bob, but Yani turned her back and strode away. In her wake, dozens more guards appeared, the new ones holding sharp, pointed spears in addition to the firearms those who had already been present carried. They surrounded the three A.S.S. officers in an instant.

Bob reluctantly raised his arms in surrender, though anger and frustration was all over his face. Kahkay casually followed suit, not all that concerned about their predicament. After all, the little people hadn't killed Flufy; they'd merely bound him and were hoisting him up, which took a lot of them. So Kahkay didn't sense any immediate peril.

They were led along a hallway and deposited into a rather drab cell, three slabs of a concrete-like substance lining three of the four walls, the last being made up of a huge, barred gate. Shoved inside, a little more roughly than Kahkay would have liked, the gate swung close, locking them in.

"This is unacceptable!" Bob was yelling as the guards departed. "We are representatives of the A.S.S. Tell Yani that I insist on speaking with her at once!" No one so much as turned their head to look at him, and they were left all alone in the barren corridor.

"Idiots!" said Bob. "We're just trying to help."

"I guess they didn't see it that way," said Kahkay. Flufy glared at Kahkay from his place on the floor, but said nothing, still bound with a gag in his mouth.

"I can see that, Dick!" snapped Bob, not at all his usually genial self. "They have to see reason."

"No, they don't, Bob," said Kahkay.

"You're not helping," said Bob.

"I was just pointing out the obvious," said Kahkay with a shrug. "If you want me to help, I can do that, too."

"Then do something!" shouted Bob.

"All right," said Kahkay. He pulled out his phone, which he'd stashed in his sock, unlike Bob, who carried it in the normal holster and had just had it taken from him during capture. "Kahkay to *Redspot*."

"This is the *Redspot*," said Lieutenant Peterman over the device. "Are you all right, Lieutenant Commander Kahkay?"

"Just peachy," said Kahkay. "Beamer us up, will you?"

"Belay that!" shouted Bob, snatching the phone from Kahkay's hand.

"Bob?" asked Peterman.

"Hold on, Sam," said Bob, who was not showing Kahkay the appreciation he'd been expecting, given his cleverness. "We can't leave yet."

"All right," said Peterman. "We'll stand by." The phone went silent.

"Why can't we leave?" asked Kahkay, not getting it. Flufy tried to respond, but the logistics officer couldn't make out a single word through the gag.

"If we just leave, Yani is never going to negotiate with us," said Bob. "We'll have lost her trust."

"Seems to me, we never had it," said Kahkay.

"But we must complete our mission for the A.S.S.!" said Bob.

"We did," said Kahkay.

"How do you figure?" sputtered Bob.

"Our mission was to offer a deal, not to force one down their throats," said Kahkay. "They don't want us, no worries. We're not going to be able to work with everyone."

"But...," said Bob, who was suddenly at a loss for words. Kahkay saw understanding slowly taking root, and wondered how this man had risen to the rank of captain without coming across a situation like this before.

"You did your best, Bob," said Kahkay reassuringly. "I'll reflect that in my report. I'm sure Flufy will, too, won't you, Flufy?" Flufy glared even harder at Kahkay, if that were possible.

"I... you're right," said Bob. "I took it too personally, didn't I?"

"Yep," said Kahkay.

"It just seemed like such a no-brainer deal," said Bob.

"Oh, it was," Kahkay assured him. "They just don't have any brains on this planet."

"Can we keep the temper tantrum just between us?" asked Bob.

"Fine by me," said Kahkay. "How about you, Flufy?" Flufy growled. Kahkay smiled. He knew he should have untied and ungagged Flufy by now, but he was really enjoying seeing the man bound on the ground. "Besides, we can just ask Teela to sign the agreement."

"Teela?" asked Bob, confused.

"Yeah, I was talking to a few of these guys at the reception this morning. Apparently Yani lost an election and Teela is going to be sworn in as their new leader tomorrow. And Teela ran on a platform that included negotiating with us. Yani was probably just being a bitch because she lost," said Kahkay.

"That would have been good information to have," said Bob reproachfully.

"Yep. Good thing we have it," said Kahkay.

Grace watched Bob and Dick laugh from her station on the bridge. Those two had gotten awfully chummy, awfully fast. Six weeks on board, and Dick had already made a positive impression on their commanding officer. That was a step in the right direction, though it wasn't enough.

Dick shot her a smile that she knew was meant to be charming, and she glowered in return. Schmoozing the captain was not what she'd had in mind when she decided to get him back on track. If he had been doing a good job all around, she'd allow him a little goofing off without complaint. But the fact of the matter was, Dick had only improved in the ways in which he wanted to.

For six weeks, Grace had been trying to figure out how to get the Dick Kahkay she knew back. The one who had impressed her and pushed her. The one she'd fallen for, though she'd never admit that to him. She knew he had been in pain, and she understood why he let the self-doubt take over, but damn it. It was time for him to grow up and move on.

That Bob had come to like Dick didn't help because Dick was going for the easy win instead of the hard one. He was impressing people with the old Dick Kahkay personality, but unlike in the past, he didn't have the same work ethic behind it. One couldn't, or shouldn't, succeed without both, and it infuriated Grace that Dick seemed to be trying to do that when he could be so much better.

Didn't Dick understand how she'd put herself on the line for him? Did he not realize the sacrifice she'd made? If he screwed up, that reflected poorly on her. She, who was on track to be captain before long. She risked everything by bringing Dick on when no one had wanted him, when A.S.S. command had been ready to force him out of the service, and she had pulled a few strings to keep him in.

To be fair, she hadn't laid all of that out to Dick, but he had to have figured it out, right? He had to know just how much trouble he'd been in. He was not a dumb man, and there had been others who followed similar career trajectories that they'd both known. He knew the next step was being washed out of the organization. He had to know that.

Grace had seen changes in him. He had come alive a bit, even if it was a bit of a hollow version of life. He wasn't the total mess she'd found him in. But six weeks later, she expected, she needed, to see more progress. He needed to at least do his job, if not excel at it like he used to.

"Whatcha thinking, Gracie?" he asked from right beside her. She started, and hated herself for doing so. She'd been so wrapped up in her thoughts that she hadn't heard him cross the bridge.

"I was thinking it sure would be nice to get your crew schedules on time for once," she said, perhaps a bit too harshly.

"Check your shared folder," he said. She gave him a puzzled look. That's how she asked for things to be turned in, but he never did it that way. Turning to her station, she pulled up the folder and, sure enough, the schedule was there. And so was every other assignment he'd been behind on.

"When...?" she asked, looking up at him with a bit of wonder. She didn't want him to get a big head, but she was blown away, impressed he could accomplish so much in so little time. A week ago, none of this had even been started, as far as she knew.

"Look," he said quietly. "I don't want to make a big deal of things, but I get what you did for me. It took me a little while, but I get it now. Don't worry. I've got your back, too."

"Good to know," she said, still a bit stunned.

Dick walked away from her as only he could, and headed for the elevator. He turned at the door. "Oh, and uh, Gracie?"

"Yeah?" she said.

"Thanks." The elevator doors closed on him in what she'd remember as an almost-perfect moment. The one where she knew she had her Dick back.

"What's he thanking you for, Grace?" asked Peterman, ever the one to butt in. She didn't answer, turning back towards her work with a smile that she couldn't hide.

CHAPTER TWELVE
2424, EDGE OF A.S.S.- EXPLORED SPACE

"First officer's log. I've heard many things about the A.S.S. Thrifty, none of them good. I think perhaps I can be useful here, whip the crew into shape, tame that snarky captain. I look forward to the challenge, and a long, long tenure as part of this ship's group. I am the Lady for the job."

Chief Engineer Colm Foley dragged his exhausted frame into his apartment. It had been a very long day. Some coolant seals had failed, and no sooner had he gotten those under control, than the primary intake manifold had sprung a leak. It was rough work.

"Aw, it's all right, Colm," said Fitzy, going around behind the couch and rubbing his shoulders. "We've had worse days, and everything's set right now."

"Been a bit o' time since we had a longer day than this," said Foley, not unhappy because he loved working on his engines, but ready to relax for the evening.

"At least you didn't refer to Lieutenant Who as a 'he' again," said Fitzy.

"One time!" grumbled Foley. "And the captain still thinks Who's a bloke."

"You should tell him," said Fitzy. "Isn't it a bit evil to let your captain look a fool?"

"Mayhaps," said Foley. "But…" His phone beeped. Sighing, wondering what was broken now, Foley answered it.

"Chief Foley," came Kahkay's booming voice, not sounding the least bit tired. "I'm heading to the ship's bar for a drink. Care to join me?"

"Right away, sir!" said Foley, suddenly wide awake. He snapped the phone shut and leapt to his feet. Kahkay had never invited him to drink before! The captain must have noticed the engineer's attempts to bond with him at long last! It was finally working!

"Mmm, hmm," said Fitzy, bemused. "I see how it is. Your boyfriend calls, and you run off and leave me all by my lonesome."

"Oh, shove it," said Foley, not unkindly, though he didn't appreciate the teasing. This was what he had been waiting for!

Foley got to the bar in record time, but Kahkay was already there, sitting perched on a stool at the main counter. Foley climbed up beside him and motioned to the bartender, Dave, who brought him his favorite scotch. Foley gave her a nod of thanks.

It had been several seconds, but Kahkay had yet to acknowledge Foley's presence. He had a faraway look in his eyes, staring at the wall behind Dave's customary tall, purple hat. She gave Kahkay a look, offended by the staring, then realizing his eyes weren't on her, she moved on to the next customer.

"You meet her yet, Foley?" asked Kahkay. Foley started a bit, not realizing Kahkay had noticed him.

"Who, sir?" asked Foley as he sipped his whiskey. Good stuff. He gave Dave a smile of appreciation and she smiled back.

"The new XO, Commander Lady," said Kahkay.

"Oh. Of course, sir," said Foley. They'd picked up Lady several days ago, right before they headed out on this patrol. She seemed all right to Foley. Perhaps a bit stiff for his taste, but she was definitely competent.

"She looks kinda like her," said Kahkay.

"Like who, sir?" asked Foley, confused.

"Gracie," said Kahkay wistfully.

"Pardon me, sir, but who's Gracie?" asked Foley.

"Never mind," said Kahkay, shaking his head and turning to Foley. The thoughtfulness was gone, and now Kahkay's trademark happy smile was back. "How are you doing, Chief?"

"Not bad, I suppose," said Foley. "A bit o' trouble in the engine room today, but everythin's smooth as silk now."

"Good, good," said Kahkay.

"Sir, forgive me askin', but I was surprised you called me," said Foley.

"Well, Foley, it's sad for a man to drink alone," said Kahkay.

"Right you are," said Foley. "But there are plenty of people in this bar. Why me exactly?"

"Because you're hilarious! Those little noises you make? They're the best," said Kahkay.

"Why, thank you sir!" beamed Foley. "I try."

"You remind me of this fellow I met once," said Kahkay. "Or maybe it was twice. Good guy. Made the same kind of noises."

"That was me, sir!" said Foley excitedly. Kahkay remembered him!

"No, I think I'd remember that," said Kahkay. "He was an Irishman. About your height, same accent, but he didn't have the beard."

"Yes, that was me!" said Foley. "I've only had the beard for the last year."

"No, no," said Kahkay. "A different man. I'm sure of it. But almost exactly like you."

"Well, that's quite a coincidence!" said Foley, making a mental note to shave his beard as soon as he got back to his apartment.

"Isn't it, though?" asked Kahkay. "I'll have to introduce the two of you if we ever run into him again."

"I look forward to it, sir," said Foley. This conversation had lots of promise. Kahkay was enjoying his company. Foley hoped it would be the first of many such nights together.

Doctor Prudence Awshucks was drunk, as was her custom. Sitting in the ship's bar, staring out the window at the stars whizzing by, she almost didn't regret taking this assignment. The liquor was good, not to mention free, and the view was pretty. As long as that cold, cold vacuum of death stayed on the other side of those windows.

A month in, this vessel didn't seem so bad. She got bored a bit, but as a senior officer, had the run of the ship, so she could always wander up to the bridge to see what was going on, which she did frequently.

The only downside to that was that damn Kahkay always hit on her. *Always.* He couldn't keep his eyes off her boobs. She'd never seen anything like it. She had to admit, it was almost animalistic, which was kind of hot, except his voice was annoying enough to ruin the effect. Ah, well. She could handle him.

Speaking of Kahkay, she saw him sitting at the bar, laughing and joking with Chief Engineer Foley. Kahkay was here almost as much as she was, usually alone at first, but calling attention to himself until a crowd had formed around him. She couldn't stand it, but that's why she had her lone table by the window. The bar wasn't huge, but it was nice to put a little physical distance between them and her.

Tonight, though, she didn't really want to deal with it. So she took a last swig of her peach schnapps and headed for the door, her bed calling her name.

Awshucks didn't notice Kahkay get up until they stood side by side next to the elevator down the hall, waiting for her ride.

"Doctor Awshucks," said Kahkay simply, nodding at her politely.

"Kahkay," she said, nodding back. There was silence between them for a moment. Surprisingly, he kept his eyes forward and didn't ask her to go back to his room once.

This behavior worried the doctor. Kahkay hadn't seemed himself for a few days, she realized as her buzz lessened. He had made fewer lewd comments, almost seeming reserved compared to how he normally behaved. Not enough to make everyone notice, she didn't think, but enough that this quiet moment in the hallway prompted her to make a conjecture: he was having a crisis of faith.

The elevator doors opened, and for a moment, Awshucks considered ignoring her conclusion. After all, Kahkay hadn't asked for her help, so she wasn't inclined to give it. But she *was* responsible for the crew's mental health, as well as their physical, and if the captain wasn't operating at peak efficiency, it could be a problem. Problems cut into her drinking time. She followed him on.

"Kahkay, you're late for your physical," she said testily.

"You're right. I'll come down to the hospital tomorrow," he said tiredly.

"I'm afraid I have to insist we do it right now," said Awshucks. "Let's go."

"Really, Doctor Awshucks? I mean, can't this wait?" asked Kahkay.

"Nope," she said, pulling rank on him in the only way she could.

"Uh. For crying out loud. I thought the benefit of having a drunk for ship's doctor was that I didn't have to follow protocol," whined Kahkay.

"I may be liquored up, but that doesn't mean I don't do my job," said Awshucks. "Come on." The elevator doors opened to the hospital floor. She grabbed him by the arm and half dragged him towards her office, Kahkay acting like a petulant child the entire time.

"Sit," she said, depositing him in a chair across from her desk.

"Let's get this over with," grumbled Kahkay. He started to take his shirt off.

"The shirt can stay on," said Awshucks.

"Oh, OK...," said Kahkay warily.

Awshucks opened her drawer and pulled out a fresh bottle of schnapps. Grabbing two glasses, she poured them each a healthy amount, then slid one over to him. "Here. Drink."

"Not that I'm complaining," said Kahkay, taking the glass and sniffing it, as if suspicious of possible poisoning. "But what kind of physical is this?"

"My kind," she said, downing her tumbler in one shot, then pouring a refill. Seeing her, Kahkay followed suit, and she topped him off. "What's the matter with you?"

"What?" asked Kahkay, frowning.

"Yer not yerself lately. You were all full o' piss and swagger, and now you're not," said Awshucks plainly.

"I'm sorry?" asked Kahkay.

"It's not good for the crew to see a captain lose his confidence," said Awshucks.

"I haven't lost anything," said Kahkay angrily.

"Good," said Awshucks. "That's all I needed to know. You can go then."

Kahkay rose and moved for the door, but then paused. He turned around and sat back down. She sighed, not really wanting to deal with this, but it had been her idea to bring him here in the first place. Might as well suck it up, Awshucks, she thought to herself. This is your job.

"Well, maybe I'm... a little off my game," admitted Kahkay.

"No kidding," she deadpanned.

"I mean, it's been an adjustment, trying to be captain," he continued.

"Of course," she said, sipping her drink. She needed more alcohol than she had available to get through this if he was going to keep doling out little tidbits at a time.

"It's just, I didn't know how hard it would be. People die when I make the wrong decisions," said Kahkay.

"Then don't make the wrong decisions," said Awshucks.

"Oh, great. Problem solved. Thanks, doc," was the sarcastic reply. This time Awshucks held up her hand because he was actually going to leave, one foot already out the door.

"Sit yer ass back down," she said. "Spill the beans."

"We do have doctor-patient confidentiality, right?" asked Kahkay.

"You need to ask?" asked Awshucks.

"Forgive me if I'm worried about you using this against me as a topic of glib conversation as you drink with your buddies," said Kahkay.

"In case you haven't noticed, I don't have any buddies, and more importantly, I *am* a professional," she said.

Kahkay sighed. "Fine. OK. I didn't deserve this job. Someone else did."

Ah. Now they were getting somewhere. "And you think this someone else would be doing a better job?"

"Probably. Yes," said Kahkay.

"Could someone else have saved your first XO? What was his name, Larry?" asked Awshucks.

"Garry," said Kahkay bitterly, real pain in his voice.

"Whatever. Could someone else have saved him?"

"Maybe...," said Kahkay, thinking about it. "Maybe not."

"What else have you screwed up?" she asked.

"I didn't see that Dirt wasn't a real A.S.S. officer," said Kahkay.

"Neither did the other seven hundred-plus crew on this starsheep. Next," she said.

"I'm the captain! I should have realized..."

"Kahkay, don't be a damned fool. You're a human being, just like everyone else. You can't know everythin'," said Awshucks.

"I guess you're right...," said Kahkay doubtfully.

"Look, I don't like the A.S.S. all that much, but they don't just make anyone captain. You musta shown a bunch of someones somethin', over and over again, to get this promotion," said Awshucks.

"Well...," said Kahkay.

"You sayin' you got this job on a lark, or because of one thing?" asked Awshucks.

"Of course not," said Kahkay.

"Then find the pair you lost and put it back in yer sack where it belongs. Now get out of my office," said Awshucks.

"Um, thanks, doctor," said Kahkay, not sounding sure he meant it. He finished his glass, then stood.

"Don't mention it. Ever. I don't want people thinkin' they can come to me with their problems," said Awshucks.

"Right," said Kahkay, head tilted as he left. Clearly, he didn't know what to make of their exchange. That was fine. Neither did she.

Lieutenant Tokaladie nodded, smiling up at the reptilian being leaning over her station. "Uh huh," she said distractedly, paying far more attention to his pale yellow, vertical eye slits than to the words coming out of his mouth.

"...and so that adjustment should help you to operate with two point six percent better efficiency," said Lieutenant Commander M-.

"Excellent," said Tokaladie.

"I am ssssorry, Lieutenant Tokaladie. I do not mean to question your professionalism, but do you understand the process I've laid out for you? Because it is rather complex, and you have not asked a single question."

"No, no, I got it," said Tokaladie. "And please, call me Michelle."

"I cannot do that," hissed M-. "It would be most improper to address a colleague by their first name while on duty."

"You're right," she said, placing a hand on his scaly, three-fingered palm. "How about we have a meal together and discuss this further?"

"Discuss the process?" asked M- confused, removing his hand from under hers. "I would be happy to go over it again right now. We do not have to wait until the designated eating time to do so."

"That's not what I meant," said Tokaladie, a twinge of disappointment creeping into her tone.

"What did you meant?" asked M- sincerely, looking her in the eyes.

Tokaladie's heart skipped a beat. This man was a roller coaster. "I just thought-"

She was interrupted as the elevator doors slid open. A tall, imposing woman in a green uniform - the version with the black pants, not the skirt – strode onto the bridge. Everyone turned to look at her and her long, dark hair, pursed lips, and severe, yet attractive, face.

"Ah, Commander Lady!" said Kahkay, legs crossed, turning in his chair at the center of the room. "How are you settling in so far?"

"Fine, fine," said Lady.

"Finding everything all right?" asked Kahkay.

"Yes," said Lady simply.

"What did you mean?" asked M- again, distracting Tokaladie from the exchange between their commanding officers.

"I just-," she started, but this time she interrupted herself, catching a glimpse of a reading at her station. There had been no one at the pilot's controls, and Tokaladie was monitoring them as well as her own work. "Captain, the ship is drifting off course."

"Lady, take the pilot controls," said Kahkay quickly, and Lady gratefully slid into her seat, Tokaladie obviously having saved her from some serious and unwanted flirting from the captain. Tokaladie really needed to speak up and let Kahkay know how offensive his behavior was. Perhaps now that the XO was a woman, too...

"Uh, Mewbiepants, what's going on?" asked Kahkay. Tokaladie was a bit miffed Kahkay had asked M- instead of her, given that she'd reported the issue. M- had returned to his desk the moment of her announcement, and was already studying his screens.

"Sir, we seem to be caught in some sort of energy vortex, pulling us towards the moon of that fourth planet there," said M-. Turbulence shook the bridge and Tokaladie grabbed the edge of her desk to keep from tumbling to the floor.

"Whoa! That's getting violent! What's causing that?" asked Kahkay.

"Hmm, I do not know, sir. It could be the tractor beam of a very advanced starsheep, one that can bend around the moon, and captained by a sole life form who intends to hold us hostage and / or kill us," said M-. After a long pause he added, "But that is just a guess."

Why did M- do that, wondered Tokaladie? As accurate as his guesses were, he had to have realized by now that that just fed into Kahkay's theories that he was evil. Tokaladie wished M- had the wherewithal to help himself and shut up.

"Hmm. The last time you made such a specific 'guess,' you were exactly right," said Kahkay suspiciously. "I ask you again, and I remind you those A.S.S. regulations you love so dearly say that you have to answer me honestly. Are you evil?"

"Of course not, sir," said M-, not sounding sincere to the human ear, though Tokaladie thought she knew him well enough by now to believe him. She smiled a little at the closeness they were developing, even if things were not progressing fast enough for her taste. "I am just a very good guesser."

"Well, if you turn out to be correct...," said Kahkay, letting the sentence dangle.

"If I am, Captain, it is merely luck. I have no foreknowledge of what is trapping us," insisted M-.

More turbulence. The bridge rocked again. Tokaladie saw Foley slip out of the elevator and take his station unobtrusively. Kahkay noticed too and gave the engineer a nod.

"Well, I've got my eye on you, Mewler. Ferris Mewler. Yeah," chuckled Kahkay to himself.

Tokaladie didn't get the joke, but she really wished the captain would take the obviously perilous situation more seriously. She saw Lady roll her eyes at Kahkay from the pilot's controls and felt a kinship. Maybe Tokaladie should befriend her. It certainly wouldn't hurt to have another senior officer in her corner.

The elevator doors opened again, and this time Lieutenant Who and Doctor Awshucks stepped out. Tokaladie checked her clock. Less than sixty seconds since the first alert and all senior staff were present. Good response time.

"Lord have mercy, what's all this shaking around up here?" asked Doctor Awshucks, stepping unsteadily forward, even though the starsheep had stopped rocking. "I spilled peach schnapps all down my front!" Tokaladie wrinkled her nose. She could see, as well as smell, that.

"Sorry, uh, Doctor Awshucks," said Captain Kahkay, glancing at Commander Lady. "Perhaps after this crisis is averted, I can buy you another one."

What was Kahkay's game? Was he trying to make Lady jealous? Why would he do that? And why would the captain try to get involved with any of his staff? Awshucks sure wasn't appreciating it, nor was anyone else. His behavior was just atrocious. She would speak up about it soon, Tokaladie promised herself.

"Foley, is this thing hurting us?" asked Kahkay. He stared at the screen intently. What was out there?

"No, Captain. Shields and stabilizers are operating within normal parameters. But we used up a lot of our budget in the first three episodes, so the defensive actions we can take are limited," said Foley.

Kahkay frowned. "Uh, episodes?"

"I believe Chief Engineer Foley is colorfully referring to the last few missions as if they were installments of an old Earth television or radio program," said M-.

"Exactly, sir," said Foley.

Kahkay frowned. It was true that he tried to add levity to serious situations, as he'd been doing by hitting on Doctor Awshucks and Commander Lady mere moments ago, but how dare his chief engineer joke around at a time like this? It was one thing for the captain to do it, projecting an air that he was in charge of the situation. It was another for an underling to do it, as it made it seem like Foley didn't care about his job.

That M- understood the joke Kahkay missed only infuriated Kahkay further. M- was evil; Kahkay was sure of it. The fact that M- seemed to know what was happening only proved that point. Between evilness and incompetence, Kahkay felt like his crew was coming apart.

That wasn't entirely fair. Most of the problems that had happened so far were his fault, not the crew's. He was just taking his disappointment at himself out on them, and he couldn't do that. Grace would never do that.

It all kept coming back to Grace. She had been all he could think about lately. It didn't help that the new XO looked a bit like her, same beautiful features, tall frame, long, dark hair... Sure, there were differences in the face; they weren't sisters or anything. But from behind, Kahkay could almost swear Grace was sitting on his bridge, and that only made his shame greater.

Immediately, though, he needed to re-establish control of the situation so he replied to Foley, "Well, look, we don't need the metaphors, Foley. Just speak plain ye old English. Or Scottish or whatever it is you speak." Nailed it.

"How about Irish?" asked Foley, which Kahkay found odd since the engineer had said he was Scottish, hadn't he? Kahkay remembered something about leprechauns. "We can't afford t' use t' guns nor beamers, but we have shields and communicators."

"So we're going to have to talk our way out?" asked Kahkay. "Not exactly my style, but I'll manage."

Kahkay heard M- mumble behind him. What was that reptile's problem now? "Excuse me?"

"I said, talking is your favorite thing!" repeated M- accusingly.

"Well, you got me. It pretty much is. I just love the sound of my voooooice," said Kahkay, trying to keep that chill air going, though getting more desperate with each passing second. He hoped the crew didn't notice.

"Captain, we're receiving a transmission from the alien ship," said Lieutenant Tokaladie. Here it was, the moment of truth. Kahkay was expecting this, but that didn't mean he was ready for it.

Kahkay couldn't just talk his way out of the situation. The last time he had tried that, his commanding officer had been beheaded. Now, he was the commanding officer, with a whole starsheep of people who didn't deserve to be beheaded, and who just might be, or worse, if he didn't figure something out quickly.

"Well, put it in the big screen thingy there," said Kahkay, gesturing towards the front of the bridge as casually as he could muster.

"Yes, sir," said Tokaladie.

Sweat was dripping down his back, which Kahkay took to be a sign that he needed to make another joke. Keep everyone distracted, and they wouldn't have time to be scared. He was frightened enough for all of them. "Commander Lady, get me some popcorn. This is going to be fun."

Lady protested, of course, but Kahkay insisted. He knew it was stupid to order his XO to do something so banal, but he wasn't about to lose face in front of the staff. Besides, verbally sparring with her reminded him of past exchanges with Grace, and that made him feel bizarrely both better and worse at the same time.

"Lieutenant Tokaladie, why isn't the call on the big screen thingy yet?" asked Kahkay.

"It is, sir," said Tokaladie. Kahkay begged to differ. The screen showed an empty room and the back of an empty chair. That couldn't be the call that was coming through.

"I'm down here!" said a high pitched voice that seemed to be coming from the vacant room.

"Where?" asked Kahkay with confusion.

"Down here!" said the voice again.

"Tokaladie, angle the camera a bit down. I-I can't...," said Kahkay, annoyed he'd have to ask her to fix the auto-zoom. If the ship displayed things wrong, surely she should know to correct that. The angle changed, but too quickly, and he saw only a brief flash in the rough shape of a being. "A little bit further though. A wee bit more. No, no, up, right. Oh, that's low. Right there. Wow. You're a short fellow, aren't you?"

The individual on screen was tiny, even taking into account the scale of the video. Either that, or he was normal-sized but riding in a giant ship, though his shrill voice indicated that probably wasn't the case. He was bald, pink, with an ugly, shiny, silver frock on and several silver flowers stuck to the top of his dome. His one eye was below a thick, bushy brow, as if all the hair that should be on top of the head had been glued to his forehead. His mouth was wide, showing three rows of jagged, yellow teeth.

"I am actually quite tall for my species!" protested the alien.

"Really?" asked Kahkay. "Well, then, why aren't your feet touching the ground?" While the camera had been moving around, he'd noticed a considerable gap between this being's feet and the floor.

"This is how my people like to sit." The response was very defensive.

"Riiiight," said Kahkay. There was no way that was true.

"Captain?" asked Who from the back of the bridge.

"Not now, Who, I'm on the big screen thing," said Kahkay, annoyed. Who's timing was terrible. Couldn't he see Kahkay was trying to save them? "I'm... by the way, I'm Captain Kahkay of the starsheep *A.S.S. Thrifty*. Who are you and why do you have my beam of a ship in your tractor beam?"

Kahkay knew he was messing up words, but he couldn't help it. It was all he could do to even act calm. The sweat now had to be soaking through the fabric, and he could feel it in his butt crack.

"I am Clint and I have your ship-," started the alien, Clint apparently.

"Did you say your name was Lint?" interrupted Kahkay, going for that levity again. It was the only thing he could think to do under the circumstances.

"I said Clint!" said the tiny man angrily. "C-l-i-n-t."

"Clint? That's a bizarre name! Has anyone?" asked Kahkay looking around the bridge. "Nope?" No one else seemed amused, and he was sure they all saw right through his act. How could they not? He was screwing this up and endangering them all.

"It is a name used by your people as well as mine," said Clint.

"It is? I've never heard of such a thing before," said Kahkay, a lie. He was stalling, racking his brain for anything that could help him get the crew out of this safely. Clint may look laughable, but with the *Thrifty* firmly ensnared, they were entirely at his mercy.

"It is, sir," said M- unhelpfully. "A number of notable Earthlings have been named Clint. For instance, twentieth century movie star Clint Eastwood, the great twenty-second century philosopher, Clint Marley, and-"

"All right, that's enough Metamuce," Kahkay cut him off. "No one asked you."

"You should be nicer to your science officer, Captain Kahkay," said Clint. "He is correct."

"Mmm, I like this being already," said M-. Evil bastard. Kahkay could feel what little control he had of this situation slipping away.

"Captain Kahkay?" asked Commander Lady. Why was she still on the bridge? Hadn't he ordered her to go get him some popcorn?

"Hush!" said Kahkay testily. "I'm speaking with a fellow captain. Executive officers are not invited. It's an A-B conversation, so F off."

That didn't sit well with Lady. "Captain Kahkay, I must insist-"

She stopped mid-sentence. Kahkay heard a brief groan, and turned in time to see her collapse, a smoking hole in her chest. For a moment, she had Grace's face. His heart dropped to his chair and he wanted to jump up and run to her, to run to Grace, but he was frozen in his seat by fear and indecision.

"Mercy me! She's dead!" exclaimed Awshucks, though Kahkay barely heard the doctor.

"Dead?" asked Kahkay, in shock. "What in the blue blazes was that?" She couldn't be dead. She'd barely been on board any time at all. And she had Grace's... No, she wasn't Grace. The dead body wasn't Grace.

"That was to show you how serious I am, Captain Kahkay," said Clint, who looked pleased with himself. "I have killed your second-in-command, and if you do not meet my demands, I will kill the rest of your crew one by one."

Kahkay stared, jaw opening and closing, but couldn't manage to get a word out. Shit. He, and by extension, the crew, were fucked.

CHAPTER THIRTEEN
2424, EDGE OF A.S.S.- EXPLORED SPACE

Lieutenant Who Grappa stared down at the body of Commander Lady, sprawled on the floor beside her. This wasn't real; it couldn't be. Who had seen her share of dead bodies; one couldn't be a doctor and avoid those. But she had only been security chief for a little over a month, and this was another big, black mark on her record. She was failing at the job miserably, and that made Who mad.

"I will kill the rest of your crew one by one," the alien known as Clint was saying from the big screen. "Starting with that huge ape there."

Who looked at Kahkay. The captain's shirt was soaked through with perspiration and he was staring at the screen dumbly. Who's opinion of Kahkay was low already, and this behavior did nothing to change it. Who's life was in this idiot's hands, though at this point Who thought she didn't deserve any better. Though, she still didn't want to die, especially not standing with Kahkay.

"Who?" Kahkay finally stammered.

"That big, furry creature standing over your deceased XO's body," said Clint. Who bristled. She knew that her species did bear some resemblance to an Earth ape, but she did not like being compared to such an unintelligent creature.

"Right, that's Lieutenant Who," said Kahkay, who barely seemed cognizant of what he was saying. "Uh, if you think your little beam can harm Who-"

"Who. Surrender," said Who quickly. She didn't know if she was going to make it through this alive, or if she could do her job and protect the crew, but she did not intend to give up easily, and certainly not because of some inadequate captain's misspeak. "No. Shoot. Who."

"Who, shut up!" ordered Kahkay. Who growled, but didn't say anything else. She didn't trust or respect Kahkay, but following the chain of command was ingrained in her enough that Who had a hard time being outright disobedient, even against those who warranted it. And Kahkay probably deserved to be listened to less than any senior A.S.S. officer Who had yet encountered.

"Thank you, Lieutenant Who. At least someone over there has brains," said Clint. For a second, Who felt like maybe life would be better serving under Clint, if the tiny alien did, indeed, accept her surrender. But only for a second.

"Who, get off the bridge," said Kahkay, whose cool had long been lost.

Who opened her mouth to reply, but Clint beat her to it. "No one can leave the bridge, Captain Kahkay, as your officers have been trying to tell you. I have sealed you in."

Who looked down at Commander Lady, who had, indeed, been trying to report that piece of information to the captain just before she died. Who took responsibility for Lady's death, but she also held Kahkay partially responsible. Who would do her best to make sure they both paid that debt.

"It's true, Cap'n," said chief engineer Foley. "I cannae get the doors open."

"Well, thanks for trying, Foley," said Kahkay. "Well, trapped or not, Who, you're under arrest for insubordination."

Seriously? *This* was what Kahkay was choosing to focus on now, in the middle of the emergency? Who surrendering without permission? Who surveyed the bridge. If she made a move to mutiny, who would support her? Maybe if she offered Kahkay to Clint, the alien would let them go.

Who quickly dismissed the notion. As tempting as it was, she knew she could never do that, nor did she want the responsibility of trying to keep the whole ship safe when she couldn't even keep officers standing right next to her alive.

"Mmm, actually, Captain," said M-. "Regulation 6521.3 allows crew members to surrender themselves when their lives are threatened, regardless of orders, and prohibits superior officers from seeking retribution." Who gave M- a small smile of appreciation. At least the science officer seemed a capable and noble being, worthy of the A.S.S. that Who believed in.

"Goddamn it, Mucifer. Do you ever shut your trap?" asked Kahkay, looking like a child throwing a temper tantrum. "I mean, come on! Crew! We are making a terrible impression in front of the company."

"Uh, company? *He killed her!*" said Awshucks, and Who grunted in agreement. The doctor seemed like a horrible person, but in the moment, even she was better than Kahkay.

"I'm clearly aware of that, Doctor Awshucks. I can see Commander Lady's body there," said Kahkay coldly, not looking in the direction of the fallen XO. "That doesn't mean we need to act like fools."

"Mmm, in your case, I do not think it is acting," said M- quietly. Who started to rethink the mutiny idea. She still didn't think herself capable of leading, but if Awshucks and M- were fed up with Kahkay, too, one of them could assume command. And it was starting to look like the spitting-mad Kahkay would need to be removed if any of them were going to get out of this alive.

"I'm not saying we'll give into your demands, um, Clit, was it?" asked Kahkay.

"Clint," said Clint, over pronouncing his name. Who didn't blame him. She was tired of Kahkay calling her a 'he.' The captain couldn't get anything right.

"Right, Clink," said Kahkay, and Clint pulled his shoulders back in frustration. Yep, Kahkay was seconds away from goading Clint into murdering the entire crew. "I'm not saying we'll do what you want, but uh, what are your demands?"

Who had only one demand in that moment, and it was for a new commanding officer.

Lieutenant Michelle Tokaladie watched the exchange between Captain Kahkay and Clint with growing dread. Never had she seen a captain act so erratically, and glancing over at Commander Lady's body, Tokaladie couldn't help but wonder if Lady wasn't the lucky one. At least she hadn't seen her death coming. The rest of them were just waiting for Clint to get tired of Kahkay and blow them out of the sky.

Not for the first time, Tokaladie wished that she were the type of woman to speak up when she saw a situation going wrong. Awshucks, M-, and Who were giving the captain grief, and seemed ready to step in at any moment if Kahkay went too far. Tokaladie wanted to be like them. She knew what was happening in front of her was wrong, and yet she couldn't bring herself to be the one to step up and do something about it.

Then again, while the other senior officers, save Foley, whom Tokaladie could never see being anything but supportive, no matter how bad the orders were, made snarky comments, none of them made an actionable move against Kahkay, either. Perhaps there was a limit to what they were willing to do. The A.S.S. bred the chain of command into them at the academy. Was this the result of such a policy? That no one could save them from a terrible leader? If they survived this, Tokaladie vowed to start questioning things and work to change that.

"I... I honestly didn't think I'd get this far," Clint was saying on the screen, in response to Kahkay asking for his demands. "Normally, I threaten, the captain blusters, I kill the crew members, and then the captain tries to attack, and then I blow everyone up, and then I go home, so day well spent. No one has ever actually asked me what my demands are."

"Well, imagine that," said Kahkay sarcastically. "You don't get any respect. I *completely* understand." Kahkay gestured around the bridge as he said it, turning to meet all of their eyes, holding each gaze for only a second. Was he flipping serious? Everyone stood by, letting the captain be an ass to all of them, risking all of their lives, and *he* had the nerve to complain about a lack of respect? Tokaladie had never wanted to smack someone more.

"You do?" asked Clint, taken aback.

"Of course I do, Clint. By the way, may I call you Clint?" asked Kahkay.

"That's my name," said Clint, confusion mixing with the surprise. Tokaladie echoed his emotional reaction on this. What was Kahkay's game? A moment ago, he had been falling apart before her. But with the last three sentences he spoke, something had changed in his eyes. Had he snapped and was going the suicidal route now? Or did he think he could somehow win Clint over to save himself, while tossing the rest of the crew under the bus?

"Great," said Kahkay. "All right, Cliff, you've seen how my crew treats me. I've been their captain for, like, what, it's been a month now, and they already make comments behind my back – yes, I heard you earlier, M- - and surrender without my permission, and refuse to make me popcorn, and whatever Tokaladie does. It's infuriating!"

"Hey!" said Tokaladie. She really didn't know Kahkay's strategy here at all. He called M- by the correct name for once, then immediately dissed everyone present. His behavior had crossed over from immature to erratic and borderline insane.

"Exactly!" said Clint, apparently deciding to take Kahkay at face value, as a peer. "All I ask is one little thing, and no one will even listen to my orders, even after I've captured their ship and taken them hostage."

"We're two of a kind. Two peas in a pod. Brother from another mother. What say you and I have a drink and complain about how *everyone* treats us?" asked Kahkay.

"That's tempting, Captain Kahkay, but I'm not coming over to your starsheep. You would just lock me up," said Clint. So the alien wasn't totally won over, eyeing Kahkay suspiciously now.

"Flint, buddy, look at me. You know me. Would I do that to you?" Kahkay flashed a broad grin, and it almost looked to Tokaladie like his old self was back. Except, now there was a dark edge behind his eyes that she didn't know how to interpret. She shivered unconsciously.

"We just met," said Clint.

"Still. I just... Look at this face? Would this face lie to you?" asked Kahkay with a tone approaching sincerity.

"I would assume so," said Clint. Whatever Kahkay was trying, it was failing, his momentary bond with the alien broken. Tokaladie edged a step closer to M-. If this was the end, she'd try to steal a kiss before they disintegrated. Then, at least she could go out with one less regret.

"Never!" insisted Kahkay. "Would you mind holding for a minute? I'm sure me and my crew here can put our heads together and figure out, yeah, how to prove it to you."

"OK. You have one Earth minute. I'm timing," said Clint.

How would one minute accomplish anything, wondered Tokaladie.

"Lieutenant Tokaladie, mute the call."

"He's on mute, sir," Tokaladie said.

Captain Richard B. Kahkay ignored the sweat on his brow and spun towards the crew. They all looked at him expectantly. He hoped against hope that he wasn't about to let them down.

Five minutes ago, Kahkay had been on the edge of a nervous breakdown. He had given up all hope, realized his limitations, and found himself wanting. He had no idea what to do, and he had been ready to throw in the towel.

Then, he'd looked around the bridge and seen the eyes of his various crewman. Chief Engineer Foley, who trusted Kahkay implicitly. Lieutenant Who, at whom Kahkay had misdirected his ire at a moment ago. Lieutenant Commander M-, whom Kahkay was sure was evil and unworthy of any loyalty, so he skipped over him pretty quickly. Doctor Awshucks - he didn't like her much either, but to lose her boobs would be a horrible thing for the galaxy at large. He also reluctantly had to admit that she saw through him in a way that no one had since Grace, though it felt more intrusive when she did it.

Commander Lady was still there, too, dead on the floor. At second glance, she didn't look much at all like Grace. That was good. Kahkay couldn't afford to think about Grace right now. He knew he'd failed her most of all, and was glad she wasn't here to see him at his worst. She'd been with him in similar straights before and helped him, and now he felt like he'd betrayed her by going back to this.

There was Lieutenant Tokaladie, young and sweet and in need of protection. A few ensigns whose names Kahkay didn't know were present, but even younger, and even more in need of protection. Yeoman Cliff was looking disappointed in his commanding officer.

Kahkay's gaze lingered on Yeoman Cliff, whose visage was familiar, and suddenly it hit him. Yeoman Cliff *Roberts*. Kahkay had seen his name in the file, and the face had some recognizable features, but it was only in this moment that Kahkay put two and two together. This was the son Captain Gene Roberts had told him about.

Gene Roberts, the man who was beheaded because Kahkay screwed up. Cliff Roberts, a young man, barely past being a boy, who had to grow up without a father these past few years because of Kahkay. Kahkay had let him down over and over again.

That was when it clicked for Kahkay. He couldn't doom another Roberts. Whoever Cliff's mother was, she didn't deserve that. Kahkay had to get Cliff through this and back home, if he did nothing else. He couldn't repeat the mistake of running his mouth off without thinking things through.

Kahkay didn't have to make the same error, not with the rest of these smart, talented people on his bridge. They were the best of the best, as far as Kahkay was concerned, seasoned A.S.S. officers who had been placed with him for a reason. Well, except for M-. Kahkay had tried to do it himself the last time, but he now realized that a captain was only as good as the people around him, hence why Gene Roberts had died, bringing along the wrong person in Kahkay. He had Cliff and Foley and Tokaladie and Who and Awshucks, though, and they could get through this together.

And so, he quickly tried to connect on an emotional level with Clint to buy some time, and when that didn't work, Kahkay managed to get his crew an extra minute. Would they help him, or had he already screwed things up so badly that they'd lost their faith in him? Time to find out.

"Foley, can we fire at him?" Kahkay asked.

"No, sir, nor are our engines any match for his beam. I've never seen such advanced technology," said Foley.

Kahkay turned to M-, unable to keep the accusation out of his voice, but betting M- would assist, rather than die to be contrary. "Mew, you 'guessed' what the danger was. Any guesses on how to escape it?"

"No, Captain," said M-. "Unfortunately, I have never heard of anyone being in this situation and surviving."

"But you've heard of someone being in this situation and dying?" asked Kahkay hopefully. "What did they do to get themselves killed?"

"Hmm, I do not know, ssssir. I only heard of the previous captives, um, when Clint told us about them a few minutes ago." M- was looking at Kahkay warily, but Kahkay believed him. Besides, he didn't have the time to press the science officer further.

"What about beamers, Foley? Would they work? We can send Who over there to rattle his cage," said Kahkay.

"Who. No. Go," said Who quickly. "Who. Already. Surrender."

"Look, no one's going to hold you to that, Who," said Kahkay, disappointed at his security chief's lack of initiative and willingness to help out the team. "You can pretend to surrender, then bash his skull in."

"No," said Who sadly. "Not. Honorable."

"It wouldn't work anyway, Captain," said Foley before Kahkay could ask Who if his life was less important than his honor. "The beamers are blocked, and as advanced as that ship is, I don't read anything like beamers on it."

What kind of super advanced starsheep didn't have beamers, wondered Kahkay, but quickly pushed the thought away. His minute had to be almost up. "Well, Doctor Awshucks, ideas?"

"Drink. A lot. Do you happen to keep a stash on the bridge somewhere?"

Kahkay couldn't blame her. He wanted to drink, too, though he wouldn't allow himself that right now. He couldn't be any weaker than he'd already been. "Of course I do," said Kahkay. "Bottom drawer on the left behind the... you know. Anything useful, though?"

"What do you want from me? I'm a doctor, not a military barbarian. I heal people, not hurt them."

"Uh, I expected as much," said Kahkay. He guessed her recent talk to try to knock him out of his funk was a one-time offer of help. "Lieutenant Tokaladie?"

"Actually, sir-," began Tokaladie, but Kahkay cut her off.

"Never mind. You know what, I don't know why I asked you anyway," said Kahkay, not unkindly. He knew she was counting on him to save her, not the other way around, and his heart went out to her naivete.

"I'll think of something. I always do," said Kahkay, more to himself than to them. While none had offered any useful suggestions, it had been helpful to speak with them. It reset his mind, and he found their presence comforting. This was what he needed from them. Now it was time for him to take it home. He'd found his strength in them.

"Time is up, Captain Kahkay," said Clint.

"Tokaladie, I thought you had him on mute," said Kahkay in surprise.

"She did. I unmuted myself just now," said Clint.

"My stars! You can do that! That is advanced, indeed!" said Foley, awed. Kahkay had to silently agree with his engineer.

"So, can you prove your sincerity to me, Captain Kahkay?" asked Clint.

"Yes, I...," said Kahkay, searching for a bluff and not finding one. Then he caught the eye of Cliff and steeled himself for a rare moment of total honesty. In this case, he measured it might buy him just a little more time, and he needed that. He also hoped it would make his watching crew proud. "Got nothing. I got nothing."

"That is fine. I used the minute to think of some demands," said Clint, simple Clint, missing all the subtext going on right now, and Kahkay's newly recommitted brain whirling. "First, I'd like six trillion bars of gold."

"But, you know, starsheeps typically don't carry more than a few thousand bars at a time," said Kahkay. A lie, but one he hoped would stretch out the conversation even more. He was disappointed as Clint moved right along, no interest in negotiating.

"Fine, I'll take what you have now, and you can write me an I.O.U. for the rest. Second, I want half of your women. The pretty ones. Like, uh... Lieutenant Tokaladie and

Doctor Awshucks there." Clint made an appreciative noise that Kahkay could only describe as creepy.

"OK," said Tokaladie quickly. Kahkay shot her a pointed look. Really? Had he already let her down so much she'd rather be with this evil alien than on his ship? Tokaladie's face was inscrutable, and she didn't meet his eyes.

"I thank you kindly, sir," said Doctor Awshucks, which was about what Kahkay had expected from her.

"You look like, what, you're ten?" asked Kahkay. "Do you even know what to do with a woman? I mean, have you even gone through puberty?"

"No, but I hope to within the next year," admitted Clint.

"OK, look, trust me," said Kahkay, taking on the tone of a trusted mentor. He thought he had a reading on Clint now, and was pretty sure he was playing the little guy. Clint was still dangerous, and Kahkay still needed a clincher, but he was feeling good that things were turning around, which let him speak more confidently. "You don't want half our women. That's too many women at once. If you took them one at a time, sure, I understand, that'd be one thing. But having a couple hundred women around you... the nagging will be incessant!"

"Hey!" said Tokaladie and Awshucks in unison. But Kahkay didn't turn around this time; he was in his groove.

"Well, OK, one woman then," said Clint, relenting. He really *was* a pubescent child, and that was the way in Kahkay had been searching for. "I'll, uh... I'll just uh... take that dead one there."

"This one right here?" asked Kahkay, pointing at Commander Lady, sure he misheard.

"Yeah. That one," said Clint, almost embarrassed.

"Uh, OK," stammered Kahkay, not seeing the harm. She was dead, after all. "I mean, that's *weird*, but uh, all right. No judging. Uh, anything else?"

"I want you, Captain Kahkay, to take off your shirt and dance like a monkey," said Clint. Kahkay could sense Clint was reaching now. The alien's limited imagination had already run out of ideas. But that was all right, because Kahkay's mind was much more expansive.

"I'll give you the gold and I'll give you the woman, but that's crossing a line and I'm not going to do that," said Kahkay as if he were in charge of the situation, which he finally was.

"Then I will destroy your starsheep!" said Clint petulantly.

"Oh, yeah? Well go ahead and try," said Kahkay. He could feel the others tense beside and behind him. They were not along for this ride, but as long as none of them did anything colossally stupid, they'd see the way out in seconds. He trusted them not to mess this up, if only because he had no other choice.

"What do you mean?" asked Clint, wary, which was just how Kahkay wanted him.

"Well, you see, I've been stalling you," said Kahkay. "I've had all my crewmen below decks move our full supply of carbonatum against the hull. If you use any weapon on us, our ship will bubble out and destroy the whole star system."

"Captain, I don't...," began M-. God! Of course he'd be the one to interfere when Kahkay was so close to saving them all.

"Yes, M-?" asked Kahkay with a level tone, catching M-'s eye and making sure to say the science officer's name correctly for once.

M- looked at him, exasperated. After a pause, though, he said only, "Oh, uh, yes. All decks report they are ready with the, um... carbonatum." Whew. That was a close one!

"I've never heard of such a substance," said Clint. "Is it highly explosive?"

"Oh, highly," said Kahkay. "This is my chief engineer, Foley. Uh, Foley, please tell Clint what the carbonatum does."

Foley looked at Kahkay, slow to catch up, but Kahkay knew he would play along, and Foley didn't disappoint. "Oh. Yeah. It's *awful*. You- you don't want to see it. It'll be all like," and here he proceeded to make a bunch of explosion type noises. Foley gestured to the others, and they all joined in, M-, Tokaladie, Who, Cliff, the ensigns, even Awshucks, though the bottle of liquor she held was half gone already.

Foley continued as the rest supplied sound effects. "In the concentrations we have, it'll take out every star system within a light year from here."

"OK, that's enough, *thank you*," said Kahkay to his crew, and they all sheepishly stopped. He was grateful that they got on board with his plan, but they were dangerously close to overdoing it. "But you get the picture."

"Hmmm," said Clint suspiciously, though with a note of fear. "How come none of the other starsheeps I've encountered before had such cargo?"

"Because we know all about you, Cling-ying-aling," said Kahkay, stepping towards the screen. "You may have killed those crews, but messages get out. I came here just to lure you into this trap and force you to leave our galaxy. Are you going to go quietly, or do we get to destroy you? Please say we get to destroy you. Please, please!"

Clint burst into tears. "Wah! I want my mommy. How dare you threaten me-e-e-e!"

"Well, your mommy isn't here, Clintstone," said Kahkay coldly. "It's you and me. What's it going to be?" He couldn't resist tossing in a quiet "Oh, I rhymed again," pleased as he was with his performance.

"I'm going home. You're a terrible person!" cried Clint.

"The transmission has ended, sir," said Tokaladie unnecessarily, as the big screen had switched to the view of space outside the *Thrifty*, though Kahkay couldn't begrudge her the sense of relief she was radiating.

"Readings indicate he's headin' outta here fast," said Foley triumphantly. "Nearest star along that course is three galaxies over, sir!"

"Well, I'd say that takes care of that," said Kahkay with satisfaction.

"Captain?" asked M-, ruining the moment. "May I speak freely?"

Kahkay braced himself. Any other time, he'd tell M- to shove it, but he knew he just put his crew through the ringer, and whatever anger M- had, Kahkay probably deserved it. He didn't like M-, but he owed him that. "Go ahead, Mew," he said reluctantly.

"That was...," said M-, leaving a too-dramatic pause. "...the finest bluff I have ever borne witness to. Excellent job, sir."

"Thank you," said Kahkay in surprise. "Foley, set course for wherever we were heading before stopping off here and go! Who, get that body off my bridge before it starts to smell."

Lieutenant Commander M- checked the readings on his panel, but there was nothing out of the ordinary. The long day was over, his shift was nearing its end, and he could return to his regular duties.

Regular duties to M- meant exploring and cataloging everything they passed. The *Thrifty* had excellent sensors, and could analyze the debris and particles around them as they traveled, even at very high speeds, which M- found fascinating. There was so much about space he had yet to discover.

"Captain's Diary," Kahkay was saying from the center seat. "Today... was just a normal day, really. That's all."

That statement was far from accurate, and M- reflected that how human beings work was one of those things he hadn't yet discovered. He was trying hard to understand their behavior, but it was just so different from his own people's that he found it most puzzling.

For instance, Lieutenant Tokaladie had dropped several hints that she wanted to spend time with M- socially. He did not understand why. The bridge, while they were on duty, was a much more appropriate and convenient locale for anything he'd care to discuss with her. Why was that not satisfactory?

M- did want to be more social, as he discovered today, but in a group setting. When the bridge staff had come together to support Captain Kahkay's lie to Clint, M- had felt like a part of something, and it felt good. He wanted to do more activities like that, be a piece of the whole, and finally belong in the A.S.S. He didn't think his fellow officers thought of him when they planned such engagements, and he set a goal to change that.

Back home, there were rarely teams of any sort. There were alliances, yes, but not ones based on trust. Those were more about achieving mutually beneficial objectives, and there was no lasting connection to come out of them. M- had always found that sad, unlike most of his people, who seemed to relish it. Which was a large part of why he joined the A.S.S. in the first place.

M- still wasn't sure how he felt about Kahkay exactly. Today, the captain had displayed qualities that M- had read that he possessed, but M- had never witnessed before. Kahkay's file, which M- had studied, had many impressive deeds recorded. However, this was the first time since Kahkay took command that M- had observed Kahkay at his best. If the captain continued to behave in such a manner, M- would enjoy serving under him.

"Ooo, one more thing, Diary," said Kahkay giddily. "I-I-I began rhyming a lot today more, and that was good, and I'm doing it off the cuff, uh... Matter of fact, uh... I've got nothing." The last bit was stated with a fair amount of dejection.

M- made an unhappy noise. That was more the Kahkay he was used to, a Kahkay he did not approve of. If Kahkay could be the legendary A.S.S. officer M- suspected he was capable of being, M- would happily follow him. However, should Kahkay continue to display these annoying tendencies, M- would have a hard time not falling back into his learned behavior of being evil, at least towards the captain. It wasn't what M- hoped for, but he was enough of a realist to see it as a possibility.

Hopefully, Kahkay would not force him to resort to that.

CHAPTER FOURTEEN
2423, A.S.S. / RUCAN BORDER

"Dick, evasive action!" shouted Bob from the center seat. Commander Richard M. Kahkay's fingers danced over the pilot controls, and the *A.S.S. Redspot* narrowly avoided some pretty nasty weapons fired at them from the nearby Rucan vessel.

"How many missiles do we have left?" Bob turned around and asked.

"Thirteen, sir," said Commander Grace Thomas from the logistics station.

"Not nearly enough," mused Bob.

"Grace'll make 'em count," said Kahkay.

"I know," said Bob. "But no matter how well you use them, thirteen isn't going to save us if the other three Rucan vessels get to us before we can get out of here."

Kahkay spared a glance at the long-range scanners. Those three blips were a lot closer than he would have liked to have seen, but the *Redspot* couldn't just flee while engaged with two warships. The Rucans would give chase, and they were a bit faster than this vessel.

The Rucans were a mysterious race. The A.S.S. had been aware of them since before its founding, but had no formal relations. The border was disputed, and usually the humans just stayed far away from it to avoid any misunderstandings or unfortunate encounters, such as the one they were engaged in now. However, a cargo vessel in this sector had called for help, and the A.S.S. didn't ignore distress calls, either.

"Bob, the cargo vessel is reporting another hull breach," said Lieutenant Sam Peterman from communications. "They don't have much time."

"Damn it," cursed Bob. "Can't the Rucans leave an innocent ship alone?"

"The cargo ship is not being targeted," said Lieutenant Flufy from security.

"Then why are they being hit?" asked Bob.

"Wrong place, wrong time," said Flufy with a shrug.

"Ideas, people," said Bob. "How do we fight these bastards off and rescue that crew?"

"I've got an idea," said Kahkay. "Grace, take the pilot controls."

"What? Now? In the middle of this?" Grace asked with shocked disapproval. "Where are *you* going?"

"I second Grace's confusion, Dick," said Bob. "What are you up to?"

"Trust me," said Kahkay. "I'll be back."

"Hurry," said Bob, not happy that Kahkay wasn't sharing his idea, but Kahkay knew Bob liked and trusted him enough not to question it further. There wasn't a good reason not to fill Bob in, but keeping him in the dark was more dramatic, and Kahkay liked to be dramatic.

Kahkay stood and hovered at his station until Grace slid into position, unable to leave the pilot console unattended for even a second, under the circumstances. Then, he sprinted for the elevator, putting in a quick call to Ensign Miles en route.

Miles was already powering up a shuttle when Kahkay arrived in the bay. "Don't tell me we're going out in that, Dick," he said with annoyance.

"OK, I won't tell you, Miles," said Kahkay, strapping himself in. "Get to the back and man the beamer." Miles groaned, but obeyed, buckling into the chair next to the beamer controls.

The shuttle wasn't big, but neither was the cargo ship's crew. There would be room for all five of them, along with Miles and Dick, with a little room to spare. But that was only if they could be beamered aboard without the shuttle being hit by fire from the Rucan vessels. The shuttle was not built to withstand an attack the way the *Redspot* was. One direct shot and they were dead.

The bay doors opened, and Kahkay dipped under the hull, trying to keep the massive starsheep between himself and the Rucans, which was hard, the way everyone kept moving around. The cargo vessel was behind the *Redspot*, but the starsheep couldn't beamer the crew aboard while keeping its shields up to fight. Which meant Kahkay couldn't even give the little boat the slight protection shields might offer while attempting this stunt.

It didn't take long to reach the vessel, and Kahkay saw right away that they had even less time than he had calculated. The cargo ship had several holes in it, vapor puffing out, pieces of metal floating near it, lights flickering. It spun at an angle in the void, looking very much like it was dying, and it was.

"Hurry up, Miles," said Kahkay, dodging behind the cargo ship to give them even more cover from the Rucans.

"As soon as you stop moving so much," said Miles testily. He was a very talented beamer chief, but had little taste for adventure.

"No can do," said Kahkay, spotting one of the Rucan warships breaking off its attack on the *Redspot* and heading their way. "We've been spotted." He deftly maneuvered up and around, aware that any cover he bought from the cargo ship risked the deaths of those he'd come out to save.

"Here come the first ones now," said Miles, working the controls. The shuttle only had beamer capacity for two. A pair of figures appeared in the confined space, but Kahkay didn't even spare them a glance as he heard Miles order them out of the way so he could grab the next batch.

"Incoming!" warned Kahkay, whipping around to port. The new arrivals hadn't made it to seats yet, and Kahkay heard himself being cursed vehemently from the back of the shuttle. He paid them no mind, more concerned with the Rucan ship that was attacking them. The shuttle only narrowly avoided the purple laser blasts.

The beamer sound filled the cabin again, and Kahkay knew without looking that Miles had rescued two more of the cargo crew. That left only one soul on board, though the Rucan warship was practically on top of them now and the shuttle was heavily exposed. Kahkay heard sobs and gasps from the survivors behind him.

"Steady, Dick," said Miles. "I'm having trouble locking onto the last one with all the interference."

"I can't hold still, Miles," said Kahkay, punching the throttle and rocketing them out of the way of another burst. It sent them too far away from the cargo vessel for the shuttle's limited-range beamers to work, and now Miles joined their passengers in cursing Kahkay. Kahkay rolled and turned back, which was a mistake because that left him face-to-face with the Rucan ship.

The enemy warship was massive, twice the size of the *Redspot*, and darkly colored to look even more menacing, Kahkay supposed. It had sharp points and what looked like daggers sticking out of it. If you asked him, Kahkay thought they were trying too hard.

"Hold on!" said Kahkay, accelerating the shuttle right at the warship. It couldn't fire at them if they were on top of it.

"Watch it!" yelled Miles, as if he really thought Kahkay would ram the enemy vessel. Admittedly, Kahkay did wait a little long to duck under, and the top of the shuttle slammed into one of the dagger-like projections, snapping it off. Thankfully, it was thin enough to do little damage to the shuttle, and now they were back at the cargo vessel.

The beamer went to work again, and a moment later Miles triumphantly shouted, "Got 'em all!" Kahkay would have smiled, but now they were trapped next to a Rucan ship that was lazily turning around to finish them off and the *Redspot* was nowhere in sight.

What the...? Where did the starsheep go? Bob was kinda spineless, but surely he wouldn't have abandoned them. Not like this.

Kahkay turned the shuttle back towards the Rucan ship, trying to do a quick scan for the *Redspot*, but not able to effectively look over the whole area while running and dodging for their lives. All he knew was that the *Redspot* wasn't where it had been and certainly wasn't in visual range.

A purple blast blinded Kahkay as it filled the entire big screen at the front of the shuttle, and the small ship rocked hard. It couldn't have been a direct hit, but it was strong enough to send the little craft tumbling. Kahkay was strapped in and he hoped the passengers were, too. Given the lack of screams of pain, he assumed that they were.

Kahkay managed to right the shuttle, but it was sluggish and smoke was coming from two panels. They weren't in any shape to try to get away now. The Rucan vessel came into view, weapons ports glowing, and there was nothing more Kahkay could do. His stunt may have been bold, but it had also cost them.

Then the cargo freighter, which was just off the engine of the Rucan vessel, exploded, knocking the warship back harder than a hit from an A.S.S. ship would have. Actually, it looked like there had been A.S.S. weapons fire just before the explosion. That was peculiar. Unless...

Yep! Sure enough, the *Redspot* came into view, having used the cargo ship as a bomb against the Rucans. The *Redspot* had more than its share of blemishes on the hull, scarred from the battle it had been in, but it had never looked more beautiful to Kahkay. It fired on the enemy ship twice, three times, four times, with laser blasts and at least six of the remaining missiles.

The Rucan ship sputtered, then began to drift. It was disabled. Kahkay gave a silent cheer, then piloted the shuttle as best he could, given the damage, back towards the *Redspot*. A quick check of the long-range showed the Rucan's back up was still four minutes away. The *Redspot* would have time to flee.

Commander Grace Thomas beamed as Dick came into the captain's office off the bridge. She rose quickly and gave him a brief hug, glad to see he was all right. Dick, for his part, seemed just as happy to see her, kissing her cheek before sitting next to her.

Grace had to admit, she hadn't been happy when Bob had raised the idea of promoting Dick to Commander and having them take turns as XO and logistics officer. It had seemed like a step backwards to Grace, and she was worried it would threaten her career prospects.

So far, though, it had been working out. She got to complete her command training, as did Dick, and she got to do it with people that she liked. She was having a lot of fun, and so what if Bob favored Dick a little over her? The record would speak for itself. She having been promoted to commander first, and all things being equal, she assumed she was still on track to beat him to the captain's chair. Maybe she would request Dick as her XO until he got his own vessel.

That center seat couldn't be far into her future now. Her actions during the recent battle with the Rucans might be just what she needed to put her over the top. She had been exceptional in the fight, and she allowed herself to admit that. Bob himself had said that using the cargo freighter had been an ingenious move, and with her overall performance against both warships, she was sure she'd acquitted herself well enough for at least one commendation.

Grace didn't know if asking Dick to be her second would offend him or not. He did always try to be the center of attention, but she liked to think that she'd seen him grow this year, settling in as more of an adult than she remembered him ever being capable of. He still made idiotic comments, of course, but he'd also been more responsible and respectful in his work, hardly ever even calling her Gracie any more.

In truth, this had been the best year of her life, working with him on this ship in their command-level positions. She was starting to rethink the way she shoved down her feelings for him. If they could work together this well, maybe they could date, too, if he wanted to. He had continued to be flirty with women, but not lecherous, the way he had been. Perhaps he was ready for a real relationship.

If so, it should be with her. After all, she'd put in the time to make him a better man. Without her, he would have been drummed out of the A.S.S. Instead, he was thriving once again. He owed her this. She deserved the fruits of this long, long, arduous labor.

Shooting Dick another smile, which he returned a bit quizzically, they both turned as Bob strode into his office and crossed to the desk they sat across from. The captain was in a cheery mood, too, having escaped death and saved the cargo crew. He had nothing but good news to report to Headquarters, and that would surely bode well for his two right-hand persons.

"Great work today, Dick, Grace," said Bob genially, spreading his hands. "Both of you impressed the hell out of me, as usual. One of you did so just a little bit more, though, and that has earned a special prize."

Grace smiled. She knew that Dick would have to pay for that ridiculous stunt of rushing off without explaining his plan. Why did he have to add the flair? Doing his job well was plenty good enough.

"Dick did a bold thing, risking his neck for the cargo workers," said Grace graciously, able to afford to be generous, given the situation.

"Oh, I agree completely," said Bob. "That's why he's being fast-tracked for a captainship."

"What?" asked Grace and Dick at the same time, him happily surprised, her pissed off.

"That's right. There are four starsheeps under construction right now, and I think one of them can be yours, Dick. You may have to stay here for another six months or so, but you're on your way," said Bob. "Congratulations."

"Wow. Thanks, Bob," Dick was saying, shaking the captain's hand enthusiastically. Grace stayed in her seat stunned. Dick turned to her, going in for a hug. "How about that Gracie? I did it! Youngest captain in the fleet! Guess you owe me a hundred gouda."

"No! This is wrong!" she sputtered.

"Grace?" asked Dick, his face dropping. She ignored her friend and turned to Bob. "What the hell, Bob?"

"I thought you'd be happy, Grace. You've always been a supporter of Dick here," said Bob.

"He's been a commander for mere *months*!" said Grace, and she didn't care that spit was flying.

"He's comported himself in a superior fashion," said Bob testily.

"He doesn't listen to you, Bob. He runs off and does whatever he wants. What about that stunt, piloting a shuttle into the middle of a firefight without even warning us? He could have gotten himself and the crew killed!" yelled Grace.

"But he didn't," said Bob, almost gently. "Listen, Grace, you're a great XO, and I'd be happy to have you serve on here. But Dick is captain material. He does best taking charge of the situation. You're better with orders and regulations. There's nothing wrong with that, and we'll get you to captain before long, too. Right now, it's Dick's time."

"Screw you, Bob," said Grace, rising. "I'm putting in for a new assignment immediately." She didn't wait for an answer, storming out of the office. She tried to compose herself as she crossed a small portion of the bridge to reach the elevator, but she was sure everyone on the command deck had to know exactly what had happened.

Before the elevator doors could close, Dick slid in with her. He was the last person she wanted to see, and she immediately unleashed on him, verbally and physically, beating his chest with her fists.

"It isn't fair!" she shouted. "You don't deserve this!"

"Whoa, hey now, Gracie," said Dick, trying to catch her wrists but missing. "If it's about our bet, you can keep your money."

"It's not about gouda!" sputtered Grace.

"Look, I know you're upset..."

"You *know* I'm upset? Really? What was your first clue?" she shouted.

"Probably the tears," he said casually. She stopped beating his chest and decked him right on the jaw. He collapsed onto the floor of the elevator and she stormed off towards her apartment, not looking back.

Commander Grace Thomas returned to her apartment in the *A.S.S. Kayak*. It had been three months since she was made first officer on this starsheep, and she didn't regret the decision one bit. Captain Mulgrew was a much more professional captain than Bob had been, one who appreciated Grace's style and skills, and Grace felt much more at home here.

The computer beeped at Grace as she entered, displaying a number of messages waiting for her. Many were from various crew members with equipment or personnel requests, and a few were from A.S.S. Command, wanting status updates or communicating with her about various projects. Six were from Dick Kahkay.

Grace hadn't spoken with Dick since that day in the elevator. Although she'd had to serve with him a couple more weeks, Bob expedited her transfer request after the assault, and she had been allowed to mostly work below decks until she could rotate off the *Redspot*.

She supposed she should be grateful. The way she screamed at Bob and the punch she threw at Dick, either one could have earned her a reprimand and possibly more dire consequences. Neither had filed any reports, though, and so her record remained clear. However, she had a hard time being thankful, considering allowing her behavior a pass the least they could do for her.

In a way, Grace blamed herself. If she hadn't had a soft spot for Dick, if she hadn't put him ahead of her own needs, she wouldn't be in this position. Maybe it would have taken awhile for Bob to nominate her to be a captain, but it would have happened eventually; she was sure of it.

This would teach her to never again put a man's needs before her own. She hadn't thought that was a lesson she would ever have to learn, having been so focused on her career for so much of her life. But when she least expected it, she'd let Dick matter to her more than she should have, and she'd paid a price for it.

In another way, though, a much larger way, Grace blamed Dick. Why hadn't he stood up for her? Why hadn't he fought for her? She had done the same for him, and he was stabbing her in the back by allowing this to happen. It was his place to demand that she be ahead of him in the line. If he were a true friend, he would have.

She didn't know what she'd ever seen in Dick. With some distance between them, it was clear to her now just how selfish and conceited he was. He had never cared for her the way she had for him. He had never even considered her in his big decisions. She deserved better than someone like Dick.

Grace deleted Dick's messages without listening to them, as she had the dozens of others he'd sent her in the past several months, both before she left the *Redspot* and after. He had given her space physically, never trying to corner her to talk, but his notes had started coming less than a week after her blow up, and she had yet to read a single one. If he truly cared, he would have said it in person, not left some voicemail like a coward.

Sooner or later, Dick would take the hint. Even someone as dense as Richard V. Kahkay would eventually realize that the girl didn't want to hear from him. She looked forward to that day, the day she'd finally be free of the thorn he was; the day she could move on.

In the meantime, she was getting herself back on track. No more distractions. This was her time.

"Captain Kahkay!" said Admiral Larry Johnson. "Welcome home!"

"Admiral Johnson!" said Kahkay, hugging the older man warmly. "Congratulations on the promotion!"

"The same to you. I'm just surprised it took you this long," said Johnson. "Though you always did do things on your own schedule."

"Yeah, I guess I still do," said Kahkay. He walked beside Johnson up to the bar, an old, charming, warm place called Tip Top in downtown Columbus that he always liked to come back to when he was on Earth. It wasn't a big place, but it was a spot where he felt at home. He was glad Johnson had agreed to meet him here.

"Something on your mind?" asked Johnson.

"You could say that," allowed Kahkay.

"Well, spit it out," said Johnson, motioning for the bartender to bring them a couple of whiskeys, which he readily did.

"Look, I'm super excited to get to the *Thrifty*, but...," started Kahkay, staring at the amber liquid in his glass. Johnson had already downed his and waved for another.

"...but you're not sure you deserve it," finished Johnson. "Same thing I hear from every captain ever, but I have to say, I'm surprised to hear it from you."

"Really? Why?" asked Kahkay.

"Yes. You were such a dick, Dick," said Johnson, chuckling to himself at his pun. "Always charging ahead, nothing seemed to bother you. Well, except for..." He let the sentence go unfinished. They silently clinked glasses in salute to Captain Roberts and drank them down. The bartender quickly poured more.

"You got past that, as I always knew you would," said Johnson. "Why doubt yourself now?"

"It's just... there's someone else more qualified than me," admitted Kahkay.

"There always is," said Johnson. "The A.S.S. is life, and life isn't fair. The promotion goes to the person that takes it, or who is someone's favorite, or who's just in the right place at the right time. It doesn't always progress in a straight, orderly fashion."

"Maybe sometimes it should," said Kahkay.

"Maybe," agreed Johnson, sipping the next whiskey rather than shooting it. Kahkay followed suit. Johnson shrugged. "Whatcha gonna do?"

"I could contact HQ, try to set things right," said Kahkay.

"Don't be a fool. Things are right," said Johnson.

"But-," started Kahkay.

"No buts," said Johnson, waving his objection away. "They are. Trust me. I'm an Admiral, so you kind of have to now."

"Yes, sir," said Kahkay.

"Don't be a smart ass. You know what I mean. You've barely been made captain, possibly by accident. No one at Command is going to listen to you," said Johnson. "And if they did, what then? You want to go back to being XO for some schmuck?"

"No...," said Kahkay.

"Damn right. You refuse a captainship, another one's not gonna come around too easily again. And even if you did refuse, there's very little chance it'll go to whoever you're thinking it should go to," said Johnson. "Command would just pick whoever they want."

"That's a good point...," said Kahkay.

"Of course it is, and it's the truth," said Johnson. "Now, you're two drinks behind me. The Dick Kahkay I know would never let me outdrink him. Unless you've changed more than I think you have?"

"Bartender, line 'em up," said Kahkay, gulping what was left in his glass and reaching for two more.

As the whiskey flowed, he pushed aside any lingering doubts about what had happened with Grace. Johnson was right. This wasn't Kahkay's fault, and there was nothing he could do about it. Grace was a smart cookie, and a very capable A.S.S. officer. She'd get there soon enough. And while she may not be returning his calls now, Kahkay had pissed her off plenty of times before to know that she would soon come around and forgive him. She always did.

CHAPTER FIFTEEN
2424, TOPLEESIA I

Admiral Jamie Jamieson sat on the planet Topleesia I, a cold, tropical beverage in his hand, shirt hanging casually open under the warm sun, topless women all around him, and he was almost happy. Almost.

Finding pretty strong evidence Janice was cheating on him had thrown him for a loop. He might have suspected it before, but he didn't really believe it until the records indicated otherwise. He was now almost positive that she'd slept with Harry Dirt before recommending him to be XO of the *Thrifty*, and Jamieson felt like a real cuckold.

The *Thrifty* was almost as big of a pain in the neck as Janice. While the reports of the senior staff favored Richard R. Kahkay much more positively in the last mission briefing, Jamieson couldn't be sure if they were genuine, or if Kahkay had just charmed his officers to the point that they were willing to overlook his mistakes now. After all, Kahkay had lost *another* first officer, the third in less than six weeks.

Which is why Jamieson was out here on Topleesia I. Or, at least, that was the excuse he gave his aide, Lieutenant Commander Buzz, before leaving. Jamieson had said that he was coming to brief the *Thrifty*'s next XO, Commander Bernard Sanders, himself. Bernie was an old friend of Jamieson's, and really, Jamie was just looking forward to a guy's trip with his buddy.

Unfortunately, Bernie was getting old, and partied out quickly these days. He'd hit the ground hard, even bought hundreds of shots for everyone around them, and then petered out in less than a day. He'd already left for his room to pack, getting ready to rendezvous with Kahkay in the next system over, on Ingleesia X.

That left Jamieson alone with his thoughts, the dark ones about Kahkay, and the even darker ones about Janice. Honestly, between the ornery captain and his promiscuous wife, Jamieson hadn't had such a bad time of things, both personally and professionally, since his son had died at the hands of the C'mons.

Jamieson didn't think about Jake much these days. He wanted to, but it hurt too much. Losing one's only child was a very deep pain, one Jamieson had come to terms with over the past several years. Now, it was easier to just pretend it didn't exist.

Maybe it was time for Jamieson to give up the A.S.S. He was younger than most who retired, but he'd had a good run, a respectable career. He'd achieved the rank of admiral, and held a position at Headquarters. He didn't think he had the will to push higher any more, to go for top brass, so this was probably as far as he was going to get, middle management. Why not go out now and find something he was more passionate about?

Yet, Jamieson knew he wouldn't do that. He was a company man if ever there was one. The A.S.S. was his life. It may have cost him his son, who was all too eager to follow in his father's footsteps, but it also gave him just about everything he'd ever been proud of. He would just as soon cut off his own arm than leave the service. Entertaining the idea at all was laughable.

Still, Jamieson needed something to change, something to go right. He didn't know what would make him happy, but he knew the large amount of alcohol he was putting away was only a temporary solution. He needed something more lasting. A new passion, or an obsession. Something he could really throw himself into, a buoy to keep him afloat in this next phase of his life, if not a big enough one to set him on a new course.

What would that buoy be? He looked forward to finding out.

Lieutenant Michelle Tokaladie saw Lieutenant Commander M- looking as sad as she'd ever seen him. She wasn't sure how she knew he was sad, as his features were not at all human and pretty much inscrutable to her. But something about his posture, the more-hunched-over-than-usual position and the stiffer back, screamed out emotional pain to her.

The rest of the senior staff had beamered down to Topleesia I, Kahkay unwilling to just pick up his new XO as ordered without at least stopping by the party planet, leaving the two of them alone on the bridge. Well, alone with all the ensigns and lieutenants who manned the other stations.

Tokaladie had been invited to go along, but Topleesa I wasn't her type of place. She didn't get into the beach party atmosphere, and she was not about to let her fellow officers see her boobs. The only one she wanted to show them to was M-, and he wasn't asked along because he spoke up and reminded the captain that they were supposed to go to Ingleesia X, not Topleesia I. No one invited the buzz kill to the party, as necessary as he might be.

M-'s staying behind had been a welcome opportunity for the two of them to spend some time together, away from the other department heads. Tokaladie wasn't sure if M- kept turning down her overtures of dinner because he wasn't interested or because he didn't understand that she was asking him on a romantic date, and this time would give them a chance to figure things out. Or so she had hoped. His bad mood was interfering with that.

"What's the matter?" she asked M- as an ice-breaker.

M- made a noise she hadn't heard him make before, something like a sigh, but not quite. "I am fine, Lieutenant Tokaladie."

"You don't look fine to me," she said, gently pushing.

"You do not need to concern yourself with my well-being," said M-, a bit melodramatically somehow.

"I *want* to concern myself with you...r well-being," she said shyly, looking over at him. He stared back, unblinking, for several seconds, then made the noise again.

"Please keep this just between you and I, but I would have liked to have gone on the away mission," admitted M-.

"You would? Really? Why?" asked Tokaladie.

"I joined the A.S.S. to be part of a team," said M-. "Yet, the captain constantly, as you humans say, picks me last. He does not enjoy my company."

"I'm sure that's not true," insisted Tokaladie, though she suspected it was.

"Thank you for trying to spare my feelings, but I know it to be the truth," said M-.

"Well, Kahkay's a... an interesting, unconventional individual," said Tokaladie, painfully aware of several ensigns glancing their way. "But don't worry about him. The rest of us like you."

"Really?" asked M-, and she could tell his query was genuine.

"Yes," she said firmly. "I like you very much, and I'm sure the others do, too. You are one of us."

"I am?" asked M-. Now he was just being needy.

"Yes," she said again.

"All right," said M-.

"Hang on a second," said Tokaladie, seeing her communications station blink. "Incoming call from Ingleesia X."

"Put it on the big screen," said M-, leaving the science post to move to the center chair. The screen at the far end of the bridge blinked, the stars being replaced by a middle-aged, balding man with fewer wrinkles than one would expect from a guy with so much grey hair.

"Hello, *Thrifty*. This is Commodore Billings of Ingleesia X."

"Hello, Commodore Billingsssss," said M-. "I am Lieutenant Commander M- of the *A.S.S. Thrifty*."

"Lieutenant Commander? Where's your captain?" asked Billings suspiciously. "Tell me the truth, are you an evil traitor who mutinied and stole the ship from your good captain?"

"No, I am not evil," said M- tiredly, and Tokaladie's heart went out to him, always battling the xenophobic stereotypes of his species. "Captain Kahkay is down on the surface of Topleesia I and he left me in charge."

"Oh," said Billings. "Good. I was calling to let you know that Commander Sanders is on Topleesia I, so you don't have to come here after all, though you are still welcome if you want to visit."

"No thank you, Commodore Billings," said M-, and the commodore's face fell. "Do you know where Commander Sanders can be found on Topleesia?"

"Yes, I'll have my assistant send you his accommodation details. Are you sure you don't want to come over here before you leave the sector? We just put in a new space bowling alley."

"Ew. I appreciate the offer, but we have a mission to attend to," said M-.

"Sure, sure," said Billings. "Everyone is always rushing over to party on Topleesia I. No one ever wants to visit Ingleesia X. We're fun, too, you know!"

"I am certain that you are not," said M-. "*Thrifty* out." The screen switched back to the star scape before Billings could respond, though he was clearly opening his mouth to do so. M- turned back to Tokaladie. "Lieutenant, did you receive Commander Sanders' information?"

"Coming through now," said Tokaladie.

"Excellent. Put it on a portable pad. I am going down to the surface and hand it over to Captain Kahkay personally," said M-, crossing back to his station. "Ah, it looks like the captain has not moved from the spot where he beamered down."

"You don't have to do that," said Tokaladie. "We can send Ensign Summers."

"I'd be happy to go, sir!" said Summers quickly from the security station.

"No, I will do it," said M-. "I am not going to be left behind any longer." He took the pad from Tokaladie's hand, and quickly strode into the elevator.

Tokaladie watched him go with a bittersweet smile. As much as she was disappointed that M- had left her alone up here (with the junior officers, of course), she was happy to see him standing up for himself, doing what he needed to do to be happy. She could draw inspiration from that and finally stand up for herself. Not right away; she wasn't ready yet. But soon, she told herself. Soon.

Doctor Prudence Awshucks felt the warm sun beat down on her bare breasts as she downed a frozen peach margarita and smacked the naked ass of a couple of cute cabana boys that sauntered past. This was the life, and definitely the break she needed from that stuffy old starsheep.

She had to admit, serving on the *Thrifty* hadn't been as bad as she'd worried it would be. She hadn't had to use the beamer again since beamering up, other than today to head down to Topleesia I, but this was worth it. She'd gotten to like the view of space through the windows, and she hadn't had to go near an airlock or the cold vacuum outside even once. The nightmares had almost even stopped, thanks to her being too drunk to consciously remember her dreams. So all in all, a pretty successful tenure thus far.

The crew was annoying. Tokaladie was far too naïve and quiet for Awshucks' taste, M- had creepy scaly skin, Who needed a haircut badly, and Foley was just far too much of a people pleaser. Kahkay was an asshole, but at least she knew what she was getting with him. So maybe they weren't going to be a bunch of chums, but she could imagine worse.

Besides, the booze was free. Not down here, unfortunately, but she earned a good salary now, and she'd gladly pay for the chance to ogle the man meat and feel solid ground again. Maybe she'd even get laid; it had been far too long since she'd had her pipes flushed out, if you get the expression.

"Are you listening to me, Doctor Awshucks?" asked a deep voice. Awhucks looked down at the man whose lap she was sitting on.

"Do you have a hotel room?" she asked him. He was pretty attractive. She found power sexy, and this man had some. But he was also turning out to be a very whiny drunk, and that was something that would only kill her buzz. Either she needed to get him naked and shut his mouth with her nether regions, or she was going to need to go find another playmate. Leaving this guy would not make her captain happy, as Kahkay had specifically asked her to keep him occupied, but she wasn't going to let his sad sackness get in the way of her fun time.

"Uh, yes...," he said.

"Good. Can we go there? Now?" she asked, grabbing another drink off of a passing tray. The server didn't notice.

"Um, yes, of course," he said, rising. She followed him, winking at a few young hunks along the way, making a mental note of where to return to when she was done with this one. Topleesia I was full of men, and she wasn't going to waste her vacation on a single sex buddy.

"Here we are," he said, leading her through a ground floor entrance into a charming bungalow. The room was plain, the bed made, no clothes strewn about. Time to change that.

Awshucks tossed aside her skirt, leaving herself naked as the day she was born, completely unconcerned with the open curtains that would let any revelers peer in. Most were as drunk as she was, if not more so, and wouldn't care what was going on in here.

"Oh, wow," said her companion, who slowly unfastened his own pants. She grew impatient, crossed to him, and ripped down trousers and underwear in one smooth motion. Then, she shoved him onto the bed, jumping after him.

Awshucks didn't leave the room for literally days, having food and liquor delivered in. She'd definitely underestimated him, a man who could keep up with even her energetic proclivities. It took a while to get him started, but once Admiral Jamie Jamieson went to work, he was quite the lay.

Lieutenant Who Grappa sat next to the tiki bar, the festive atmosphere not matching her mood at all, as she nursed her drink, overdressed, on a stool.

"Who! There ya are!" said Chief Engineer Foley, taking the empty seat next to Who. "We wondered where you had gotten off to."

"Who. Right. Here," said Who.

"I see that. Are you having fun?" asked Foley, motioning for a drink for himself.

"Loads," replied Who.

"Was that sarcasm? I can't quite tell with you yet," said Foley.

"Yes. Sar. Casm," said Who.

"Oh. Well, there's lots o' fun to be had here. Look around!" Foley gestured broadly at the joyous pandemonium all around them. They didn't call Topleesia I the party planet for nothing.

"Not. My. Style," said Who.

"Mind my asking what your style is?" asked Foley.

"Why. Do. You. Want. Know?" asked Who.

"Well, we're crewmates now, aren't we?" asked Foley. "Might as well be friends, too."

"All. Right. Who. Likes. Good. Book. And. Good. Brandy," said Who.

"Excellent. I can get behind that," said Foley. "Another question for you. Why are ya down here if you don't enjoy it?"

"Need. Ed. Dis. Traction," said Who.

"From what?" asked Foley.

"Se. Cur. Ity," said Who.

"Oh. Gotcha," said Foley. "Something specific about your job got you down?"

"Yes."

"Want to talk about it?"

"No."

"Fair enough. But I'm here if you need me. Or rather, I'll be over there with Captain Kahkay, but if you need me, I can be back over here," said Foley, tipping a salute, then heading back over to the captain, who had attracted a bevy of beautiful bimbos around him.

Who watched Foley go and sighed. She appreciated his attempts, and she did think he'd made a good friend. The next time he approached her, she'd probably even be more responsive. But not today.

Commander Sanders had turned out to be dead before the *Thrifty* had beamed down to collect him, presumably of natural causes because he was very, very old, and while this one definitely wasn't Who's fault, losing four first officers in less than two months did not look good.

Who wondered if maybe she should go back to medicine. As much as she wanted to be out having adventures, she didn't want to cost the crew their lives doing it. She had a pretty low mortality rate as a doctor, being one of the best around. She'd have to transfer off of the *Thrifty*, as they already had a chief medical officer, but it might be worth it.

Then again, maybe she should give things another chance. Kahkay and Foley were waving her over. *They* didn't blame her for failing to protect the XOs. Maybe she was being too hard on herself. Maybe she should allow a little time to pass, see how the next couple of months went. Who had never been a quitter. She didn't want to become one now.

Richard Z. Kahkay sat in his apartment back on the *Thrifty*, exhausted from his non-stop week on Topleesia I. It had been just what he needed after the long rough patch he'd been through, and it gave him a chance to bond with some of his crew, who were pretty awesome, once he got to know them.

Being captain wasn't what Kahkay thought it would be, but maybe that was all right. He was learning now what his limitations were, and how to make up for them with all of the great people surrounding him. If he couldn't make it with this crew, he wouldn't make it at all.

M- was definitely evil; Kahkay had no doubt about that. But the rest of the senior staff were great, and, given time, Kahkay was sure he could get M- to expose himself. In the meantime, he kind of enjoyed matching wits with the reptilian being.

Strangely, Kahkay seemed to be having an attraction to Lieutenant Who. Kahkay didn't mind hooking up with dudes on occasion, but they weren't his go-to. He'd never met a guy he found so attractive before, but every once in awhile he'd catch himself glancing at Who's butt, or noticing his silky fur. Kahkay wondered what was up with that. Was he turning gay?

That would certainly make things easier. As much as he had tried to put Grace out of his mind, he couldn't stop thinking of her. He had to have sent her hundreds of messages in the past year, and every single one of them went unreturned. He'd thought she'd cool down by now. Didn't they have enough history together to make up for whatever slights she might be feeling?

Then again, maybe it was time to let her go. He had his captainship now, and a new crew of people to befriend. Doctor Awshucks could serve to put him in his place, if he let her, like Grace used to do. And her breasts were way, way, larger than Grace's, who had a slim frame. Kahkay liked boobs of all sizes, but he certainly wasn't going to complain about massive mammaries. Not when Awshucks was considerably sluttier, and much more likely to eventually give in and sleep with him.

No one could ever replace Grace, but maybe that was just how life was. They said you never forgot your first love, and while Kahkay had screwed many, many, many people, Grace was the only one he could describe as having loved, even if they'd never officially been together. She was the standard he'd come to measure any potential partner by, and also the reason why he'd never seriously dated anyone. No one was as good as Grace.

Could Kahkay be happy in a world where she wasn't part of his life? He hoped so. It was looking more and more like he wouldn't have a choice anyway. But if he could figure how to captain a starsheep, he could surely figure out how to get along without Grace Thomas.

He decided to make one more attempt to reach out, and then he was leaving it up to her. She could decide whether to make contact again. He would respect her choice.

Kahkay picked up a stylus and wrote:

'Dear Grace,

Congratulations. I knew you could do it and I couldn't be happier for you. You deserve this, deserved this before now actually, and I'm glad the A.S.S. has finally recognized you for it.

You are the best, smartest, most capable person I've ever known. Period. You are the person who challenged me, who pushed me along, who saved my life when it was over. You are the woman to beat all women, and no one could ever hold a candle to you.

I know I screwed up. I'm sorry for that. I never meant to hurt you, and I certainly never intended to be in your way. If I could change the past, I would. It's unforgiveable that I let my ego get in the way of us, and I regret what I did every day.

What I'm trying to say is, I love you. I only want you to be happy. If you need to be happy without me, I understand, but just be happy. And if you think you can be happy with me, I would do my best to make up for my mistakes and try to be worthy of you.

Yours forever,

Dick'

Instructing the note to be added to a basket of cookies, he sent it away, and with it, his heart.

Captain Grace Thomas stepped onto the bridge of the *A.S.S. Meru* for the first time, surveying her crew. Lieutenant Flufy, her security chief, was present, as well as several faces she recognized only from their files. She sighed in satisfaction, all feeling right with the world, and headed for her center seat.

She stopped short. A massive basket was in her chair. That shouldn't be there. "What in the hell...?" she muttered.

"Sir?" asked Commander Hannah Meyers, her new XO, turning around from the pilot's station.

"Sorry, Commander, I was just wondering what the hell this basket was doing on my chair?"

"I don't know, sir," said Hannah, turning back to her console.

"Er, uh, actually, I do," said Lieutenant Simon, stepping forward from the science station. "It was delivered with express orders to bring it to the bridge and put it there."

"Who the hell would..." Grace trailed off. She knew who would do such a thing. Only one person she'd ever encountered would do this. What was he trying to do now? Get in her head before she'd even assumed command? And with oatmeal raisin cookies? Everyone knew you shouldn't put raisins in baked goods. Yuck!

"Never mind," said Grace. "Lieutenant Simon, will you please dispose of these?"

"Yes, sir," said Simon, grabbing the basket. "Do you want to keep the card?"

"No. Trash it, too," said Grace, settling into her chair. Dick had already delayed her getting here long enough. She wasn't going to waste another second of time on him. "Commander Meyers, take us out."

For the continuing adventures of Captain Richard Kahkay and the A.S.S. Thrifty, subscribe to It's All Been Done Radio Hour on iTunes and other podcasting services. Also, check out our website at itsallbeendoneradiohour.com

ACKNOWLEDGMENTS

When I conceived of *It's All Been Done Radio Hour*, a modern geeky comedy show in the style of old-timey radio programs, *Universe Journey* was the first of our rotating series that popped into my head. I'd always loved *Star Trek*, and always wanted to do my own version of it.

Our future isn't as neat and optimistic as *Star Trek*'s, but it's not dreary, either. We have laughs, but there's also drama. The characters aren't cartoons, they're complex individuals, which I strive to show in each and every episode, even if they are short comedies.

To that end, I could not do it without an amazing cast. Nicholas Arganbright makes Richard Kahkay his own. Shane Stefanchik is gloriously "not evil" as M-. Katie Boissoneault has developed Tokaladie into far more than the intended, one-note character. Seamus Talty brings the whole ship to life as Foley. Chase McCants can convey a great deal for Who with a single syllable. Amanda Iman makes Awshucks likeable, despite her many flaws. Keith Jackson plays Jamieson with a powerful innocence.

Those are our core group, but an ongoing series like *Universe Journey* wouldn't work without the rest of the ensemble. Joe Morales portrayed Commander Garry Marshall. Dallas Ray is Harry Dirt and Lieutenant Commander Buzz. Dan Condo is Captain Yeez and Lieutenant Simon. Ryan Yohe is Janice Jamieson and Lieutenant Flufy. Addie Peelle is Fitzy. Katelyn Hamilton is Commander Lady. Samantha Stark is Clint. Nathan Haley, Wendy Parks, Virgil Von Hartzel, and Kristin Green don't play any characters from this novel, but are also invaluable in future episodes. And, of course, our wonderful narrator, Chris Allen, ties it all together.

Katelyn Hamilton probably had the hardest job as it pertains to this narrative, though. She had to bring Grace Thomas to life in a single episode, amid the story going on, and convey a depth of backstory that wasn't on the page. This novel had been conceived, but not yet written, when Grace first appeared in *It's All Been Done Radio Hour*, and Katelyn and Nick did a masterful job of establishing that relationship. I look forward very much to exploring it with them further in the future.

Much of the cast and crew helped me polish and fine-tune this book, conducting a read thru to better capture their voices. Thank you all.

I also have to thank both Packrat Comics and MadLab Theatre. Packrat was where we got our start, and there would be no series without them. MadLab has been where we've grown, and we couldn't ask for better, more generous hosts.

All of these people have been amazing, and changed my life forever, for the better. I cannot thank them enough, and they are all responsible in some way for this novel making it to you.

While some of what is covered in this book is echoed in the first few episodes of the show, I wouldn't have written it if I didn't feel it would tell something entirely different than what the radio show does, and with a different purpose. I thank all of those who supported me and this project, and look forward to the next one, whatever it may be.

About the Author

Jerome Wetzel grew up in West Jefferson, Ohio, near Columbus. An avid reader and writer, he has produced many works over the years, mainly of the fictional variety. He recommends you check out G.O.D. is my B.F.F. on IABDPresents.com. He does not recommend you check out his older, self-published novels on Amazon, at least not until he gets the chance to rewrite them.

Currently, Jerome is the impresario and founder of It's All Been Done Presents, a multi-platform entertainment network based in Columbus. He is also the creator and writer of It's All Been Done Radio Hour, a modern geeky comedy in the style of old-timey radio serials, performed live monthly and podcast out weekly. It is the flagship show of the network. He hopes to write more books, but isn't sure when he'll have the time.

Jerome resides in Galloway, a suburb of Columbus, with his wife, Morgan, two cats, Kali and Snugglebunny Fucktard (the latter predates the wife), two guinea pigs (hers), and very soon, a human infant. *Very* soon. Like, his wife could go into labor any moment soon, so he'd better go ahead and finish this book.

About the Network

Please check out iabdpresents.com for podcasts, written work, video series, and more!

Made in the USA
Middletown, DE
06 July 2018